I0564604

THE GOSPEL OF Z

THE GOSPEL OF Z

Stephen Graham Jones

OPEN ROAD

INTEGRATED MEDIA
NEW YORK

Oh You Pretty Things
Words and Music by David Bowie
Copyright © 1971 EMI Music Publishing Ltd., Tintoretto Music and Chrysalis Music Ltd.
Copyright Renewed
All Rights on behalf of EMI Music Publishing Ltd. Administered by Sony Music Publishing (US) LLC, 424 Church Street, Suite 1200, Nashville, TN 37219
All Rights on behalf of Tintoretto Music Administered by RZO Music
All Rights on behalf of Chrysalis Music Ltd. Administered by BMG Rights Management (US) LLC
International Copyright Secured
All Rights Reserved
Reprinted by Permission of Hal Leonard LLC

ISBN: 978-1-5040-9948-6

This edition published in 2025 by Open Road Integrated Media, Inc.
180 Maiden Lane
New York, NY 10038
www.openroadmedia.com

for Rane and Kinsey

THE GOSPEL OF Z

All the nightmares came today
And it looks as though they're here to stay.

—David Bowie

BEFORE

Thing is, she could have been any one of us.

And was.

All of us, really.

The pirate DJ waits a breath or two before delivering that last part, so that you can just about see his stubbly chin down there in his dark bunker, his lips close enough to the mic that there's some definite scratch there. Because he doesn't know radio so well yet.

It's that kind of voice, that kind of broadcast.

And this woman he's remembering out loud, what she's doing, what he's telling us she's doing, it's just driving her mom-car through some residential place like there used to be. A completely innocent day in heaven—that's what the past is, now, to us: the good place. Where we all want to be.

And, because this is heaven, there are children.

One of them chases a red ball out into the street in front of this mom. She could be changing the station, she could be digging through her purse in the passenger seat, she could be looking in the rearview mirror, she could just be spaced out, bulleting through some mental to-do list. But no. This mom, because she's a mom, she knows to pay the right kind of attention on these kinds of streets.

She stops, her tires chirping, coffee sloshing into the floor-board, her purse spilling on top of it, a pen lid rattling into the defroster again, but no matter.

The young boy—what is he, four? must be: not in school on a Tuesday—he's oblivious to anything but that wonderful red ball. He's just leaning down for it, now trying to stand with it. It's nearly as big as his torso, so he has to hug it to his chest.

This mom in the car, she does check her rearview mirror now, maybe just for somebody to share this picturesque scene unfolding here, on this Rockwell afternoon. Because it's almost too much for one woman to try to contain, yes?

She covers her mouth so the boy won't think she's laughing at him, her foot still on the brake, and in that moment, from behind the same brick mailbox, something else darts.

No, it *flits*.

A man, but not.

He's dead, but not, his chin and chest black with blood, one shoe gone, half that foot gone as well, his eyes not so much vacant as just more focused than anything else this mom's ever seen.

There's not even time for her to scream. Not even time to breathe in to scream.

This is how fast they are.

The dead man, the undead man, the zombie—you have to say it—he flashes across the road, scoops the boy up, and is gone, all in a heartbeat, that red ball still bouncing there. On an other-wise normal day in human history.

The last one ever.

We didn't know what they were then, either, these zombies. Not really, not like we would.

The movies, the DJ says, his voice still too close to that mic, the movies had been trying to tell us for years, but we didn't take them seriously. We didn't cue in fast enough, to that first shuffling form at the stadium on game day. To the panic at the airports, on the interstates, on the airwaves. When we could have contained it, sacrificed this city, that state, we didn't.

And so it became a flood, washing across the land. Locusts consuming the crop we were, had always been. Night falling, body by body. Couples shuttered into their houses to wait it out, the husband always coming back from the kitchen with a cup of soup the wife isn't sure she asked for, the wife watching his reflection approach in the television screen. The map over the newscaster's shoulder going red. Airplane pilots circling until their tanks dry up, teenagers wrapping their bodies around each other, big sisters standing over little brothers, telling them to run, run. Last stands at burger huts and shoe stores, tollways blocked for miles, a ferry afraid to come back to shore, afraid to get too far from it too. Survivors crashing through blockaded church doors, only to find the priests in there hungry.

We were in those movies now.

Every one of us was that mom, racing through Residential, crashing across the manicured lawn of her daughter's elementary school, parking across the hug-n-go lane, leaving her car running behind her, the door open.

Rushing across the field now is a horde of zombies, their faces slick with gore, mouths open for more.

The mom makes it to the wide blue doors, is the last one, gets pulled in by the other parents.

"What—what's happening?" she says, but it's still too early for any of that.

And then you can see it in her eyes, that where's-my-baby-girl look.

The DJ lets that hang for a bit, like he doesn't want to have to be the one telling this, what everybody out there already knows—that those movies, they all got it wrong, didn't they? They were only worried about people trying to make it through this one night. When what they should have been teaching us, showing us, is how to live like that for nearly ten years.

And counting.

DAY ONE

CHAPTER ONE

So, nearly a full decade after the plague, there was this guy, Jory Gray, early thirties, more or less white, maybe a little more complected than most, the usual scars and burns and hollowed-out eyes we all had, and he could have also been any of us as well, any single one of us. But he wasn't.

He was Jory Gray.

There were no prophecies about him—society was still too scattered for that, hiding in pockets, going cannibal—no songs announcing his arrival in this new world, but isn't that the way history works? Our heroes, they don't come onto the scene with trumpets blasting, with handbills fluttering down from the sky. They just kind of ease in, not making a lot of eye contact, because they don't know what they are yet either. What they can be.

But you can see it in him a little, if you try. The way he stood against the outer wall of J Barracks that day, right at the heart of the base, his legs crossed at the ankle like a guitar player on an album cover from the past. The cigarette in his hand a complete afterthought. One he nursed for ten minutes. One last smoke before his shift, his eyes steady on the cinder block plant before him, the factory. Staring right at it but not really seeing it at all.

His problem was he couldn't get this one girl's name out of his head.

Or out of his hands.

At the outer gate of the plant minutes later, trying to scan his notched ID through the reader, he dropped the stupid useless card, stabbed his hand down after it. Ended up knocking the card through the gate, so he had to suffer the guards, just ten feet away—*inside*—licking their lips to try to keep from smiling. Jory knelt at first, then squatted, and finally had to lie down to make his arm long enough.

This is how legends are born, yes.

At the next gate, this one tangles of barbed wire, current sparking from razor strand to razor strand, he just stood there, daring the guards to *not* confirm his face, *not* hit that lift button.

They looked away, the grin still there in their eyes, and the wire creaked up.

Jory ducked under, his shadow crisp below him.

At the tall, windowless door to the factory, almost there, almost in—he flubbed his passcode three times (her name, her name), until a disgusted guard did have to come over, process Jory through the roundabout.

The joke was over, done with. Another morning trashed by a puke. Jory could read it in their glares.

He lifted his arms for their scans, their prods. Offered his scalp for their fingers and luxuriated under it so that they pushed him away, through the last door, into the silence of the long hall.

Jory closed his eyes, breathed in the sterile air.

Because he'd stood across the road for so long, deciding whether to do this again or not, he was a quarter hour late for his shift now. Not counting the locker room.

It didn't make him walk up the long hall any faster. Fifteen

THE GOSPEL OF Z

minutes could become twenty-five, if he played it right. Maybe a whole half hour.

Not like he was getting paid anyway, right?

Jory zeroed in on the locker room door a full city block down—every building on base was a cavern—and didn't look to either side. Not because he didn't want to see, but because he didn't need to, not anymore.

To his left, like always, would be the same endless wall, obviously military. Spaced regularly down it at an unimaginative height was a line of upright rectangles of pale green. Where pictures of push-broom-mustached generals had once glowered down. When he first started here, his eyelashes still balled into nubs from Disposal, Jory's knee-jerk call was that the sun had faded around those pictures, that those generals had won this important battle with the sun, saved their little parts of the wall. Except those parts were lighter, not darker. Meaning some soldier in the before had painted darker green all *around* the frames, instead of lifting them off. Probably because he didn't want to have to remember whatever stupid order they were in.

Good for him, Jory thought.

The other wall, to his right, would be mostly glass, the bulletproof kind. A series of windows opening onto the assembly line that, if it worked like the labcoats said, was supposed to save the world.

Maybe the view through that glass was why those wall generals had been taken down. Not so they couldn't see the world being saved by somebody other than them, but so they couldn't get all judgmental about *how* it was being saved. Because no way could anybody from the old world agree with what was being assembled here now. Giants. Atrocities. The first new creature to walk the earth for thousands of years.

Handlers.

It still made Jory kind of sick, thinking about them, about what the posters said they were able to do, the punishment they were built for. They were tanks on two legs. But the razor wire outside would stop them, if they ever clambered off the assembly line before they were supposed to. It had to.

He told himself this every day.

Not that any of them had sat up on the wide belt so far, looked around with their dead eyes.

But still.

Seven and a half feet of seriously augmented killing machine? It was the stuff of nightmares. Like that wasn't enough, add in their regiment of hormones and chemicals like Jory had to do every shift, and take into consideration their grafts and fiber optics, their implants and nuclear fibers, their circuit-driven consciences and steel-shanked bones, *then* put a zippered gimp mask over their heads, case the rest of them in double-plated leather, and what you've got is what you never would have wanted to get, if the world didn't need it so bad: handlers. For the dead. Giants strong enough to keep a zombie on a leash, walk it through a room, then drive to the next place, do it again.

This is the future.

One Jory never asked to be a part of.

Just on the hunch-shouldered shuffle from his housing unit to here, he'd seen six ways to end it all. Six casual methods of suicide. The big reset button. Game over, erase all memories, please. All he'd have to do would be to climb this fence, step into that road, hide behind that one dumpster for the rest of the morning.

Except her name had still been in his mouth then. And he didn't want to risk taking her with him.

Meaning, even gone, she was still saving him.

Stupid, stupid.

He might as well just walk into J Barracks, sign up to be a torch. That was the seventh way to die that he'd seen. And it was probably the quickest, all told. The most sure anyway.

In the ten minutes Jory had stood there with his cigarette, two jeeps had pulled up, and two baby torches had walked out to them, their flamethrowers loose and jaunty under their arms, like they thought they were going to live forever. Like they fully expected to come back. Like they hadn't already left the key to their footlocker on top of that footlocker.

Jory'd ground his cigarette out under his boot, saluted those torches away.

The idea of J Barracks had been to feel better, to at least not be on *that* track.

But he was still himself too.

So far, the postapocalypse was pretty much sucking.

Jory straight-armed his way through the door at the turn in the hall, into the locker room, his eyes narrowing to adjust to the light from the few bulbs left. It was empty for once. He was twenty minutes late. Everybody else was already out there on the line, building tomorrow.

On Jory's locker, courtesy of some joker—Timothy probably, Jory's shift mate—was a black-marker happy face. Tiny like a whispered secret, no more than a half-inch from round crown to rounder chin.

Jory stared at it, stared at it, and finally licked the pad of his thumb, pressed it into the face. He studied the face grinning up at him now through the whorls and vortices of his print then pressed it back into his locker door beside the other face. It was the same, but paler. He pressed it again, and again, until the ink was dry.

Ten minutes later, most of it spent sitting on the bench, watching his hand shake or not shake, Jory pushed into his assigned clean room, his scrubs pungent with disinfectant, so that his eyes kept trying to water.

Another day in paradise.

"Hey hey hey," Timothy sang from the other side of the stalled belt, his scalpel following the guide line drawn on the handler's massive bicep, "thought I was going to have to save the world all by myself."

"Gonna need more than me for that," Jory said, their usual call and response. But his voice was creaky from not talking to anybody today. From the half pack of cigarettes he'd sucked down before he even stood from the chair in his kitchen.

"What?" Timothy went on, angling his head down to see through his plastic goggles. "You catch the virus, man? It make you sleep late? I mean, in addition to, like, eating people, running around on all fours. Having kick-ass bad breath, all that."

"Sorry."

Timothy shrugged, angled his scalpel deeper into the muscle, the handler's oversized middle finger twitching. "Hunh," Timothy said, and did it again, a line of the handler's metal-flaked blood seeping down its massive forearm.

"Don't," Jory said, hooking his eyebrows up to the camera in the corner.

"Player piano," Timothy went on, digging deeper with the blade, then pressing it to the side, the middle finger going up-down, up-down. "C'mon, get the other side, we can do chopsticks."

Jory looked away.

"Like they have time to watch every room," Timothy said, letting the nerve go. "So?"

"So what?"

"So you."

Jory rubbed his nose with the side of his hand. "Had to

sneak into H for some smokes," he said. "Machine on my road's jammed."

"Dirty habit," Timothy said. "Lying, I mean."

Jory looked up to Timothy. Timothy didn't look away.

"Other people's business," Jory said. "That's another bad habit."

"So don't tell anybody else," Timothy said. "But I'm not exactly anybody, am I?"

"More like nobody."

"Just wait, man. Working on my demo tape, yeah?"

"You don't even play anything."

"Working on that too. And on there being a radio for me to play it on."

Jory pressed the heels of his hands into his eyes, rubbed them up into his hair, then held his hair back, like trying to stay awake.

"It's Linse," he said. Out loud. Finally.

Timothy eeked his mouth to the side, cocked his safety goggles up onto the leather aviator ones he'd always worn on his forehead, like he was about to fly away to some better place.

Jory nodded, telling Timothy he'd heard right—Linse.

"As in no more?"

"As in gone, yeah."

"Shit, man," Timothy said. "Sorry? Would say there's other fish in the sea or something, but—what's our population these days, do you know? Was she the last woman on earth, or just the last hot one?"

"C'mon, T. Don't, not today."

"I'm just saying. You leave a couch on the curb, it's not outside the realm of courtesy to give your good friend a call. And by *couch* here, I don't mean couch, yeah?"

Jory took his apron off the hook, shrugged into it, his lips tight, his hand falling to the scalpel in the apron's pocket.

"What does *couch* sound like though. . . ?" Timothy went on. "I know there's something, it's right on the tip of my—no, I just *wish* it was right on the—"

"She went up the Hill," Jory said, almost not loud enough.

But it carried.

The Hill.

"No *way*," Timothy said, leaning back from the half-built handler in mock shock. "Only guy I know with a steady . . . the last piece of tail on base, practically, and you make her feel dirty enough she has to go to *church* now? For the rest of her *life*? Congrats, dude. Serious"—fake-licking his middle finger, smearing it on an imaginary chalkboard—"score one for the perverts."

"I never should have told you."

"I'm just saying, man. We've got limited resources these days, right? Forget about yourself for once. Think about maintaining the species, yeah? Give the rest of us a heads-up, let us play a little Adam and Eve with them perky little apples . . ."

"Don't."

This is how much you can regret coming in to work.

Timothy smiled, the wheels turning in his thick head now. Cutting and talking, talking and cutting, guidelines be damned. "I mean, even if she's bad in bed, does she shave her legs? Because, I've gotta say, here in the twilight of humanity and all, that's about all I really—no, no, this is A-material time. Yeah"—his voice going water-cooler casual—"so you say you lost your basement girl, that one you pulled from her hiding place whenever-ago? Oh-oh, I'm sorry, not basement girl, excuse me. I didn't realize. Backdoor girl, of course, I forgot who I was—"

If this were one of the old-time movies, the close-up here would be the floor by Jory's boots. His scalpel *tinking* off that hard surface, the handle and blade starting to seesaw away from each other, but that process taking such a torturously long time.

Timothy looked up, to be sure this was happening, and it was: Jory coming across the table for him. Across the handler. The three of them spilling down onto the floor on Timothy's side.

"Dude! You—" Timothy tried to get up, holding his scalpel high, out of the way. Jory's hands were already at his throat, driving Timothy's head back, Timothy's work goggles snapping off. Spittle, grunts, teeth. Jory's eyes too wet, too full, too much.

This was another reason why the long cigarette break by J Barracks. Because he was afraid he wouldn't be able to ignore everybody.

"*Don't—say—that—about—her!*" he grunted, slamming Timothy's head back with each word, his thumbs on Timothy's skinny-man Adam's apple. Then Jory raised his right hand high, to start the punching. Timothy peeked, not wanting to see it come.

It didn't.

Jory let go, leaned back. Pressed his hands into his eyes again and held them there, trying to will time backwards. Start this scene all over.

But why stop there, right?

Why not go back to this morning. To the front door closing with him in bed, a note waiting for him at the kitchen table.

Or even farther, to Z Day, Jory in the backyard of what had been his house. A perfectly normal day. One he didn't appreciate nearly enough. One he should have been documenting with his camera, every single moment.

Maybe if he held his hands on his eyes long enough, he could go back, start over.

Please.

"Dude, dude, *dude*," Timothy was saying under him, at a whisper almost, except five hundred times more urgent.

The cameras weren't miked though. Why whisper?

Jory pulled his hands away, the room swimming with what looked like paramecium. Angel paramecium, made from light. Fireworms.

He smiled.

"She went up the Hill . . ." he said again, trying to laugh about how stupid it was.

"*Dude*!" Timothy said then, wriggling, trying to buck Jory off in the softest way possible.

Jory focused on Timothy's work goggles in the corner before zeroing back in on Timothy's face.

It was washed pale, unable to make words anymore.

"What?" Jory said, craning his head around on instinct, to follow where Timothy was looking.

The handler.

Standing. And then standing some more.

It was terrible. It was majestic.

Jory slumped away, not so much out of fear as out of reverence, and Timothy pulled him the rest of the way down then kicked the two of them back under the belt, into the places where life could keep happening.

"No, no," Timothy was saying, reaching up on the wall, Jory following his hand with dream eyes, the kind where everything makes sense, where you don't have to stop to make connections, just accept, accept.

The button.

Timothy wanted the button. And now he had it, was slapping his hand onto it, the room flashing emergency red, the vents sucking closed, the bulkhead on the other side of the room creaking down.

And then the handler angled its head, saw the two of them in its dim way.

"Eight," Jory said to himself, "eight ways to die," and this *was* funny, but then Timothy was dragging him all the way under the belt, through the wires and cables. Where nobody would have thought two people could fit. But nobody thought a handler could ever wake on the belt, either.

Jory only looked back when the huge hand clamped down on his foot. His boot.

Timothy could tell, pulled harder. "Help, help!" he yelled to Jory, setting his feet and jerking Jory forward by the armpits, Jory looking up at Timothy, at how hard he was pulling, like all of this mattered, and, just because it would be rude not to, he pointed his foot.

His boot slipped off, the handler falling against the back wall.

The bulkhead was almost down now, its huge gears or cables or whatever grinding in the ceiling, dust shrouding its descent.

Jory'd always wondered what it would be like, this safety measure.

Loud. It was loud.

And big. Shaking the whole building.

He smiled again, and then Timothy's hand hooked under the bulkhead so he could pull himself under, live.

Not Jory.

You can see him here even better than when he was smoking by J Barracks, probably. The way he gets up from the floor of the clean room. The way he studies this handler, just standing itself. Its all-black eyes registering Jory in an instant, its weight rolling up to the balls of its great bare feet. The ghost of a grin starts on Jory's face, and then he's sinking, falling, Timothy's hands on his ankles, dragging him through, under, an instant before the door—

Before it *should* have slammed shut anyway.

But the handler was already there, its fingers hooked under the door, three or four tons of pressure trying to close it, finish that process. The handler's muscles rippled all along its frame, its extra veins surfacing, even the incomplete ones, its lips drawn back from its teeth in impossible effort.

Jory and Timothy were at the opposite wall in the control room by now, their backs to that wall, Timothy holding Jory down, Jory just watching through the foot-thick plastiglass window in the bulkhead—why a window?—the handler's face there.

"He—he can't—" Jory said, watching the door inch back up.

"He doesn't know he can't," Timothy said, his hand absolutely clamped on Jory's wrist.

And whether Jory would have tried to stand again, to help that handler, loose it on the world in its raw state, none of the fail-safes wired in yet, it doesn't matter.

Two guards crashed through the door, assessing the situation in a flash, sliding on their knees to the bulkhead, to spray bullets underneath for what felt like minutes, finally cutting the handler off at the knees, its face sinking from the window, even when the window jerked lower, the bulkhead locking into the floor at last.

The guards fell back, breathing hard.

The first one turned around, raised his visor.

"So," he said, "which one of you's the—" he started, then flinched back.

The handler was at the window again. Slamming its hands— the fingers just meat under the door now—into the glass so thick it was almost a cube.

"No," the second guard said, reaching to his belt for another magazine, "no, he can't, he can't . . ."

"How long you think he can go on like that?" the first guard said, kind of amazed now too.

"Until we're all dead," Timothy said, when the first impossible crack shot through the glass.

"No!" the second guard said, angling his barrel at that glass, about to spray it, except Jory was close enough to guide that gun down.

"He doesn't understand," Jory said. At which point the guard ripped his gun back, settled it instead between Jory's eyes.

"Whoah, whoah," Timothy said, standing, holding his spidery hands out, the rest of him shaped like a question mark.

It's all recorded.

The way Jory smiled, that barrel leaving a crescent burn against his left eyebrow. His right hand, rising slowly and not threatening, to his side, to a spot on the wall just over Timothy's shoulder.

The second red button.

Because he couldn't see, couldn't turn his head *to* see, Jory found the wall with his fingertips, pressed the button with his thumb, the room going jet-engine hot, instant crematorium.

It's all there if you want to see it.

All except that, on the red of that plastic button, now, there's a faint happy face, from the ink on Jory Gray's thumb.

And then the rest of it happened.

CHAPTER TWO

As for how the plague started, there were nearly as many theories then as there are zombies.

No, correction—there were nearly as many theories as there are people left.

At the height of the plague, the best estimates had six or seven walking dead for every uninfected man, woman and child. That sounds kind of positive when you run the numbers, do the math to figure how many people that meant were left to fight the good fight, have more babies, start things over. Except you can't do the math like that. It wasn't a case of a sixth or seventh of humanity still hiding somewhere, waiting this out, it was a case of each zombie taking down twelve or fifteen citizens, leaving them cracked open in the street, steaming. Moving on to the next one.

And, though these numbers are more of a guess, of those twelve or fifteen victims, usually one would have been an incomplete meal, would rise to join the horde, to get *its* twelve or fifteen meals, and infect one *more* person, bring him or her over to the dead side. The worst game of Red Rover ever, pretty much.

So, taking all that into account, maybe five percent of the

North American population was making it through that first decade. Probably way less.

And of that less than five percent, isolated in clumps all over the map, there was maybe one kid for every fifteen adults. Not because they couldn't run faster, couldn't hide better—they could, they definitely can—but because they get scared of the dark, out there alone. Because they call out for other people, for just another voice. Because they go back for pets, and dolls. Because they don't know how to drive cars, use guns, open cans without a can opener.

Maybe it's better that they went first though. They didn't have to grow up thinking this world was the real world. They didn't have to see the things their moms and dads were having to do to survive.

Not that there were that many moms.

Like Timothy was telling Jory, there was maybe one woman for every five men. It's not that the women were slower or weaker, any of that, but that the majority of women tended to work in places thicker with people. The malls and schools and high-rises that the dead just slit down the side, ate from until their sides burst. Literally.

The men who tended to live were the linemen, out on a call alone, watching a curious plume of smoke thread its way up through the horizon fifty miles away. The truckers, taking a shortcut on some back road they hoped didn't have any scales. The poachers out in their boats, sitting on a bench of stacked alligators. If there were any hang gliders up in the clouds somewhere, they probably lasted a while too, could land out where nobody was, then take off again, and again, until they starved up there, never came down.

You'd think the men-to-women numbers would have all been balanced out by the *im*balance in the military, how male it was, and how the dead just swallowed line after line of troops, overran tanks and transports and everything else we could throw at them, but no. At least as far as base was concerned, Timothy was right—Linse had been the only woman in Jory's housing unit, and each housing unit was eight apartments back to back.

So, yes, Jory had extra locks on the door, a chair under the knob most nights, and a looted pistol by his bed. He'd had to ask a neighbor how to pull the slide back, and then, out on Disposal, he'd tested the gun against a wall, to make sure the neighbor hadn't been lying.

It had kicked in his hand so hard he nearly dropped it.

This is Jory Gray, yes.

He even laughed at himself that day, so don't feel bad. From the least can come the most, right?

And, like everybody, he tuned in to the late-night radio broadcasts as well, to listen to the out-there theories of zombie genesis—okay, at *least* as many theories as there were pirate DJs—but it was just entertainment. Because there was no television anymore, and not enough servers to make a network, and no way to plug into a network anyway.

So you laughed where you could. Jory and Linse would sit in the living room, in chairs that didn't quite touch, their scavenged little radio throwing out theories so outlandish it made them feel like maybe this world was the good one after all. It was better than that other one the DJs were talking about, anyway.

Jory would always be watching Linse too. And he never knew she was looking up the Hill the whole time.

CHAPTER THREE

When the flames died down in the clean room, anything remotely biological burned away, those toxic ashes flushed down the drain, the guards stood, delivered Jory and Timothy to the guards in the hall. They hooked their arms under Jory's arms, their faces stone, and dragged him and Timothy to the showers, for scrubdown.

"Three hundred eighty-eight days without an accident . . ." Jory heard Timothy singsonging from somewhere behind him, and Jory wanted to smile, wanted to be like that, to just be able to take the next thing in stride.

In his former life, Timothy had been an elementary school custodian. Maybe that had conditioned him to deal with messes.

Jory had taught high school biology. There, life was messy, sure, but there were organizing principles. Textbooks with the answers in back, at least.

That was all over. Now you made it up as you went.

But that handler—Jory closed his eyes.

The way the handler had wanted to get out. To get *off* this assembly line.

Jory'd never asked where they came from, but always imagined some max-security lockdown kind of prison way out in the Midwest, or down in Louisiana, or Arkansas, one of those places where the inmates would be especially brutal, hard to kill.

The prison would be tall and grey, Jory knew. A medieval castle, the walls slick-poured concrete, the tops dripping barbed wire. Guard towers, the trees all buzzed down for a half mile all around it, no major highway even close to close.

That kind of place. Where the guards in the breakroom—a hairsbreadth from being inmates themselves—would have seen the first reports of people eating people, of the dead walking the streets, and would have gotten on their internal radio system, shut that mother of a place down. Because it was a prison, one for the worst offenders, locking it down wouldn't take much. Just cutting the phone lines, the shortwave. Pulling the draw-bridge up and keeping it up for the next eight, nine years, until the military came knocking, asking for some men who knew how to use their hands, and maybe weren't afraid to.

The line of volunteers—especially considering what they had to have been eating for years now—would have wrapped all the way around the yard. Not a single one of them expecting that part of this big escape they thought they were making, it was getting a chrome spike to the brain stem. Living for months in a vat. Forgetting your name. Laying down on a wide black belt as a man, getting up a monster, not even able to think for itself.

Once or twice, Jory had seen crude tattoos on the arms of a handler, the ink faded and, now that the arm was juiced to twice its size, the anchor or woman or name all stretched out, smeared.

They were children, though, the handlers. Enormous infants.

In the public demonstrations, the faith sessions—manda-tory on base—Jory had seen the soldiers handling the handlers. Showing how they could drop them to their massive knees with the touch of a button. How they could slap them back and forth, get no response. How they didn't even feel it when a blade cut into the thick meat of their shoulder. The handlers just kneeling there, head down, built to please.

Built by Jory to please.

It had been a step up from Disposal though. From trolling the restricted zones, knocking down any building that looked like it was falling down anyway.

It was good, Disposal, most of the time spent on the truck, really, but there was always the chance of flushing a leftover zombie too. Of not coming home to Linse. Of Linse just sitting there waiting for him to come home.

So he'd taken the promotion to the shiny new factory, learned the procedures. Met Timothy. Probably not even by accident, both of them being from the school system.

The military took everything into account, when it came to handlers.

Everything except pushing one off the belt.

Jory shook his head, half in wonder. What had he been thinking?

In the shower with him and Timothy now were the two guards who'd slid into the clean room on their knees, saved the day.

Jory squinted, went rag doll so his clothes could be peeled off. So the brushes-on-poles could be scraped across his skin.

Beside him, his showerhead already on, already steaming, was Timothy, some amateur inkwork on his back Jory'd never have suspected—tic-tac-toe lines. A grid of blue from scapula to scapula, then a crude handprint on his shoulder, like he'd just been pushed.

The tattoo wasn't about resistance, Jory knew. It was about solidarity. A we-will-never-forget kind of thing, for all the children sacrificed to the plague.

Jory closed his eyes.

"Dudes!" Timothy was saying beside him, to the two guards scrubbing them down. "It's not like—he wasn't even *infected,* right?"

"It," Timothy's scrubber corrected, his voice a dial tone.

"Handlers are inoculated with a nonvirulent strain of the virus," Jory's scrubber recited. The handle of his brush was six feet long.

"Exactly," Timothy said, wincing from the water, ducking the wire brush.

"It's supposed to make them taste bad," Jory's scrubber went on, Jory submitting to the brush. Hoping it would hurt worse, even.

"And you *weren't* inoculated," Timothy's scrubber said to Timothy. "Now turn around."

"But I was, we were, we were holding our breaths the whole time, see? We were—"

"Just shut up," one of the naked guards said, getting the scrubdown as well.

Timothy flashed his eyes up, started to step across to that guard, but Jory stopped this naked fight from happening, turned Timothy around like the scrubber wanted.

"Let it go," he said to Timothy. Both of them leaned against the wall now, legs spread, forearms pillowed between the tile and their foreheads.

"He better hope I don't see him on the street," Timothy mumbled.

"Guy who saved your life, you mean?" the guard said.

"I'm sorry," Jory said then. To Timothy. For all this.

Timothy just smiled his jangly smile.

"She's not coming back, man," he said. "Not from there, not from them. Nobody does. But that doesn't mean you have to kill yourself either. Now, just—" but for a moment he couldn't talk, could only grind his teeth, sway his back in. From the brush. "Yeah, yeah," he called back to his scrubber, "definitely, you're right. I probably *did* get some virus there in the crack of my ass, let me just spread a little, like, yeah, yeah, you mind if I call you Sheila? That work for you?"

Ten more minutes of that, and then the locker room again. Jory and Timothy each shave-headed now, their skin raw and angry.

On each of their locker doors were reassignment slips. Just blank, not filled out.

Timothy crumpled his. "Man," he said, looking sidelong at Jory. "Guess I'll see you in the next life, yeah?"

"Think I want to come back?" Jory said, letting his slip fall. Not saying anything about the razor cut on Timothy's head. A mole or something gone. One thin line of blood, stopping no time soon.

"What say we skip a few, then?" Timothy said. "Get ahead of all this?"

Jory opened his locker door one last time, and by the time he looked up he was in the back seat of a topless jeep, crawling across base.

Is there a pit to throw defective survivors in, he wondered, or do they just get escorted over the fence?

He smiled, covered it with his hand, then forgot he was smiling.

They were in Housing. At the front of Jory's block.

"Five, four, three . . ." the soldier at the wheel was counting. Staring at Jory in the rearview.

"What?" Jory said.

"Oh-seven-hundred," the soldier recited. "Right here."

"Thought I was being reassigned?"

"Oh-seven-hundred," the soldier said again, enunciating very clearly, then let the clutch out so Jory had to plant a hand on the spare tire behind him, vault over the side. Run for a couple of steps, then lose it, the unmaintained asphalt tearing into his knee. But good asphalt would have done just the same.

So.

Home again, home again.

It had to be a trick of some kind.

You don't screw up like Jory did and get a ride home, right?

Oh-seven-hundred, though.

Maybe this was part of the punishment, having to spend the night not knowing what kind of hammer was going to fall.

Definitely that. Jory could already feel it. Like the evil jailer in that old story, telling his prisoner he's going to be executed in the morning of one day next week, he'll know when, when it happens, ha-ha.

Jory was the guy in the cell here. His own living room.

He sat there until dark, smoking cigarettes, no radio, no Linse, no nothing.

At midnight, not able to sleep, coughing up tar, he shouldered a pack—an unopened carton of cigarettes in it—and took a place under the second-to-last light before the gate.

Soon enough, a transport rumbled to a stop. Jory swung his pack around, held the carton up to window level.

Like always, the door opened.

It didn't make base feel any less like a prison.

CHAPTER FOUR

The rest of night for Jory Gray—it's him, walking out past the edges of the history books. No feeds, no secondhand sightings.

What he would tell the jeep driver—not in the least interested—when he dragged ass back to base at 0900 the next morning was that he'd started out just at the canteen. One last night before judgment, all that. But then that canteen turned into another, and another, and finally he was off base, in old downtown, that one lobby-turned-bar with that glass casket on wheels. Inside, a zombie, supposed to be not just first wave, but Typhoid Z itself, Patient Zero. Without labs to run the virus, though, there was no telling.

And the glass around it was shatterproof, of course, and doubled up, and the zombie was shackled, its arms, legs, and the rest of its bones obviously broken, its face burned down to the white, but, like all of them, it wouldn't die. It didn't know how.

For four quarters, if you could find them—galvanized washers worked too, and were worth more—you could grind the steam-paddle-looking wheel around by the wooden handle, send that blue spark into the zombie's shackles. Make him dance.

Jory's story to the driver would be that he'd fed every round piece of metal he had to that zombie, and then gone looking for old pay phones to loot, just to turn that wheel some more.

The driver would just stare ahead, maybe tongue his lower lip out.

Where Jory more likely spent his night—backtracking from later events—was on top of a parking garage Disposal hadn't got to, for lack of big enough equipment.

The parking garage was the kind where you could take the ramp, spiral right angle by right angle up into the sky. Finally get deposited up into those stars. Four stories closer, anyway. Large portions of the concrete retaining wall were crashed through. Maybe this was one of the places people bunched up. Another mall, another elementary school, another bad-idea church.

It never mattered.

This particular parking garage, it was within the new city limits, so was supposed to be virus-free.

That's not why Jory Gray might have been drawn there though.

The parking garage was at the edge of downtown, where the land started to slope up. Where it started to turn into the Hill.

It was as close as he could get to Linse without actually stepping into the light.

For three hundreds yards all around the Church—tall white walls, no windows—the ground was razed. The only things standing were seven thick pillars, holding nothing up. The Weeping Poles. Where, when you were passing by, giving your life to God or whoever, you would pin your most prized possession. The best marker of your former life. What you were leaving behind, forever.

Then, on a schedule—every eight days, like a grace period?—the poles would burn, severing your most important tie to who you'd been.

No matter how hard Jory tried to tunnel his eyes through the night, though, he couldn't make out any detail on the poles. Couldn't zero in on whatever Linse had left.

Maybe just him, sitting up here.

If he could, he'd walk in, trade something for her. Trade everything for her.

But nobody went in there, not even the military. Especially not reassigned assembly line workers, their hands still bloody with the abominations the priests hardly approved of.

Bloody with that, and worse.

That had been the only good thing about the line, really. That, cutting here, inserting this, it existed in the now, didn't bring the past with it like Disposal had. On the line, you could just pretend you were a goldfish, moving from moment to moment. You never had to think about the rest.

At least not until one day you wake up alone in your housing unit.

Jory stared at the Church. Trying to make sense of it all.

Even before the plague, it had been some kind of religious place, Jory had heard.

As long as he could remember, though, it had always just been the priests up there. He'd never even seen one up close. But everybody knew about them. That question of how the plague had happened? They'd changed it just a little. The *how* was immaterial, as far as they were concerned. All that mattered to humanity now, it was why.

This, they could answer.

Man was being punished for his own appetites, his many over-indulgences. It was that easy, and that poetic, at least to the God they pushed. Man's stuffing himself full of material things? So, so what if he had to see, and *live with,* his own worst sin—ceaseless, all-consuming appetite—would he maybe learn his lesson then?

So the plague was punishment, pure and simple. A divine judgment being visited upon the world, a flood to wash away the sinners, open the eyes of the elect.

And, that elect—they all lived at the top of the Hill, behind those tall white walls.

Up there it didn't matter what you'd had to do in your own kitchen on Z Day, the Day of the Dead, the Bloodbath, whatever you called it. It didn't matter if you were trapped in a nursing home when the first wave crashed, and had to cut your way out with a chain saw, and it didn't matter if you were in a day care. The Church could wash all that away.

For a price: the rest of your life.

What Jory had told himself nearly twenty-four hours ago at the kitchen table, smoking half a pack down to the butts and grinding them out on the Formica, was that that had to be why Linse had gone up the Hill.

She was guilty.

Where he'd found her was in the ruins of her own house, trying to dig down into the basement. Back then she was mute, nearly catatonic. Had been living on who-knows-what for who-knows-how-long—Jory never asked. Her eyes were shot a very specific red, that got Disposal's military escort for the day antsy. But Jory had shielded her, taken her hand, brought her back to base. Towards the end she'd even smiled a time or two, he was pretty sure.

The second time it had happened, her maybe-smile, Jory'd had to fake his way into the bathroom, so he wouldn't scare her by crying.

When you smoke enough cigarettes, though, when you sit up in the night and trainsmoke yourself into something not quite bliss, not even close, then you can pretend that your eyes are like this from the smoke.

And nobody's close enough to ask, either.

From a lower level, three tinny radios were on the same station but somehow not in sync. More like a chain of echoes. It was a pirate broadcast, this particular DJ talking about—*whispering* about how what nobody wants you to know is that it was hamburgers that started the plague. Cheeseburgers. Double-meats.

Jory—if he was up on that parking garage at all—studied the cherry of his cigarette, blew it redder. Looked past it to the Weeping Poles. To the Church. He flicked his cigarette out as far as he could. It was a promise he would keep.

DAY TWO

CHAPTER FIVE

Where the driver dropped Jory off was a long, low bunker, one Jory had never even considered. Like the mouth of some huge metal snake, its body underground for eons.

The front doors were thick, deep, tall. Built for cargo.

No, not for cargo. Built for a holocaust. For an apocalypse. For *this*.

"So . . . so I work here now?" Jory said to the driver.

The driver laughed in spite of himself, shook his head in something like thanks to Jory, then chirped his tires, was gone.

"You're the one?" a guard squatting by the door said, studying the curious specimen Jory must be.

Jory didn't answer. It smelled terrible here. Snake breath.

Instead of cranking the huge doors open, the guard shuttled Jory around the side, delivered him to a portable building tacked on to the main structure like an afterthought, the miniblinds a dead giveaway of the office inside. The office *work*.

"I'm not very good at keeping files," Jory said to the guard.

The guard just heaved his arm ahead of them to pull the door open, then didn't say goodbye, good day, good luck, any of the things Jory was wanting to hear.

So.

A waiting room. A real one, from out of the past. Completely out of keeping with the bunker it was tied to.

Jory took a seat, the soldier behind the desk just staring at him.

"Magazines are all kind of out of date," the soldier said.

"I'll be sure not to fill out the subscription card then," Jory said back.

The soldier appreciated this, and the minutes ticked by, Jory trying not to construct a story from the address labels on the magazines—dentists, a woman named Molly, her last name discreetly markered over—finally thumbing up a snapshot of Linse. He'd gone back to her house for it, months ago. Sifted through the ash and ruin, the white leather album it was in mostly gone.

"You can't cut up the magazines," the soldier said in his bored voice, about the snapshot.

Jory pocketed it, one smooth motion, like he'd never been holding anything.

A red light buzzed on the soldier's desk.

"That for me?" Jory said.

"It means you're done," the soldier said. "It means dinner's served."

Jory stood, his heart hammering.

"Any advice?" he asked, moving for the door on the far side of the soldier.

"Say 'sir' every chance you get," the soldier said, and then Jory's hand was at the knob, pausing for a flash too long, the nameplate on the door finally registering: *Scanlon*.

Shit.

Without General Warren Scanlon, humanity might have just gone under with the first wave, never thrashed back to the surface.

Everybody knew that the only thing that finally killed the dead was fire, but Scanlon was the first to start baiting them into the high-rises, then burning them from the ground up. Five hundred and a thousand at a time, falling like torches thrown from a cliff. Scanlon counting them as they fell, his eyes crinkling into a grin.

Tallish, white mustache, jagged scar on his neck, skin leathery from standing in the heat of so many bodies burning, that kind of warhorse.

All he needed was a stubby brown cigar, really.

Jory knew he had captain's quarters on base somewhere, but he'd always just been a rumor. Somebody you say you might have seen, pulling his cover off as he stepped into a building. Somebody who never smiled, because there was nothing to smile about. Because this was war.

Or maybe he never smiled because of the other rumors, about *how* exactly he'd baited those hordes into those high-rises.

He needed his own *church*, really, Jory thought. A legion of priests praying for him around the clock, then more priests praying for those first priests, and maybe even a third ring, just to contain the sin.

If Jory had known his oh-seven-hundred was with Scanlon, he might have been on time. Or just never come back to base at all.

For maybe half a minute after Jory walked in, Scanlon kept reading from whatever folder was on his desk. The only sound the door's piston hissing closed. Jory didn't dare sit down, not without explicit permission.

"Suicide, right?" Scanlon finally said, leaning back now. Angling his head over so Jory's answer could funnel in. "You're the one with the death wish?"

Jory swallowed.

Scanlon cracked his face into a grim semblance of a smile, leaned forward, his elbows on the table so he could steeple his hands under his chin.

"Let me explain. My colonel . . . Roberson. Colonel Roberson here"—the file—"who I don't even think is *alive* anymore, who probably died saving citizens like you from themselves, he tells me he found you up on a, on a water tower, is that right? Nearly ten years ago? He was on recon, I believe. Helicopter? Any of this coming back? Said you'd climbed all the way up just to jump off. That the only way he knew you weren't one of them was the hammer in your hand."

Jory was just staring at a place beside and behind Scanlon.

"Because they don't use tools, Gray," Scanlon finished. "How he knew you weren't a desiccate."

Jory tried to breathe out, couldn't get it done.

That hammer. Spinning down into space.

His heart writhed in his chest. Threatened to come up his throat. Leave him altogether.

But it already had. Ten years ago.

"Sir," Jory managed to get out. Just that.

"But"—Scanlon fake-reading the file open on his desk—"you weren't a carpenter *before,* were you? What were you, son? Just asking, because you *damn* sure aren't any kind of soldier. Not two and half hours late like this. Not in my army."

"What was I?"

"You didn't always fuck up other people's medical assembly lines, did you? Was that even a job, back before the Flood, or was it more like a hobby?"

"Flood?"

"The dam broke, Gray, damn near drowned us all."

"Yes, sir."

"Well?"

"Teacher, sir. Biology. High school."

Scanlon stared at Jory. "Good," he finally said. "We might need some of that again someday."

"Biology?"

Scanlon chuckled. It wasn't pretty. "No, no, son. I believe we've got about all the *biology* we can handle out in the restricted zones, don't you? High school though? Don't have any of that."

"Or kids," Jory added, inflecting it just like an indictment. Half on accident, half not.

Scanlon cocked his head the other way now. As if confirming he'd heard Jory right. That Jory would talk like this, to *him.* On *purpose.*

"My colonel make a mistake, plucking you off that water tower, Gray? Because we can fix that right now, if you want. Put *you* on that table, on that belt. Make you into something useful, something productive. That what you're looking for here, that how you're going to help the cause? You *still* a suicide, Gray? That why you didn't crawl ass under that bulkhead like a sane human being yesterday? I've seen the tapes."

"I'm not—I don't think I'm tall enough, am I? Sir. To be a handler."

"Don't you worry about that."

"That's not what it was anyway."

"That's not what it was, *what*?"

Scanlon stood, to better hear this answer.

"That's not what it was, *sir.* It wasn't suicide, yesterday."

"You saying you can't even do that right? That you're that much of a fuckup?"

There was no good answer. Jory just sucked his cheeks in, his eyes a cool thousand yards off.

"Say we did put you on that belt, Gray," Scanlon went on, "you know how long until you're useful? Four months, son." Holding his old-man fingers out to show. "Four months for each one of those bad boys. And"—coming around the desk—"do you know what it all depends on? On people not bringing their petty little lives to work. Did you know that by the time a handler's ready for service there's more than half a mile of circuitry running through it? And that's aside from the hormones and drugs and chemicals and radiation and grafts and implants and boosters and vaccines and fail-safes and kill switches. None of which are easy to come by these days, I might add. All of which you"—chest tap, chest tap, his index finger blunt—"*incinerated.* Poof, up in smoke, gone. Goodbye."

Jory mumbled that he understood.

Scanlon lifted his chin to let this prime humor back in. Savor it. "I don't think you do, son. Because of your little mishap yesterday, we may very well end up with a whole new plague. All it takes is one, right? Just one hot case out there in general population."

"This one wasn't hot, sir."

"I'm not talking about the handler, Gray. They can't *get* infected. I'm talking about the desiccant that's going to slip his leash now because we're short staffed, are having to push the handlers we have *left* harder than they can take. If you'd pulled your little stunt a year into the program, well then, we might have some reserves. Some back stock, something in cold storage. As it is, though, we can't roll them off the line fast enough to keep up. Unlike the desiccates. Their manufacture is . . . significantly more efficient, you could say. Like fucking wildfire."

Scanlon stopped, studied Jory again. "Know how old the oldest handler in the field is now?" he said.

Jory did, but didn't think he should say.

"Two months," Scanlon filled in, holding his old-man fingers up again. "And that's just the showroom model we had to recommission. Which is what makes what happened yesterday in your clean room especially . . . what's the word?"

Scanlon stepped away, his hands together behind his back.

"Tragic?" Jory said.

"Unforgivable," Scanlon corrected, and chuckled in his chest, shook his head. "Now," he went on, "infractions at your level aren't something I bother to step on, even when they're on the way to the can. Except when they're this *egregious*. That a biology word?" Scanlon laughed at his own joke. "You're my special case of the day though. Getting the personal touch, as it were. God reaching down to Adam, all that. Reaching down and asking why the *hell* didn't he crawl under that door faster, at least *pretend* he wanted to live?"

It was the second time he'd asked—the real reason for the face-to-face, Jory was pretty sure, so Scanlon could understand what he'd seen on the recording—but there still weren't any good words for why he hadn't left when he should have. It had to do with the way a dad or mom will stand by a lost kid at the mall, waiting for the kid's parents to show back up.

Except, here, the kid was an unholy killing machine, born and built.

Maybe "death wish" really was the best way to say it.

"I know, I know," Scanlon answered for Jory when it was obvious Jory wasn't going to come up with anything, "you hate this place, miss your whoever, can't take it anymore." He shook his head as if disappointed. "And here I thought you might be interesting, have some steel to you, some David against Goliath. Just another civilian though, right? Another ant. Worker bee. Drone."

Jory lifted his right shoulder in response, completed Scanlon's list with, "Zombie."

Scanlon chuckled, had to look far, far away.

"So," he said, bored with this now, "what do you think might be adequate discipline for your mistake? Aside from the world dying all over again, I mean."

"Sir?"

"It's easy, son. Your live-in charity case chose eternal salvation over you, so you decided to come to work with a broken heart, destroy four months of concentrated effort. Every action has an equal and suck-ass reaction, Gray. You ever teach your students that?"

"That's physics. Sir."

"Well let me put this in biology terms then. Big fish, they eat the *shit* out of the little fish. Day in, day out. And you're square in my pond now, son. So what kind of hell do you think I should rain down on you?"

"Other than the hell of the past ten years?"

"Yeah. Other than the last nine years, eleven months and twenty-seven days, Gray. If you want to split hairs."

"Banishment," Jory said. "Exile. Drop me off in a hot zone."

"So you can get infected, take advantage of some weakness in the fences part of your brain somehow remembers? No thanks. Think a little less melodramatic, if you can."

"Demotion then. Sir." Jory said then, "Just for me. Timothy, he had nothing to—"

"Demotion to what? There something lower than making the same cut in the same damn strip of meat day after day, for the rest of your life?"

Jory bit his lip now, on the inside. To keep it there. And then said it the hell anyway. "Runner, sir. *Bait.* You are still doing that, right? Out there somewhere?"

Jory pictured the waiting-room soldier, listening. Holding his breath, his eyes wide, impressed.

Scanlon's other name, the one nobody else would ever call

him to his face, was Triple Threat. It stood for the three *T*s of tic-tac-toe, like Timothy's homemade tattoo. It's what Scanlon was supposed to have played, with a razor, on the backs of hundreds of runners, in order to get the scent of blood up into the air. Turn the dead on to them.

Hundreds of runners who never got to confirm or deny these *X*s and *O*s. How deep they were or weren't cut.

Children, if the stories were true.

Scanlon leaned back in his chair, his hands a steeple again, and something like a laugh shuddered through his frame. Mostly his shoulders. Not at all in his eyes.

"What do you think you know about any of that?" he said to Jory.

"Guess I'm not young enough anyway, am I?" Jory said. Just loud enough. For three, maybe four hundred dead kids to hear. To stop what they were doing and look around, wait for Scanlon's response.

The whole world was waiting, really.

Not even one muscle in Scanlon's face gave him away. What he had or hadn't done.

"Were their mothers really up there, at the tops of those buildings?" Jory said then. "Sir?"

Scanlon leaned back, had no choice but to shake his head in wonder, it looked like.

"You may turn up interesting after all," he said. "If they *had* been up there, would that make it all right with you, son?"

Jory assumed he was about to die. And he assumed that would be a good thing.

"Roberson had it right the first time, didn't he?" Scanlon said then, leaning down to Jory's file again. "You are a walking suicide. It's what you're asking for right now, isn't it? Not to be here anymore? World not living up to your expectations, that it?"

"Sir."

"Know what? You want to throw your life away so bad, I've got just the ticket."

"Sir?"

"Poetic, even," writing with flourish on Jory's file. "You can gain an intimate understanding of how important one of these new handlers is to our cause. To our *survival*. How important each one is to the creation and maintenance of this grand social experiment. A tour through the real world, such as it is. And *then* come here, question my actions. Does that work for you? The ones that allow you to be standing here in the first place, I mean. This all acceptable to you, Gray?"

"I'm not field rated, sir."

"You are now. Class four, graverobber."

"Preburial?" Jory said, maybe grinning just a little. "I've lived all this time to—to end up in J Barracks?"

"We're all getting processed down to J sooner or later, son," Scanlon said. "Like it or not."

Jory nodded, kept nodding. Just to keep the vomit down, his voice steady, or close enough. "I a driver, a torch, or the dead guy?" he said, though he already knew the life cycle of J Barracks.

"Humor, yes," Scanlon said, huffing air out his nose. "Make it through twelve calls holding a torch, and you graduate to driver, how's that?"

"Otherwise I'm the dead guy."

"You already are the dead guy, Gray. Now get the hell out of my office. I'm trying to save the world here."

Jory dipped his forehead to this, a gesture he didn't remember ever having made before. But it felt right—you bow to the person who's just killed you, don't you? Does that get you your soul back?

The air was syrup. The carpet, tar.

"A father," he said at last, somewhere in the twenty minutes it felt like it was taking him to get to the door.

"Son?"

"You asked what I used to be. Before. A father, sir. Just so you know who you're sending out there. A father, for eleven years."

"Good, good. Take that, use it in the field. Think of this assignment, think of it like when you started to jump off that building—"

"Water tower."

"Think of it like, when you jumped, we caught you. Held you by the hand for nearly ten years. But now it's time to let go, son. See if you can fly or not."

"And what if I do?"

"I honestly hope you do, Gray. Lord knows we need something."

How far Jory made it before he collapsed was through the waiting room, down the ramp, and around the corner of the portable, under the window unit.

Not throwing up like he wanted to, like he needed to, but leaned over, just in case. Leaned over on one hand, his left. Because his right—

With his right hand, he fumbled up the snap of Linse, to anchor him, but instead—no no no—instead it was the hammer. Matted with hair, matted with blood.

And then his stomach did empty itself.

It didn't help.

CHAPTER SIX

So.

Jory had used a hammer, those ten years ago.

Like all of us. Like every single one of us.

This is important.

Nobody lived through the plague by just running away. At some point in the chase you got backed into a corner, got sniffed out hiding in the cooler at the grocery store, got heard knocking wrenches down in the pit at the lube shop around the corner.

Or, like Jory, you were trying to get an oversized eyehole screw into the fence in the backyard, not even sure if this was your fence or your neighbor's—the screw was supposed to go deep enough into the post to hang the hammock he'd gotten for Christmas, but it had been too cold to give it a test run until now—and then something clicked in your mind. In his.

The mail.

The whole day, he'd been sad in a stupid kind of way that there would be no mail. But it wasn't a federal holiday. It was just another Friday. Only, for his district, a snow day they still had to burn.

The mail *was* coming. And, because his wife was at work, he'd get to get it himself. Could even let it sit in the box a while *before* getting it, if he wanted.

Jory smiled, twisted the eyehole screw one more time, waiting for the dry wood of either his or his neighbor's fence to split. He'd been using the screwdriver, its shaft ran up through the eyehole, but then the wood had started creaking, he'd squinted in response, held his breath, turned a smidge more—the usual home-repair story.

The hammer, it was just hanging by its claw on the top of the fence. It hadn't been necessary at all.

And the mail—why was Jory thinking of the mail?

Of course.

At some level he'd registered that faded post-office blue, flashing between the houses up the street. Danny, the same as it had been Danny for the last two years.

Except, you always *heard* Danny first, right? His rattletrap little postal van thing.

It was sunny, though, the first hot day.

Maybe Danny was taking advantage too.

Neither snow nor sleet nor rain, right? Nor a perfect day either.

The last perfect day, as it turned out.

Jory gave the eyehole screw another last twist, just for good measure, and that was when he heard the first scream.

At first it could have been the dry wood, complaining, but then, when he wasn't twisting, the scream came again, got cut off.

"Hunh," Jory said, and looked over his shoulder, across into his other neighbor's yard, to see if there was anybody to visually confer with about this.

Nope.

It was a Friday, a workday.

Jory shrugged, hooked his index finger into the hook and pulled, giving it gradually more and more weight, trying to keep half an eye on the fence line, to see if it was swaying in.

And then he saw it again—that flash of postal blue, just one house over.

A siren blaring across town now.

Jory unhooked his finger. He studied his house for any movement—any small face behind the glass, asking him if everything was okay.

He didn't know if it was. Not yet.

And she'd go to the front door anyway, wouldn't she? Hadn't he said he was going to work on the flowerbeds, then found the hammock there with the garden tools, decided it was fate, that this day had actually been *designed* for him to hang it in the backyard?

"Danny?" he said. Mostly to himself.

On cue, that postal blue darted across the front end of the fence line. Moving from next door to Jory's. Running on all *fours* from next door to Jory's, its movements so slick, so graceful, so focused.

Human, but not. Not even close.

Jory fell back into the new red mulch spread in a circle around the tree that was going to have been the foot tie for his hammock, if the fence held.

"Danny?" he said again, much quieter. Much louder in his head.

And then a scream from his own front yard and Jory was scrambling up, falling uphill, a new hollowness in his chest. Not even aware of the hammer in his hand until, in the upstairs hall ten minutes later, he needed it.

CHAPTER SEVEN

Because he didn't know where else to go, that night Jory went back to the parking garage. His plans were unspecific. Just to be close to her maybe. In case she walked along the balustrade up there, or rampart, whatever it's called when the fort's a church.

To be close to her and to smoke a lot of cigarettes. To look at each one as if it were a new thing. Study its silhouette, taste its roundness.

J Barracks.

"I'm going to be a torch," he told Linse, across all that distance.

A torch.

It was a joke.

He might as well just step off the parking garage, four levels up. See if he could land on a mattress two guys happened to be carrying from one doorway to another. His chances in the field were just about as good. *Preburial* was the absolute right name for this assignment, yes.

At least it would be fast. That was something. In the postapocalypse, Jory guessed, you take what you can get. The toilet paper still in its crumbly plastic, that you hide for two weeks, ration out. That tube of face moisturizer you smuggle back onto base, leave behind the medicine cabinet mirror to make somebody's day. The wine cellar you fall into, don't tell anybody about.

The fact that your death is going to be a fireball, not a feast.

Jory tossed another butt over the edge and tracked its descent, the orange sparks crumbling into the night.

"Very melodramatic," Jory said to Scanlon. To the idea of Scanlon, standing behind him.

There were worse things you found out in the field though.

Mummy families sealed into a room so well you have to break in, and then spend the rest of the day caught between a running apology in your head and a guilty sense of jealousy.

At least the radios up on the parking garage were all off tonight, for whatever reason. DJ holiday, Jory told himself. Big DJ party across town. DJ wake, DJ funeral, DJ wedding.

More likely there'd been a raid, or a battery had failed. Or there was nothing left to say.

Jory cupped a new cigarette close, sparked it alive. Stared through the smoke, very dramatically, at the Church. Flicked his cigarette over the edge long before it was a butt.

Five minutes later and four stories down, the cherry of that cigarette still glowing, Jory ground it out under his boot, was still studying the high Church walls. Like gauging them.

In his belt was the pistol he'd looted, the pistol he'd taken from a living room where one skull had a hole in each temple, where the other, slightly smaller skull had a small hole directly in back, a larger one where the eyes had once been.

Again his plans were unspecific.

But he was already dead, right?

Jory shook another cigarette up, not sure if it was a firing-line smoke or not.

It lit on the second roll of the wheel, and in its wavy nimbus of light was one of the Weeping Poles.

Jory breathed in again, brighter, and looked behind him.

This was the pole you passed if you were coming from base, most likely. If you'd started walking just before dawn, no duffel over your shoulder, no shoes on your feet, no carton of cigarettes to catch a ride through the gate because, if you're wearing white all over, the guards know where you're going. That they're not going to have to let you back in.

Jory'd seen the penitent walk through base before, seen them drift out of one life, into another, the guards averting their eyes, the trucks idling behind, waiting too.

Everybody waiting. This holy walk.

Jory blew smoke at the pole.

When it cleared, there was just the usual torn-out pieces of maps—hometowns, probably—the curled-at-the-edges photographs, the medals and the earrings and the pages of books, the car keys people had held on to for nearly a decade. The dog tags.

Mostly dog tags. At least on this pole.

Not for pets, but for soldiers who never came back. Or who came back dead. Who came back hungry.

Jory rubbed the heel of his hand into the exact center of his forehead. Closed his eyes. Said her name into his chest. Told himself he wasn't blubbering. That his lips were steady. That his voice wasn't breaking, wasn't broken.

When he could see through the blear again, he checked over both shoulders, ran his eyes along the skyline, along the silhouette of the Church walls.

He was alone.

Jory found Linse almost immediately. What she'd left was still close to the surface—her ID card, tacked up with an earring stud. The one you had to have to live on base.

Jory slipped the ID into his pocket, looked up the Hill.

"You did it," he said to her. "You really did it." Then, quieter, sucking his cigarette bright, "Good for you."

When he finally turned his back and shuffled off, twin lung-fuls of smoke trailing around his head, his cigarette was clamped under a rusted staple, the cherry pointed down but smoldering, climbing, catching, the whole pole flaring up minutes later, a candle in the night, novitiates spilling down from the Church with buckets of water, but it was already too late.

This is Jory Gray.

DAY THREE

CHAPTER EIGHT

Because he hadn't had the nerve to use the looted pistol on himself, and because the cigarettes were taking forever—before the plague, he'd been down to a pack a month during the semester—Jory made it to training at 0900, in some Quonset-hut hangar kind of building way out by the fence.

He was one of fifteen burnouts milling around, flicking their eyes to all the dark places in the warehouse.

Jory, his hands working on automatic, pinched a cigarette up to his lips.

Before he could light it, a hand came around, pulled it from his mouth. Crumbled it.

The other fourteen burnouts were watching now. Half smiling.

Jory turned, beheld their drill sergeant. Their Scanlon-in-waiting.

"What?" Jory said, licking his lips where the paper had been.

The drill sergeant—*Voss* above his pocket, in handsewn thread—stepped around, moving at all right angles, like this was a dance, and squared off in front of Jory.

"What, what?" he bellowed, somehow in a speaking voice.

"What, sir," Jory mumbled.

Voss laughed to himself, the sound roiling up from his barrel chest, his lantern jaw. His polished boots. Then he looked around at the sorry state of this batch of recruits and lost his chuckle.

Cueing in, eight of the nine who were already smoking dropped their butts to the slick concrete, ground them out. The ninth, the youngest reprobate of them all, just stashed his.

"Well," Voss said, turning so that it was for everybody, "one or two of you might live to the end of the week yet, taking into account this is Thursday, of course. You"—singling out a wiry dude—"what do you think happens when a spark from one of these bad habits drops down between the frame and the compression tank of your torch?"

"Sir?"

"Just take a flyer. An educated guess. Insofar as that might apply to you."

"Boom."

"Boom, yes." To all again, "The torches each of you will be issued, their reservoirs, when full, have enough jelly in them for sixteen hours at full throttle. Sixteen hours wide open, not counting the autocool. Let me say that again now. Sixteen *hours*. In a can the size of your hand. Now tell me"—in Jory's face again—"your nicotine fix, is it worth turning the building you're in into a mushroom cloud?"

Before Jory could answer, Voss was spinning on his heel to face the rest of the class. "And it's not you I'm worried about here, don't get me wrong. And it's not the torch either. What—what is it that you think I'm worried about here? And don't say the dezzie."

This last part to the reprobate who hadn't crushed his cigarette, but had rubbed the heat out instead, threaded it behind his ear.

Voss was very aware of that cigarette.

The reprobate smiled with half his mouth, looked to the class, and shrugged. "You coming into the field with us, then, sir?"

Silence. Dead, dead silence.

Voss reached up, gingerly plucked the cigarette from behind the reprobate's ear, then crushed it into the reprobate's forehead, the tobacco flakes catching in the reprobate's eyelashes so he finally had no choice but to blink, lose their important little staring contest.

"You're in the right place, son," Voss said to him, *just* to him, then turned, targeted another burnout. "You, Glasses. If you blow your torch up, take the whole room out, who are we going to miss?"

"The handler. Sir. Even if the explosion doesn't kill it, we can't use it again, because some of its safeties might have been compromised in the concussion wave."

"Good, good. Yes. Did we all hear that now? The *handler* is who we'll miss. Now, do any of you know how much work goes into building these insults to nature?"

Voss was speaking right to Jory again. Close enough for little flecks of cold alien spit to be on Jory's lips now.

"Four months," Jory answered.

The reprobate snickered. Looked away.

Voss nodded, kept nodding. "Four months and more dollars than any of us would ever see, if dollars still existed. Which isn't to say you can't be charged for one of them, am I right?"

Again, he was speaking to Jory.

Jory just stared back at him.

Voss nodded, liked it. He turned, surveyed the group again. "Now, I'm going to need somebody to be dead here. Wait, I know, I know, you."

The reprobate.

"Not a short-finger, boss," he said, waggling his fingers to show.

Half the fingers snipped away was how you could tell an enlisted zombie from a regular infected. Not that they knew the difference.

"We can fix that right here," Voss said, unsheathing a short utility blade from his belt.

He slashed forward with it, angled it against the back of the reprobate's neck, guided him down to the concrete none too gently.

"Yeah, that's about perfect," he said, placing his boot between the reprobate's shoulder blades, flipping his knife back into his own belt. "Consider it practice for the show, why don't you?" With his knife hand, then, he pulled a black silk hood from his rear pocket. "Now, I know most of you haven't seen one yet, except maybe in your nightmares, but do we have a handler in the house?"

A commando-looking farm boy took one official step out, his right eye swelled shut from whatever had gotten him on this detail. Voss had to look up to see that shiner though. And then look up some more.

He smiled, threw the hood into this commando's chest.

"Good, good. You'll do fine, son. All we need now's a dezzie to—"

"That'd be me, sir."

Everyone craned around to the wiry dude, waggling his arm in the air, a coil of homemade Zs tattooed up from his wrist, and coming out the collar of his shirt, a ward against the plague maybe. Or camo.

Before Voss could say yes or no, the wiry dude was on all fours by Commando's leg. Panting like a dog. Lunging in place. Snarling.

64

THE GOSPEL OF Z

Hesitantly, Commando lowered his hand to the wiry dude's shirt collar. The make-do handler and his eager zombie dog.

Voss shook his head in wonder. Maybe disgust. Then he turned around to address the rest again, "Now, since, as you all know, the Church has asserted what it takes to be its God-given—"

"We need one of those too, don't we?" a punk said, casting his eyes around for support. Finding none.

"A god?" a bald recruit with a fishnet on his head said, smiling around it.

"A priest, yes," Voss said, staring Fishnet down. "I was just getting to that."

Jory laughed in his mouth, keeping his lips as slack as he could.

Voss turned to him, stepped in. He licked his thumb, an especially slimy, string-hanging lick, and pressed that wetness into Jory's forehead.

"A volunteer, good," Voss said. "There, you're ordained. Now stand there and be condescending, think you can handle that?" Spinning back around, pacing. "As I was *saying,* since the Church has asserted itself into what should be military operations for the good of all mankind, since they put their noses into it last year, we can no longer just cremate any dead we find, contain the potential infection the obvious-ass way that's been saving our asses for ten years now. No. They're pansies, gentlemen. They want to *bury* them now, if they're dead. 'Honor their remains,' 'Get back to the normal cycle of life,' all that. But, of course, how can we know which stiffs are going to come climbing back *out* of that grave, right?"

Glasses: "Send a tissue sample to the lab. Sir."

"Sure," Voss came back, "if you want to wait two weeks. In which time PFC Ass Hat here has reanimated and bitten thirteen people on the face. Let me ask this another way, geniuses. Why have the dead been such a thorn in our side these last ten years?"

"More like a rhinoceros in our side," the reprobate said, from the ground. Not hiding his smile very well at all.

"Nine years, eleven months," Jory said to himself.

Voss pretended not to be hearing any of this. But it was definitely taking some effort.

"You, Glasses. Go."

"Because their species has no built-in mechanism for population control. Sir. They're locusts. They ravage their environment down to a nub. Actually, there are theories that we all carry the Z gene, that when there gets to be too many—"

"Okay, okay, this is fill-in-the-blank, not essay."

"The dead don't eat their own kind," Jory said, before Glasses could continue. "If they did, that would be their population control mechanism."

"Cannibalism," Glasses chimed in.

"Yes, the first taboo," Voss said, making his point. "Cannibalism. So I'm not the only one here who read the training manuals. Or lives in this world."

"Second, really," Jory said, to Voss's back. Which then became his front.

"Excuse me, Father Smartass?"

"The second taboo is cannibalism. Sir. The first, it's incest. With zombies it's the same thing though, eating and sex. They do both with their mouth."

"He's right, sir," Glasses said.

"Jesus Mary and *Joseph*," Voss said, punctuating it with his feet. "Well, can a six thousand degree plasma firestorm still *kill* them, you think, and not leave anything infectious for somebody to step on?"

Feeble nods all around.

"Good, good," Voss said, exasperated. "So glad it's all right with you. Thank you. Now, if we're all through showing off our big brains, is everybody *simpatico* with learning what it is that you're supposed to do here to *keep* your brains from getting eaten?"

"'Simpatico'?" the punk mouthed to himself, squinting to try to track the word down, Fishnet mumbling about how they don't just eat brains, Jory looking past all this for a moment, to the far wall. A guy there, just real casual. Making a pistol of his hand, putting it into his own mouth—his answer to how to keep your brains from getting eaten, maybe?

"Well?" Voss said, cueing in himself to Jory's inattention.

"Yes," Jory said, coming back. "Yes, fire can still kill them."

"Well, with our Father's blessing here, then," Voss said, and walked them through the demonstration—the commando leading the zombie-on-a-leash to the 'dead' reprobate on the floor, the zombie sniffing, and, if he starts to take a bite, meaning the corpse is clean, uninfected, then the handler jerking the zombie back, denying him that one bite that *would* infect the corpse.

"And," Voss went on, "if dezzie here *isn't* interested—happens more than you'd expect lately—then that's when it gets fun, right? When you get to earn your bed and board, ladies."

Jory looked up to the guy standing against the far wall. Still just watching.

Voss hauled an old leaf blower up, crenellated red paper taped to its nozzle.

"This is where you do what you do," he said, and yanked the pull cord, fired the leaf blower up. Voss directed the paper flames down onto the reprobate, sweeping them back and forth three times, slowly. "Ten count plus two. Eight's supposed to be plenty, according to specs, but we aren't taking any chances, right?"

"Why not just muzzle them then?" the punk asked, more just out loud than *to* Voss. But Voss spun on him anyway, clamped the punk's neck in one hand and pinched his nose shut with the other.

"Open, open," he said, and finally the punk parted his lips. At which point Voss hawked something vile up, spit it into the punk's mouth, pushed up on his chin. "What'd I have for lunch, private?" he said then. For everybody.

Instead of answering, the punk threw up through Voss's fingers.

Voss hauled him up by the hair. *"What did I eat?"* he said.

"Something with . . . pepper," the punk got out.

"Exactly," Voss said, and pushed the punk away. "Smell *and* taste, pukes. Cut off the dezzies' airflow, their olfactory system's compromised. What, you don't think we thought of this? Pulling their teeth, sewing their lips shut, anything instead of building these, these handlers, they're calling them, these—"

"Abominations," Commando said, having to concentrate to recite this complicated word, and lift his hood to get it out.

Voss nodded *yes, that—abomination.*

"But what if he does bite me anyway?" the reprobate said, the paper flames in his face. "In spite of all these, um, these heroics?"

"As far as we know, the virus needs a beating heart to circulate it," Voss said. "So you should be okay, so long as you don't get bit *in* the heart. But, like I said, we're not taking any chances, are we? Assume infection, burn it off the face of the earth. Good question. Now, heaven forbid, but if the dezzie"—guiding Jory-the-priest's hand across to the wiry dude's undead mouth—"happens to infect somebody *living,* then how long until that person dies and reanimates?"

"But they can't get it, they can't turn," Fishnet said, like a question.

THE GOSPEL OF Z

"Excuse me?" Voss said back, his voice dripping with insult.

"The priests, they—"

"They're human, son. Don't believe the hype."

"But the video," Fishnet said, his eyes all imploring at Glasses, "in the video—"

"This is the army, everybody got that? We don't have Sundays here, when we can believe whatever we want. Until we know otherwise, if you walk on two feet, you can be turned."

"Like . . . monkeys?" somebody said, his dimples giving him away.

"Kangaroos," somebody else whispered.

"Ostriches," the reprobate tossed in.

"*People!*" Voss yelled, throwing his leaf blower away hard enough that, at the end of its long, shardy skid, there was silence again. Just Voss's own exasperated breathing. Then he came down, came down some more. "Okay. Okay. Now. If Father Smartass gets his ass bit, how long until he reanimates?"

Commando shrugged a guilty shrug, said, "Took my—took her four days."

"You *waited?*" the punk said, still wiping at his mouth.

"I thought she was—that she could—"

Voss interrupted, "Re-an's been clocked at thirty-seven seconds, private. And, yes, that includes the dying. So, torches, if somebody gets bitten, does that mean you have time to inspect the wound, call back to base for a decision?"

"Ten count," Glasses said. "Plus two." Pulling his hand away from the wiry dude, snapping at him.

"Good point," Voss said, stepping into this near miss. "Should you yourself become infected, and not have the balls to torch yourself—and you won't, nobody ever does—then your driver, stationed outside, he'll have no choice but to code the scene. Handler, priest, fancy gun and all." Voss mimed a missile whistling in over his shoulder, exploding at his feet. Another mushroom cloud. Then he smiled. "Even if he just *suspects* something irregular's going down, I mean, then"— tapping his fingers on some imaginary keypad, launching another missile. "Constant contact, ladies"—touching his own ear. "Your voice, it's how your driver knows you're not infected, right? How he knows you're still human. Otherwise, he's all that's standing between you and another plague. Easy decision there."

The guy against the wall across the warehouse seemed amused by this.

"Shouldn't I have a knife?" Jory said.

Voss turned to him. "Yes, if you were a real boneface, you'd have one of their Church-issue KA-BARs. To"—taking a knee beside the reprobate, guiding him down to prone again, none too delicately—"to open the body up, let the decomp really waft out. Dezzie loves that shit."

Commando cut his eyes back and forth, from the wiry dude to Voss. "But, but what if it gets away, sir? Gets free."

"The handlers never let them go," Fishnet answered, looking to Voss for confirmation.

"Handlers don't know *how* to let go, son," Voss said to Commando.

"And they're really immune to the virus?" Glasses asked.

"Don't believe that," Voss said, not turning around to Glasses this time. "Like I was saying, *no one's* immune to the virus. Handler's systems are intentionally polluted though. Hormones, chemicals, radiation, juice, AC, DC. There's not enough room for the virus to take hold. Everything in them's already spoken for. Their dance card's full."

The reprobate, sitting up again, his arms looped over his bent knees, chuckled, no real mirth there at all. "Hell yes," he

THE GOSPEL OF Z

said. "What could be safer than walking into a room out in a hot zone, a room with a, a probably infected dead guy, some Halloween priest with a crazy knife, a zombie that hasn't been fed in weeks, and a pro-wrestler on hallucinogenic steroids?"

"Said the dead guy," Voss added.

"He's got a point, sir," Glasses said.

Voss looked up to the ceiling. For patience, tolerance, serenity. "And none of you have a *choice.* Show of hands. Who volunteered here?" No one. "Thought so. But, yes, consider this assignment your death sentence, kiddos. It's why we invest such a rigorous afternoon-training session in you. Because you're worth it, each and every one of you. Because you're all going to be back to teach this class with me someday. Now, any questions?"

Punk: "So—so what's the third taboo, then?"

Voss: "Class dismissed."

"Suicide," Jory answered. Watching the place on the wall where the smiley guy had been standing.

CHAPTER NINE

The video Fishnet had been talking about—you wouldn't say it had gone viral. Not just because that word had a whole different charge after the plague, but because when the grid went down in the first wave, got propped up again just to get swatted down again the next year, and the next, it took the Net with it.

Communications blackout. Ham radio operators, these unexpected heroes, the only ones able to whisper into the void, maybe get a voice back.

Always the same questions though:

Where are you?

How many of you are there?

Is the army coming?

Do you have food? Water?

Have they found a cure yet?

Is this really happening?

Have you seen a boy, about fourteen, kind of carries himself like a second-string weakside tackle—

The real literature of humanity, it wasn't in the sixteenth century, it didn't happen in the twentieth. It was nearly ten years ago. It was these radio operators blockaded in their attics, knowing full well they were about to starve, about to be eaten.

It was these radio operators, delirious with life, halfway dead, telling stories about cruise ships moving from port to port to pick up the uninfected. Telling people the stories the people needed worse than air.

But the army was never coming, and nobody had food, and there was no cure, and there weren't going to be any more football games. This was really happening. All over the world.

And into the middle of all that came one grainy recording, passed hand to hand on whatever media there was, and finally just going oral, becoming a story everybody knew had to be true, because they'd heard it nearly the same so many times.

It goes like this:

Used to—this would have been about two years in—we had holding pens. These epic corrals that went for acres and acres.

Packed behind those tall walls—the dead.

Because they were our mothers, our brothers, our wives and our husbands. Because it wasn't their fault.

That was the propaganda anyway. That there were labcoats toiling away at a vaccine somewhere. That that vaccine could be grandfathered into the horde.

Wrong.

There *were* labcoats toiling away with the virus, but not to cure it. The idea was to engineer some retro affair that could hitch a ride on the *Z* bug, end the whole plague, and all its carriers.

And, according to the pirate DJs—and they make sense— good old planet Earth wasn't going to be taking too many more nuclear strikes before it would just huddle into a long winter, wait this infection out. The last resort in the first wave—it had been to nuke Manhattan, to make a crater out of LA, to sink Miami and San Francisco into the sea, to burn Houston down over and over, until it wouldn't *stop* burning.

It was never enough though.

What was needed, what was finally *done*, was to herd and bait as many of the dead as possible into the most parched pieces of land they could find, and then sacrifice that land with a serious missile.

It's what finally ended the first wave. For about six months.

But, of course, if even *one* crawls away from that radiation, if even one didn't get herded up in the first place, then—isn't that how the plague started in the first place? With just one Typhoid Z? As far as the pirate DJs were concerned, after the first wave, each wave after that's been the direct result of the labcoats doing Nazi experiments on the dead, and then some clean room getting compromised, some tech forgetting to strap a wrist down tight enough.

It's got to be a lie though.

If it's not, then the Church is right, and we deserve all this.

And, as for that famous recording Fishnet was talking about, like most of us, Jory had never even seen it. The story he'd heard was enough though. A version of what we all knew—what, when we told it, we didn't use our whole voice for. Just the reverent part.

It's those sprawling zombie pens from the second year.

It's these three tall priests on a security camera.

They're standing at one of the gates in the wall, the ones that fry anything that touches it. Twice-dead corpses stacked waist-deep around it, because they don't learn.

Wading through this, let in by some true believer of a guard, come these three spindly priests, walking in what looks like a ritual triangle, an arrowhead pointed into the writhing mass of the dead. It's like they're going to sacrifice themselves, like they've chosen to trade their lives for the rest of ours. They've got that kind of serenity, that kind of purpose, that kind of resolve, their eyes set not on this world, but the next.

Except—except when they walk into that snarling darkness, another security camera picking them up, the dead are *parting* for them.

The three priests here, they're so tall, so thin, so white, their ceramic masks giving nothing away. Their long fingers extending to each side, to brush the heads of these zombies, these—to them—children.

And then, with maybe a mile left to cross, the security camera loses them.

But you know they made it to the other gate.

No doubt at all.

After Jory had the story whispered to him during break, out on Disposal one day, he carried it with him for nearly a week, checking it from all the angles, replaying it, and then, one radio-free night, just Linse on the couch, him in his chair, the door locked, he told it to her, a grin in his eyes the whole time because only a fool would believe this, right?

At first he didn't even think she was tuned in.

The same way he'd once looked up, thought the mail was coming.

Behind the medicine cabinet mirror in their bathroom were the tubes of moisturizer and face cream and makeup he'd been spiriting home for days.

None of it had been touched.

CHAPTER TEN

For too long after training that day, Voss's bellow still ringing behind his eyes, those paper flames roaring, Jory stood in the doorway of his housing unit. Waiting for that fabric scrape of slippers, coming up the worn-flat carpet in the hall.

It was just him though.

He touched his fingertips to the wall just above the light switch and balanced there, the night pressing in behind him.

He still couldn't get her name out of his head.

He tried to laugh at himself. At how stupid he was being.

It didn't help.

In the kitchen minutes later—pure willpower—he held the back of his fingers to the coffeepot, then unplugged it, went around the apartment unplugging everything, ended up breathing hard behind the couch. The front door just yawning there at the end of the hall.

Had it really only been three days? Seventy-two hours.

But still.

Jory felt around in his head again for that reset button, was standing in the open doorway of J Barracks twenty minutes later, a bag over his shoulder.

Inside was radio chatter, card games, the edge of a knife being drawn across a whetstone.

The punk—it was the grown-out blue mohawk, black at the roots now, but it was the sneer too—was the first to look up.

"Thought you had housing, kimo?" he said.

"It's haunted," Jory told him.

"Whoa, whoa," the wiry dude said, coming up all at once from his bunk, holding his hands out for silence. The reprobate's knife scraped to a stop. Fishnet reached for the volume knob on the radio but The wiry shook his head no-no, then an evil grin spread across his face. *Lab wars*," he said, the idea sounding better, now that it was out loud. "Everybody in? New guy?"

Commando looked from his hand of cards to Jory, like Jory had brought this in with him.

"Battle of the AM bands . . ." Glasses explained, not so much folding his hand as laying it down, faceup.

The reprobate chuckled, drew his edge along the stone again, wiped the grey dust on his shirt front. "It's educational," he said, pulling his lips away from the word.

"It's where you weigh the merits of disparate theories of zombie genesis," Glasses went on, "and whoever can tune in to their theory first wins."

"And I'm the tuner," the wiry dude cut in. "Cool? Totally random, man. First signal that dials up."

"For real?" Jory said.

"Got a TV, a video game, a blow-up doll?" Fishnet asked.

Jory shrugged his bag off, had nowhere to sit.

"I think it's locusts, like he said," Commando started, nodding to Glasses.

"Oh, bullshit on that," Fishnet said, standing to make his point. "It's fucking eggheads up in geosynchronous orbit, waiting all this out. Their cure for the population boom. I heard it the other night on 1190. Conservation of resources by way of—"

"You even know what 'geo-whatever' means?" the punk asked, the wiry dude pressing his ear to the radio, dialing for the first voice, the tip of his tongue ghosting in and out.

The reprobate shook his head, held the knife away from himself so as to look down along the edge. "What time is it anyway?"

"Three?" Jory said to the reprobate. "Two forty when I left my place."

"What time do they come for us?" somebody got the nerve to ask, his tone not nearly so light as he was obviously trying for.

"Drivers don't get here till seven," Fishnet called back to whoever was worried.

Reprobate finally looked away from Jory, blew dust from his blade and narrowed his eyes like digging for a memory, like leaning on luck. "It's *hamburgesas*, losers," he said. "Double-meat with cheese, times six billion." Then he pointed to the wiry dude with his knife, made a circle with the point for him to dial deeper.

Glasses cleared his throat, breathed deeply, serioused up his eyes, and took a stab. "We—we finally developed the cure for AIDS and weight gain and loneliness and aging and sadness, only it had this one kind of negative side effect . . ."

Jory grinned that weak-sister effort away, turned around as punctuation, giving this idea his back. When he came back around, everybody was waiting. "Bubonic plague plus rabies," he finally spat out, "hiding down in some monastery cellar in Haiti for two hundred years."

"Wait, wait, shh . . ." the wiry dude said, finding a voice in the static.

"Hamburgers . . ." the reprobate called out, not even looking up.

"Divine retribution," Fishnet tried, smiling.

"Wrong channel for God," somebody said.

"Wrong crowd," the reprobate added, barely loud enough to hear.

"A comet passes a thousand years ago," Jory said then, feeling his way through it, "and we—we're just now drifting through its tail, and it's all sparkly with frozen organic matter that only thaws with the heat of passing through an atmosphere."

"Nice, nice," Glasses said. Then, "Our Pacific fishing trawlers had to start casting their nets wider and wider, deeper and deeper, and finally dredged up something from the sedimentary layer associated with the Bikini Atoll experiments. Clay, sludge. It glows at night, is hot enough to cook shrimp over. Three weeks later that trawler drifts into port. Infection Point Z."

"No, no, I heard that one," the punk said. "That's the way it really happened in—"

"What would those people in space eat for ten years?" Commando said, mostly to himself.

"Each other," the reprobate said back anyway.

"Shut up! Shut up!" the wiry dude was saying, trying to wave the theories away.

But Jory wasn't done. He was smiling now, finally, not looking away from Glasses. "The earth finally reaches a tipping point, spits up the virus as antibody, to cleanse itself of the infection we've become. The biological nuisance. Or—or, two kids nobody likes, they find an old book in the library, make the proper sacrifices, intone the right incantations—"

"But zombies are evil, right?" Commando was saying. "God wouldn't have done that to—"

"Not two kids, two *hikers*," Glasses went on, over the wiry dude's cease-and-desist gesticulations. "They're up on some glacier, fall into a crevasse, see this leathery hand coming up from the ice. They carry that body back to civilization, and the radiation from the scans the university does, it kick-starts something unholy in its bloodstream, and nobody even knows they need to lock the door behind them yet . . ."

"No mixing science and religion," Fishnet said, halfway sullen from not making it to what's sounding like the final round—Jory and Glasses.

Glasses pushed his glasses back up onto the bridge of his nose, said, "It doesn't mix—"

"*Unholy*," the reprobate told him. "You said 'unholy.' About a lab experiment."

"Wait, wait!" the wiry dude begged, pawing for the volume.

"Why can't you mix them?" Jory said to the punk. "You can believe in penicillin, you can believe in—in evolution, right?"

"That mean they're not true?" Fishnet said.

Jory didn't answer. He was back on task, back in the game. "So—so this one kid with cancer, he survives it, it's a miracle, only he's addicted to medicine, to the idea of medication, so gets hooked on meth, which these guys are making with water from a pond that truckers have been dumping waste in for—"

"No, the cooks, they've been using runoff formaldehyde as a stabilizing agent," Glasses said, liking it. "From the hazardous waste drum behind the mortuary."

"So when the kid's teeth and skin start falling out, off, whatever," Jory said, in the rhythm of the theory, "at first nobody notices, because they're all like that."

"But then," Glasses fell in, "if you look at the booking logs down at the station—this is Arizona, some place dry—you see this kid showing up month after month, looking worse and worse—"

"Guys, guys!" the wiry dude was saying.

"Until he finally gets killed, something undeniably fatal, like a bullet to the chest," Jory said, "only that tweaker with the gun, part of his mania that week was werewolves, so the bullets were cast from silver, only this batch of silver was impure, he'd melted it down from his mom's jewelry she got from her grandma, the silent-screen scream queen, and it's a mix of, of platinum and costume paste, and that *unholy* chemical, pharmaceutical, radiological time bomb, it lodges—"

"Festers," Glasses corrected.

"*Mixes* with what's left of the brewery his spinal fluid already is. So then, six months later, there's another booking photo, only, in this one, you can like see the kid's cheekbone through his skin, you can like look into his sinus cavity and see maybe like a spider living in—"

"*Over!*" the wiry dude finally insisted, stepping between Jory and Glasses, pushing them apart, then crossing the room to the reprobate, pulling the reprobate's hand up in victory. "We have a winner, gentlemen!"

"What?" Fishnet said, rolling to the edge of his bunk to see better.

In answer, the wiry dude held the already halfway-through-it radio out.

. . . and can it be any kind of coincidence that at the exact same moment the plague first started being reported, there were also reports that the fast food industry was failing, was collapsing, not due to lack of customers, but lack of product, lack of converted South American jungle to sustain their precious cows? What does that tell you, people? Picture this. Obese American pulls up into the fast food lane, already dying on the inside, just trying to pack dead cows around his mortality, dead cows if he was lucky, *and then—*

"Preach it, brother," Fishnet interrupted, taking the radio from the wiry dude, to hold it higher, but rolling the tuner instead, losing the sermon.

The reprobate laughed through his nose. "Double-meat with cheese, ladies," he said, coming up to a sitting position on his bunk, his legs hanging down now, the knife easy in his hand, then gone. "Now you know the rest of the story."

"His name is Dalton," Glasses said, sickened. Nodding down to the radio to show who he's talking about. "Self-styled Buddha of the apocalypse. Ex-dungeon master, onetime big-name hacker, back when there were servers. This is one of his better ones. They run it every night at—"

"—just after three . . ." the reprobate cut in.

"You cheated," the punk said.

"I won," the reprobate corrected, then jumped down, his biker boots heavy against the concrete floor.

"Won what?" Jory asked, squinting with his whole face.

The reprobate crossed to the bulletin board, the stack of names in a line from top to bottom, first to last. "This," he said, and took his name out of the third slot, tacked it back on at the very bottom.

"I up there?" Jory asked. "Gray, Jory."

"We all are," the reprobate said, scanning the room.

Then everybody was at the board, looking for their places in line.

Except Jory. And Glasses.

"Circus animals," Jory said, at a conversational level. Just talking. "Circus animals. There's a guy comes on at four who says it's circus animals, all doped up six ways from Sunday. That they were getting loose, mixing genes that never should have been mixed."

"There's really some out there, I've heard," Glasses said, watching the mob at the bulletin board.

"Some what?"

"Giraffes, lions, whatever there used to be. Monkeys."

"Popcorn."

Glasses smiled, said, "Music."

Jory nodded. Looked down to his hand. Shaking.

He held it tighter to his leg.

"Zebras," Glasses said then. "Remember when *Z* was for *zebra*?"

Jory nodded, did remember, then the punk was holding two fingers to his lips, asking around.

Jory hooked his head for the punk to follow him to his bag on the floor.

Inside, carton after carton.

"Shit," the punk hissed. "Think I can kill myself on these before seven o'clock rolls around?"

In answer, Jory lobbed cartons out to the rest of the room and then the radio was up again, music this time, Fishnet strutting out with some serious Eastside swagger, the whole bunkhouse whooping and catcalling, trying to prove how alive they still were, like they could stave off the morning if they laughed enough, if they smoked enough cigarettes.

Twelve hours later, three of them would be dead.

CHAPTER ELEVEN

Picture this. It's important.

A house deep in suburbia, before the plague.

No, no, the *approximation* of a house, lost in Residential. Just one of many, like the huge mother-house ambled this way a few years ago, dropping model after model in these curving, maternal lines that keep branching out into the horizon. The kind of neighborhood where you can slip up, walk through the wrong front door. And where it might not even matter that much, because everybody's already trying to be like each other anyway.

How long would dinner go before the mistake was apparent? Before the kid smiled, mumbled an "oops" and slipped out, to his own house. How long before the husband really looked at this woman who wasn't quite his wife. How long, not before the wife noticed this wasn't the man she married, but how long before she said something about it?

That kind of place.

And names aren't important here. Faces either.

Mannequins. This is the mannequin family. Bland, feature-less, right off the showroom floor. Fresh from the window display, in their street clothes, their creaky everyday wear.

The four of them sitting around the dinner table—mom, brother, sister, the tall, tall, awkward dad.

By the dad's plate is his cell phone, a device both slender and bulky, so his molded plastic fingers can handle it.

The dad's got his mouth open, is about to relay some interesting story from work, or the drive home, when that phone burrs, becomes a bug flipped over on its back for him to stare down at. For him to not be sure if he wants to touch it or not.

And if he hadn't?

The mom's smiling pleasantly, expectantly. Like it's painted on.

"Just a—" the dad says, holding up the smooth index finger of his left hand, so he can open the phone with his right. He cocks his head theatrically at who could be calling at this hour, then licks his lips to answer, only catches the Caller ID as the phone's rising to the side of his head.

He doesn't complete the motion. Locks eyes with his wife instead, across the table.

"It's XXXXX," he says, a high-pitched whine where the name's censored out. Not because it's important—it is, or would be—but because it's lost, because it's been redacted.

Brother and sister look to Mom for the answer to the obvious question here, and she smooths her napkin across her lap, comes through like always. "It's your Uncle XXXXX." So chipper.

The dad completes the motion, pulling the phone to his ear and standing in one motion, turning away, motioning behind him for his family to eat, eat, don't wait.

XXXXX.

"That really you?" he says, instead of hello.

"Dude," the voice comes back, maybe even stoned right now, "you know I was in Jakarta? Rocked. I mean—I might be technically married now, right? Anyway, I don't have . . . I'm coming back stateside for a few here, get some paperwork ironed out, figured I might, you know, that my niece and nephew haven't—"

The rest is cut off by the dad's plastic thumb on the End button.

His wife comes in behind him, hugs him from behind, her posture somehow getting across that she understands how hard this was for him. Putting his family first. Not getting involved.

Her face here, it's completely expressionless. Absolutely real.

"XXXXX," the dad mouths to himself, and, because the name's been lost to history, it's just a long, flat tone, whining out. An apologetic tone.

This is the Bible, yes. The Genesis of the new world, buried in the last few weeks of the old one. A phone ringing by a Pfaltzgraff blue plate on meatloaf night, a hand reaching down to cover it.

It's where Jory Gray was going.

For all of us.

DAY FOUR

CHAPTER TWELVE

By seven the next morning, the radio in J Barracks had died.

"So you were really a teacher?" the wiry dude was saying to Jory. The two of them sitting outside, squinting against the sun, a pile of butts crushed out beside them.

Jory licked his lips. "Science," he said. "Biology."

"That's how you knew all that stuff."

"Or I don't sleep so well."

"Then you should have known about the hamburgers then, shouldn't you have?"

Just then a jeep pulled up, the driver grim, right hand casual over the wheel.

"Who's up?" the wiry dude called into the bunkhouse.

"Williamson, T.K." came back.

Wiry shook his head, his stare more blank now. His breath more measured.

"That's you?" Jory said.

The wiry dude stood up as if he were older than he was, and studied the jeep. The driver fiddling with something by his leg.

"What do I need?" the wiry dude said, barely out loud.

From inside the bunkhouse, a twine-wrapped cube of the heat-resistant body armor tumbled out, rolled to a stop. They were stacked under the bulletin board like bricks.

"I'm playing hockey against them?" the wiry dude said, hooking a finger under the twine, working his footlocker key up from his front pocket, slapping it into Jory's hand.

"You'll be fine," Jory told him, and licked his lips again.

The wiry dude walked backwards for a few steps, launching a salute from his forehead, and then his driver for the day was ferrying him out to the field, to the restricted zones, to whatever corpse had been detected, still fresh enough to be a threat. Still fresh enough to kill the world, if left to rise.

They found the dead by snapping anklets on scavenger birds, Jory knew. When three of the anklets congregated for a certain amount of time, it rang the bells on base, fed them coordinates, got a driver to J Barracks in under two hours.

There was supposed to be a coyote version too, Jory had heard.

He faked a salute back to the wiry dude, though they were already a plume of dust. From inside, spilling out the door, "Dude, no they *don't!* They carry *two* knives, man."

It was Fishnet. Arguing with the punk, the punk's mohawk drooping to the left like a rooster comb. The rest of the crew was pushing through, out into the morning.

"They're priests," the punk said, lighting up. Registering the receding jeep. "They're priests, not ninjas, cool?"

"They really cut into them?" Jory asked. "The corpses or whatever?"

"They're dead already," the punk said, charading his idea of a knife in, giving it a sneery twist.

"It's one blade," Glasses said, leaned in the doorway. "One's ceremonial. Two would be for defense."

"Dude!" Fishnet said. "You think I'd make this shit up just for laughs? Like they're not freaky enough already, *without* a knife in each hand?"

"And they don't need defense," Glasses went on, sucking on a cigarette, coughing all the smoke back out. "They're immune, can't catch it."

"They're not immune to being stepped on," Jory said.

"Handlers," the punk offered.

"So you're saying they have a knife especially for dispatching handlers?" Glasses said, just considering it out loud.

"Man, what if one of *them* went hot, yeah?" Fishnet said, casting around for support, somebody to share this doomsday with.

"Handlers can't reanimate," Glasses said. "They've already died and come back once, kind of."

"Oh, there's rules?" the punk said.

"But they're immune to them*selves* anyway, right?" Fishnet said.

"Zombies?" Jory said back.

Fishnet shrugged *sure, yeah.* Like this one *had* to be a slam dunk.

Glasses laughed through his nose at this. At them.

"What?" the punk said.

"You haven't seen the videos, have you?" Glasses said.

"Which one?" the reprobate said, there all along somehow.

Glasses looked up to the approaching jeep.

"Who's up?" Fishnet asked, holding his fist in front of his mouth, to breathe into it.

Reprobate leaned back into the bunkhouse, holding on to the doorframe with his fingertips, then came back with no eye contact, just a name, said as flatly as a name can be said, "Hernandez."

Fishnet looked back to the jeep. Swallowed.

"Just burn 'em all, right?" he said, the corners of his mouth ghosting up into a smile.

Nods all around. A clap or two on the shoulder.

Fishnet leaned down for his cube of armor, stood with it, and didn't look back.

"Feels like a funeral already," the punk said.

Jory licked his lips again, hated himself for it. It was an old habit, from some late-night movie twenty years ago, that he wasn't supposed to have snuck back into the living room for. *Friday Night Chiller, Saturday Scare Fest,* something like that. This group of refugees trekking across the Himalayas, it slowly becoming obvious that one of them isn't like the others, the rest of them finally figuring it out when one of their group, his lips aren't raw like theirs. Because he—it—had some other way to keep them wet, evidently.

They'd driven it off a cliff, kept on with their very important trek, the movie going to commercial on a ragged hand coming back over the cliff's edge.

Ever since then, just to show how human he was, Jory had been a lip licker, until he hardly even thought about it anymore.

Except for some times. Some days.

And it did feel like a funeral, Fishnet easing away, holding on to the fold-down windshield with his left hand, his face still not turning back.

The video Glasses finally hauled up from under his bed— ancient laptop, cobbled from three or four other laptops—it was surprisingly clear.

Definitely not first wave. More like from the last couple of years.

It was a zombie strapped to a dolly, its lower legs broken, to the side because the dolly wasn't tall enough. Strapped enough that the only skin left visible was its midsection.

"How'd they catch it?" the punk asked, but Glasses shushed him.

Another zombie was in the background, strapped to a concrete picnic table. This was an old rest stop. Jory reoriented his head, like, if he looked more from a few inches over, he could get a different angle on the scene.

It had been maybe six years since he'd seen anything on a screen. The brain forgets.

"Oh yeah," the reprobate said, nodding like he was remembering this show—two men in full camo and elbow-high lineman's gloves were cutting up the picnic-tabled zombie. Like a turkey. Slice, slice, pull.

When they had maybe a pound or two of the rancid meat, they swept it down to the concrete pad under the table, ground it to mush under their boots, their fingertips to the tabletop so they wouldn't slip.

Meanwhile, in the foreground, the dolly zombie's eyes were wheeling, but it was strapped in tight enough it couldn't even push a shoulder forward.

"Here it comes," Glasses said, angling the laptop screen back slightly, to cut the glare.

"I don't—" Jory said, but then he did—the two camo men were scooping the mushed-up zombie meat into the top of a metal funnel, the kind with the articulated tube at the bottom. This one was rusted, two feet long.

"I heard about this," the punk said, ten years old again.

After a camera reposition, for close-up, the camo men wrenched the zombie's mouth open enough for the funnel tube and jammed that tube down into its throat, the zombie's throat engorging with it.

"They won't eat of their own kind," Glasses said, adjusting his glasses. "Not willingly, at least."

The reprobate laughed a sick little laugh, and, on cue, one of the camo men held the tube in place, the other started jamming the pestle end of a wooden bat into the top of the funnel, forcing the meat down.

It clumped down the tube, oozing out some of the spaces between the segments, something black coming up around the corners of the zombie's mouth, the zombie in a panic now, fighting so hard it tipped the dolly backwards.

The camo men just followed. Better this way.

More meat, more meat.

One of the camo men held the zombie's mouth shut with a pipe under the chin, his boot on the top of the zombie's head, but he didn't have to. The zombie wasn't going to puke, probably didn't even have that reflex anymore.

And, besides, the meat had hit its stomach, its insides, its blood.

It shrieked, bucked—the zombie on the picnic table too—and, with this meat inside it, the dolly zombie was able to lift a shoulder now. Get some space under itself.

"It makes them stronger, right?" the punk said, definitely not looking away. "Faster?"

"Like an eight-ball for the walking dead," Glasses answered, not looking away either.

"Eight ball?" the reprobate asked, the whole room looking over to him.

"How old were you when New York fell?" Jory asked.

"Ten," Reprobate said back like a challenge.

"Too young to know," Glasses said, directing them all back to the screen, to this coked-up zombie.

First one strap popped, uncoiling the two below it, and then another.

The camo men looked to each other theatrically—all for the camera—then one brought a machete down, de-legged the zombie. De-armed it.

And still it bucked, great black gouts of its tar-like blood slinging around, spattering the camera lens.

"Now," Glasses said.

The camo men were dragging a killed woman into the scene, somebody they'd found in a ditch, probably. They got to slicing filets off her as well, holding them up for the zombie to snap at, gulp down.

"What?" Jory said, almost pushing away.

"Everything gets accelerated," Glasses explained. "Metabolism, activity, strength. But appetite too."

"They don't know when to say when," the punk said.

Glasses nodded.

Ten cued-through minutes later, most of the dead woman's right leg was down to the bone, and the left was disappearing fast.

"Three, two—" Glasses led off, and on what would have been "one," the first contusion showed on the zombie's unstrapped middle section. The only place it *could* bulge.

The camo men laughed, fed it more, more, until the bulge split, started spilling, one of them evidently chanting, "Push, push!", and still the zombie kept eating more, snapping the air for it, the two men completely unaware of the zombie behind them, rising from the concrete table, trailing the straps it had been able to pull its now-meatless self through.

"This is the last in the series, right?" somebody said, and was answered an instant later by the rush on-screen—teeth, a forearm—the camera tilting at the sky now, just blue, slipping past.

"Holy shit," the punk said.

"Why don't we just feed them like *that* to kill them?" Commando said, back from the bathroom, or prayer, wherever he'd been.

"Because they'd only kill themselves by eating all of us," Jory said, looking up to Commando to see if this was taking.

It was.

With a keystroke, Glasses closed the player, had his hand on the top of the laptop screen to pull it closed, but the punk stopped him.

"What's that one?" he said, pointing lower down the menu.

Filename: *gymboreenauseum.*

Glasses smiled, clicked, said, "Classic first wave, man."

While the player organized itself around the file type, the image locked on-screen was a hallway. With lockers. Lockers with combinations. A ceiling like inverted terraces, the bottom side of staircases all meeting in the middle, at these blunt sky lights. Artwork on the walls, probably by class.

"That's a school," Jory said.

"Nobody's seen this one either?" Glasses said, looking around. "This one even played on the news."

"When there was news," the punk added, leaning in, his hand on Jory's shoulder, and then the video came on. A bright gymnasium. The cameraman up high, so the whole floor's in the shot, slat after slat of laminated board. Parents and teachers on one side, making a wall in front of the few classes of kids they've been able to get this far.

"That you?" the punk said back to the reprobate, about the kids.

"Shut it," Glasses said, holding his hand up as, on-screen, from the other side of the gym, the locker room doors, the dead came, some of them running on all fours. They were falling over each other to be first to this magic feast.

The moms' fists are curled around pens and brushes and high heels, and the dads are looking up to the banners on the walls, like they're supposed to be ladders, or ropes. Or like the dads' names are up there. And then, the zombies spreading across the shiny floor like a black stain, purses and basketballs raining down on them, one of the dads in back of this last stand, he picks up the kid closest to him, the child dearest to him, and he hurls her as far as he can up into the stands, and then the other dads start doing this too, even as the zombies are crashing into them, and what the camera can barely see is that there's a teacher up there, a coach in the blue chairs, and he's catching every kid he can, and slinging them higher, up to this old man of a janitor, at the announcer's booth.

It's made of cinder block, but with glass windows.

Jory reached forward, pulled the screen down. He kept his hand there.

Nobody tried to open the laptop again.

"Everybody thought schools were the safest places," the punk said.

Jory was still seeing it. Breathing harder than he wanted to be breathing.

A horn honked outside, just once.

"That'd be me," Jory said, standing as if in a trance, hooking his finger under the twine cord of an armor block. Not even licking his lips once.

"Gray, Jordan, right?" the reprobate said, just because somebody had to. Because Jory was already through the door, out into the sunlight. Just a shadow, receding, losing his edges.

"I think so, yeah," the punk said. "Jory. Biology teacher. Mr. Gray."

"Mr. Gray . . ." the reprobate said, letting his eyes linger through the doorway a bit more, in something like appreciation, then turning away from it.

"He wasn't up for three more calls," somebody said.

"Right after me," Glasses added, pinching his glasses at the bridge, taking them off, his face so naked now. His eyes so small.

"How—how old would those kids be now?" Commando asked then. "On the movie. If they'd lived."

"They didn't," Glasses said, and pulled a trembling, unlit cigarette to his lips. Tried to draw smoke from it.

Tried again.

CHAPTER THIRTEEN

Verse two, the mannequin household. Where it all started.

Where it keeps starting.

The dad's down in his corner of the basement, the columns of teetering junk so generic, so poorly suited for surviving horde after horde, wave after wave.

Lamps, skateboards, hat racks?

But maybe it would be comforting to dawdle your last week away down there. Shuffle through your memories, shake the flashlight for more battery juice. The house above you inhabited, slobbering.

None of that yet though.

None of that without this, without the dad squinting into his vintage computer monitor, the light from the letters bleeding out onto his plastic face, no real sweat there.

His search term in the default engine is *Jakarta*. All the usual, useless data reeling past—economy, climate, social customs. History, geography, exports. Relative size. Livestock. Malaria, tuberculosis, leprosy. Agriculture, art. Photo galleries, sightseeing suggestions, airfare.

The husband clicked deeper, deeper, was getting nowhere.

"Where are you?" he said into the screen, coming even closer so the screen's right there, caught in his work glasses.

Then his wife's voice, calling down, "Hon? What are you doing down there?"

The husband looks up as if through a pool of murky water. Blinks, blinks. Remembers he can speak too. "Nothing, nothing. Just, you know. Work. Busy bee, beaver . . ."

Upstairs the wife angles her head to the side—she's cutting carrots, has an apron on—then looks across to their son at the table, with his homework. She smiles pleasantly.

"Dinner in twenty, 'kay?" she calls down, cutting the carrot into coins again.

"Great, yeah," the dad says back.

"What's wrong, Mom?" the son says, his pencil stalled in the middle of some algebra.

Cut, cut, the carrot slices leaning over against each other like dominoes. One of them the exact shade of her skin.

"Nothing, dear. Just—nothing. Your Uncle XXXXX, remember him?"

"Dad says he's maybe married now."

The mom smiles, sweeps the carrots onto a plate. "I'm sure he's maybe something," she says. "He's always maybe something . . ."

The dad is quiet at his post now. Maybe hearing this transaction upstairs, so close. His hand hovering over the mouse.

But then footsteps. Heels. His wife walking across the living room, it doesn't matter why.

The dad nods to himself, fumbles his cell phone up from his pocket, has to stand to do it, the basement too short for his circus self. The sound his head makes hitting the two-by-twelve joist is the sound a good cantaloupe used to make. The sound a child's toy bowling ball could make against a coffee table.

The dad sits back down rubbing his head. He scooches his chair in closer, for privacy.

"Okay, okay," he says to himself, his nerves obviously why he hasn't been promoted at whatever fake job he has.

That's lost too, though.

What isn't—or, wasn't, early on, before anybody knew what it was—is the image that resolves on-screen when he plugs his phone into the port.

It's a fortune-cookie strip of paper, but not. Hand-torn, tiny, tiny little rips, like you get when pulling something from a bulletin board.

Sideways on the strip of paper, *Volunteers Needed—Six Weeks—All Bills Paid.*

The husband rotates the image, zooms in on the mimeo-graphed font. Says it again, to his brother, "Where are you?"

CHAPTER FOURTEEN

Fifteen feet from the jeep that wasn't really for him, Jory stopped. The driver. It was the same guy from the training session. The guy who'd been cocked up against the back wall, punctuating Voss's walk-through with sneers. The distant chuckler, up close now.

"You," Jory said.

"Me," the driver said back, burning the clutch a bit to show they needed to be gone.

Jory kept his eyes on the ground in front of him, then on the side of the jeep, then on the dashboard.

"Mayner," the driver said, offering his hand.

"Jory Gray," Jory said, not taking the hand. "No need to commit it to memory, right?"

"Think I picked this job?" Mayner said back.

"Said the ferryman."

"This is your first call, right?" Mayner said, and backed them up, jerked them forward, onto the road that led to the gate.

"Don't give up, do you?" Jory said, holding on to the dash.

"Yeah, *I'm* the stubborn one," Mayner said back, taking the first curve too fast.

"Everybody's new in there," Jory said. "J Barracks. Attack of the rookies."

"That a question or an answer?"

"Observation."

"J is for ghost . . ." Mayner nodded, anticipating Jory's next line. "Last week's been"—his signature chuckle—"unfortunate."

"For torches."

"For humanity."

"Humanity?"

"Reason you had your pick of the beds in there's that everybody got coded, the last few days. The dead aren't staying dead anymore. Even less than usual, I mean. Like a whole 'nother wave." Another turn, another near-death experience. "Bonefaces are even making some special robe to protect themselves, I hear."

"From the dead?"

"From us. From you. From getting coded."

Mayner rested his forearms on the top of the steering wheel, mimed a small explosion over his instrument cluster.

"Have to believe in a robe pretty hard for it to protect you in a firestorm," Jory said, turning to watch base slip past.

"Got to have faith, faith, faith."

"I don't even have a key."

"Key?"

"For a footlocker. They never issued me one."

"You bring something valuable? What?"

Jory touched the small pocket Linse's ID was stashed in.

"What were you?" Mayner said, braking hard for the gate. "Before?"

"Does it matter?" Jory said, his hand on the fold-down windshield now. He turned, studied Mayner. "What were you?" he asked.

Mayner saluted their way through the gate, said, "So you know how to use the torch, right?"

"Feels like a funeral, doesn't it?" Jory said back.

"Funerals have this?" Mayner said, and popped the glove compartment, a tangle of wires and circuits, a chrome disc spinning in there, its skeletonized player resting on a bag of sand. Some kind of pop music lilting out at them. A girl, maybe sixteen, trying to reach into her soul, pull out a hit.

Jory couldn't help but smile.

It was his first call.

Like Jory had been told to expect, their destination was deep in one of the restricted zones. The places that hadn't been cleared yet. Nowhere you'd want to be after dark.

A derelict public restroom, the landscape around it so reduced that Jory couldn't tell if this had been a park, a rest stop, or what. The only reason the restroom was still standing was that it had been built like a bomb shelter. Even so, it was creaky, tilting, had a year left, two at the outside.

Lined all along its roof, and high-stepping it on the ground like old men with delicate feet, were the Pharaoh vultures that had shown up again not long after the plague. Before, there'd been rumors of maybe three breeding pairs. With the feast the postapocalypse had been for them, these rumors were like pigeons now. Just with wingspans of eleven to fourteen feet, the grandfathers reaching out nearly to twenty. Black feathers oily to the touch. A digestive system able to process whatever fell down into it, evidently. The best survivors.

The two on the ground raised their wings in warning, but Mayner pulled right up to them anyway, leaning forward for the jeep's dust to drift past, Jory only clueing into this at the last moment, the last gritty breath.

"Thanks," he said a few moments later, coughing.

Mayner smiled, his face right up against the steering wheel.

"Helmet's behind you," he said to Jory, then sat on the hood while Jory strapped the armor on, fitted the helmet down, adjusted the strap on the torch and moved his arm on that side, to be sure he still could. Then his fingers. Then the tips of his fingers.

Stall, stall.

Finally Jory stepped in beside Mayner, and the two of them studied the broken-down restroom. Its shifting black wainscoting watched them back.

"They can't get in," Mayner said, about the vultures. "They can smell it, but they can't get to it. They don't want to be anywhere without the sky above them."

Jory didn't say anything. Four of the vultures had metal bracelets on their right ankles, those tiny lights blipping green with radio signals.

"Just one?" Jory said, about what he was apt to find inside.

"Probably," Mayner said, shrugging one shoulder. "Out here, it's—why be *out* here, right? Unless you're smuggling."

"Black market," Jory filled in.

"Probably a grocery store buried out here somewhere. Find that storeroom, grab as many cans as you can, and"—with his sideways hand Mayner zipped a fast path back to the fence.

"You've seen that one they have in the glass box in old downtown?" Jory said, pawing his pocket for his pack, hitting armor instead.

"The mime?" Mayner asked, looking over, then playacting he was lying down in an invisible box, testing its limits gingerly.

"More like a coffin," Jory said.

"You've seen it, like with your own two eyes?"

Jory shrugged.

"It's not real," Mayner said. "Control'd never let the virus circulate like that."

"They're pretty good at keeping expired canned goods off the streets too?" Jory said, trying to unstrap his chest plate, to get at his cigarettes.

Mayner stopped him, threaded a red-striped straw up from his shirt pocket, the straw tied at both ends.

"Menthol," he said, at important-whisper level.

Jory took the straw reverently. It was one of those milkshake ones, from back when milkshakes were real. Just, with a menthol preserved inside now. He ran it under his nose, trying to smell that green taste.

"Serious?" he said. "Where?"

"Just don't tell Voss."

"Because I'm definitely seeing him again."

"Toss the butt out when you and his holiness are ready for the big boy. I'll be watching for it. Won't give him the signal until then. Not that they always listen so well."

"'Big boy'?" Jory said.

"And his pet dog," Mayner answered.

Jory got it—the handler. Throw the menthol butt out when he was ready for the handler. When the *priest* was ready for the handler and his walking, slobbering bad idea of a laboratory rat.

"What if I'm not done with it yet?" Jory asked, holding the straw out before him.

"You can save the world or you can smoke a cigarette, right?" Mayner said.

Jory studied the straw again, considering. Inside was maybe the only menthol left in the postapocalypse. Maybe his last smoke ever.

"It'll help with the smell," Mayner said, nodding inside.

"So we're the first ones here?" Jory said.

"Except Señor Deadalo in there," Mayner said back.

"And whoever made him dead."

"Unless he died of happiness," Mayner said.

"Lot of that going around these days," Jory said, then pushed off with his butt from the jeep.

Mayner chin-pointed down to Jory's torch. "You know what to do with that, right?"

"Pull the trigger. Point. Spray."

"Maybe in a slightly different order, but, yeah. Okay. And"—keying his own headset on—"you can hear me, right?"

Jory flinched from Mayner's voice in his helmet, dialed it down.

Then, leaning away, into his own unlit funeral pyre, Mayner's hand on Jory's shoulder kept him there for one more moment.

"Don't make me code you," he said. "Be the one that lives, this week."

Jory looked around at the ravaged sky one last time. The jagged horizon. Then he clapped his hand down on top of Mayner's.

"Thanks for the—" he said, lifting the red-striped straw, walking backwards into his story, his torch at port arms, the Pharaoh vultures lumbering up into the air behind him, fifteen birds at once, so that for a few moments Jory was in shadow.

And then he ducked through the door.

CHAPTER FIFTEEN

A spark, a burble of light, and Jory's torch lit, the flame bobbing against the darkness.

"Hunh," Jory said into the decrepit restroom, then recoiled from the stench, covering his nose with the back of his left hand.

"Cool?" Mayner said through the helmet.

"Very *un*cool," Jory said back, coughing hard enough that he took an involuntary step forward, the tile floor giving under his weight, suggesting a cavity under there. A cavern.

Jory held the lit end of his torch up, stepped to the side, skirted whatever septic labyrinth was waiting under that part of the floor.

But the smell.

He gagged some more, managed to unknot one end of his straw, shake the sacred menthol out.

Again, he pawed his chest for his lighter, and, again, he was wearing plate armor.

"Got a light?" he coughed into his mouthpiece.

"Serious?" Mayner said, and Jory got it, looked down to his torch. He pulled it as far back along his waist as the strap would let him, leaned down, and when he strained, could just reach that precious flame.

He held the first drag in, held it, blew it out in a long grey line of relief.

Across the room, facedown in a pool of his own dried gore, was the smuggler. Fallen into the urinal and, alongside him, his contraband—cans of peaches, their labels hardly even faded.

"It's peaches," Jory said into the headset.

"Still good?" Mayner said back.

Jory didn't answer.

The rest of the restroom was the typical rusted stalls, torn-off doors—they can be shields—and animal droppings. Years of guano sloping up one of the back corners.

"What were you doing in here?" Jory said to the peach smuggler.

Though the wound that had been fatal for him was obviously on the front, like he'd fallen onto it to try to stanch the bleeding, still, there was a palm-sized circle of black blood between his shoulder blades. Meaning knife, probably, not gun. All the way through. Up close and personal.

So as not to attract attention, right?

Let the birds do that, once the smell came.

Jory sucked deeper on the menthol. He kind of wanted to live now, just to get the chance to smoke another.

Outside, Mayner looked up from the video feed—Jory's helmet—to the armored transport rumbling up the road. Shaking the ground. Shaking the whole world.

The handler.

"What's it smell like?" Jory asked, his voice breaking up. "You know, when you burn them?"

Mayner grinned like he had the perfect answer here, then swallowed it when a tall white figure swept past.

"Look busy," he said into the mic, covering it with his hand. "This party's about to heat up."

* * *

Though the video from the old holding pens was the conversion point for most of the people who sleepwalked up the Hill, the Church's real power was that, in uncertain times, it was providing certainty.

The *illusion* of certainty, Jory would have told Linse if she'd asked, but still. The illusion, it's got to be better than its opposite, right?

For the first six or seven years of the plague, it had been the military in control. Because people needed fires against the night. Because society needed some fences. Tall, sharp fences.

But now—it wasn't like the old world, and it never would be again, not after the dead had gotten up and walked one especially black Friday. That Friday was gone though. It was Sunday now. Sunday, and people were going to Church in what passed for droves in the postapocalypse. Maybe for some version of the same reason Jory was pretty sure Linse had made that walk—guilt. For what they'd had to do, in order to survive. What they knew they had inside them, now, and were afraid of. What they wanted cleansed, wiped away, forgotten. Mostly forgotten.

Where the military was just an extension of themselves, what everybody would do and do happily if they had guns and tanks and organization, the Church, it was a bridge to somewhere else. Not the past, but a place not this, not here. A place not so tooth and nail.

Which isn't to say the Church's walls weren't at least as tall as the military's. The big difference was that the military used see-through chain-link, with electricity coursing through, when it could be had. The Church, its walls were solid, so you could pretend the world was only this big, this clean. And they didn't need electricity, they had the priests, right? The dead couldn't come in if they wanted. This was a place of life.

As for where the Church had come from, Jory had no idea. He'd never been close enough to a priest to hear any accent or intonation. What it felt like was that they'd grown up *with* the dead, almost. Like the dead had created some void in the world, for the priests to step calmly into. Like the priests had been waiting centuries to do just that.

And of course they weren't the only religions to get kick-started by the plague. There had been the Church of Z in the early days. Graduated snake-handlers, pretty much, except their holy animal, the animal that sent them into a spiritual frenzy, it was the zombie. To be infected was to have the spirit course through you, take away all semblance of human speech, human thought, replace it with something so much more pure, like you'd been unburdened by greed and envy and the rest, could exist now as perfect desire, as a hunger more pure than the world had ever known.

Those congregations fell as soon as they all met in one place. But for a while there'd always been another group of believers willing to meet. Less a church than mass suicide. Which was maybe how they dealt with their own survivor's guilt.

The Bottleneckers had been next, and, of all the upstart religions, they had seemed the one most likely to keep their foothold, just because their articles of faith—they *wore* them. The reason they were called Bottleneckers was the collars the military had issued the third year. To everybody who wouldn't come onto the make-do bases. And you had no choice. If a patrol saw you out in Restricted, you were put facedown in the dirt, a silver band strapped around your neck, its sensor in lockstep with your jugular pulse, so that, when it stopped—when you got infected, like you *would,* out here without the military to watch over you—then the collar would contract all the way down to your spine, decap you. Eliminate the threat you were about to become, and thus contain the plague that much better. It was supposed to be the humane solution.

So these Bottleneckers, the Collared, as they were called at first, they started meeting once, twice a week, just to talk about it. More a resistance than a religion, really.

But they all fell down too, when somebody figured out how to jack into the collar's radio signal—they were also tracking devices, surprise—and fool the sensors into registering death. Two hundred people sitting in rows, losing their heads all at once. Maybe two or three of them still sitting there, a live mouse thrust up between their neck and the sensor, the mouse clawing and scratching, its heartbeat so alive, too undeniable for the jacked signal to override.

So, into that space left by the Church of Z, by the Bottleneckers—Christianity was tame now that the dead were walking, and if any of the other religions had made it through, they didn't have temples around here, anyway—into that void, stepped these priests. Quiet, demure. Tall. Their long fingers crossed over their navels like saints. If they even had navels. Their faces covered by ceramic masks, those masks so serene, so patient. Three crosses or plus marks or sideways *Xs* on their lapels.

All of which Jory knew, but just secondhand.

"'Heat up'?" he said back to Mayner, holding the mic close to his mouth, eyes focusing down on nothing, and then the light from the doorway blotted out and he got it—God was in the house. His representative anyway. "Oh," Jory said, a not-completely-voluntary response.

The cigarette went slack in his lips.

Where Jory had ducked through the doorway because he was still too aware of his helmet, his torch, the priest had to gather his white robes and bend over just so his head would clear.

And then he stood up, and up, turned his alien white face down on Jory so that Jory felt he was being studied by a praying mantis.

"Soldier," the priest said, then uncurled his white-gloved fingers, touched his own sternum. "Brother Hillford," he said slowly, deeply, properly. No accent of any kind coming through.

"Hillford?" Mayner whispered into Jory's helmet.

Jory was registering this in some place he couldn't quite speak from.

This priest was every bit as tall as any handler.

And, his robe, it was so white it was glowing.

Breathe, breathe, Jory told himself.

"No, not a soldier," he said, about himself. "Jory. Jory Gray."

The priest just kept on with that stare, took a step forward, time speeding up all at once, Jory reaching forward to stop the priest from falling into the septic caverns below them, but the priest's foot, it had already directed itself around the weak spot in the floor. Was putting its gossamer weight near the wall instead.

Jory nodded about this, waiting for it to register as well. But it wouldn't.

How could this priest have known where to step? Did they have some extra sense? Were the soles of his sandals that thin? Was there a shadow, giving that slight concavity away, or had he been watching Jory through the doorway, taking note? Or were his steps just divine?

"You're the special one," Hillford said then, cocking his head over, the mask so blank.

"Special?" Jory said.

"The one your general hand-picked."

"More like hand-punished," Jory said.

Outside, the handler's transport was making the earth quake. Jory studied his menthol—not even half-gone. A travesty.

Or not.

Jory stepped forward, flipped the menthol backwards, offered it to Hillford.

"You don't find these ones every day anymore," he said, keeping his face tilted down like he felt respectful.

The priest kept his hands up his sleeves.

"The world outside of us is so polluted already, Jory Gray. Would you have me pollute the inside as well?"

Jory took the menthol back, drew deep on it.

"Are you taking care of her?" Jory said then, looking at the priest's long, seemingly exaggerated shins. His shin *area*, anyway. The shin *part* of his robes.

"Her?" Hillford asked.

"My . . . her name, it's Linse," Jory said. "She went up the Hill, up to *you* about three days ago. Four. Here, she's—"

Jory fumbled up Linse's ID card.

Hillford leaned forward, as if studying it, especially the earring hole, top center. But he wouldn't take it.

"What are you being punished for, if I might ask?" he said instead, the ghost of a grin in his voice. "Starting unauthorized fires, perhaps?"

Jory pulled more smoke in, studied the menthol again—how could Hillford possibly know about the Weeping Poles?—and then Mayner coughed into Jory's helmet, made him flinch, fumble through the air after the menthol.

He had to go to his knees to catch it. He never saw the ID card, fluttering down beside his leg.

Another drag.

"I just want to talk to her," he said up to the priest, Hillford looking down to Jory like a child, and before Jory could hear the excuse, whatever it was going to be, he rolled the menthol around to the nail of his middle finger, cocked it over his shoulder, and flicked it doorwards.

A direct miss. Not even close.

The sparks popped like a firework on a still night, hung in a burst of orange, and by that time Jory was diving for the butt. He caught it on the way down, the cherry hot against his palm so that he just shook it through the door, let it fall on what passed for a stoop in this broken world.

The instant it hit, a gigantic insulated boot crushed it out— with or without the signal, the handler had been coming—and in that same instant, the zombie was in the doorway, its gimp-masked face right up against Jory, close enough that, in spite of the iron grate over the zombie's snapping mouth, in spite of the field there supposed to sterilize the virus, still, Jory thought he could taste that rancid breath.

He fell back onto his elbows, trying to kick deeper into the restroom, then came back with his torch, the flame bobbing right at the zombie's mouth grate, his finger already—with or without Jory's okay—pulling.

At the last possible moment, a cold hand came down on Jory's left shoulder, pulled him slightly around. Just enough that when his torch opened, it opened onto the wall, the flames flattening out, curling at the ceiling and floor, rushing across the doorway, leaving the zombie's leather singed.

Jory turned around, was face to mask with the priest, close enough to see the skin around Hillford's eyes. It was wrinkled, black. Scarred? That why they wore masks, some kind of nightmare initiation?

"Gray, Gray!" Mayner was yelling, both into Jory's helmet and outside, from the jeep.

Jory backed off the trigger. The priest pulled him a step or two deeper into the restroom, as if Jory weighed nothing. Jory shook away, clambered to an unsteady stand.

"Cool, cool," Jory said into the mic. A complete lie.

This is why so many torches never came back from their first call, he knew now—panic. Being in the same room with a zombie, with a freakadillo priest. Having a weapon that can make all that go away. Your driver having a weapon that can make *you* go away.

Jory's breath caught up with him. It was raspy, shallow, not enough.

"Confronting your own sins made manifest is never a simple matter, is it?" Hillford said, tucking his hand back up his sleeve.

An instant later, the zombie was all the way through the door, the massive form of the handler leashed to it, the zombie pulling on all fours for Jory, the most obvious food, the handler not seeming to even notice.

Like the zombie, the handler was in leather. And zippers. Circuitry, wires. Blue electricity coursing up and down the chain, from dog to master, and back again.

The zombie had been bad, but this, the handler, it was—Jory'd never seen one suited up for the field. In action.

He didn't believe in them, but he could tell that didn't make a shred of difference, either.

One step farther, and the zombie's front leg—arm, whatever—reached through that weak part of the floor. It came up with a squealing black rat, one almost able to squirm through the stumps of the zombie's fingers.

It pressed it against its mouth grate before it could wriggle away. The rat kicked, sizzled, died in clumps that the zombie reached for with its dry black tongue.

The handler looked down to this, made a *henh* sound

somewhere in its throat, and jerked once on the chain, a casual flick, really. It was enough to slam the zombie bodily into the wall Jory had just torched.

For a moment the zombie stuck, its leather cooking, the flesh under it smoking, and then it arched away, was pulling for Jory again.

"Elegant, no?" Hillford said to Jory, studying this zombie.

"No," Jory said, taking a careful step to the side.

"Don't look at it," Mayner was saying to Jory through the helmet.

Jory couldn't help it though.

It had been nearly ten years since he had been this close to one.

He thought it would be easier. That he was prepared. That working the assembly line, it had prepared him for this.

He was wrong.

He couldn't get his breathing right. Couldn't get his head right.

"So it begins," Hillford said then, brushing past Jory. For the peach smuggler. "Inform your escort," he said, taking a knee by the urinal. By the body.

"We're a go," Jory said into the headset. Not looking away from Hillford for an instant, Hillford's head back in some kind of silent ritual, a glistening white blade suddenly in his left hand, from up his right sleeve.

"No," Jory said, though he knew what was going to happen.

His prayer over, Hillford slid the blade easily between the lower ribs on the left side of the peach smuggler, Hillford not looking down, like he was going by feel.

What Voss had told the group was that the clergy would puncture the heart, when possible, because, if there was any virus, it would necessarily have cycled through there, and lodged.

Under his heavy robes, Hillford's shoulder and arm movements were so precise, so clinical, so devout.

When he finally must have pushed through the dense cardiac muscle—Jory had seen one in lab, in grad school—he stopped, angled his head back to Jory, to the handler and the zombie, and, just like in the demonstration, except fifty thousand times louder, he wrenched the blade sideways, wedging the ribs apart. Letting the air from the heart circulate into the air in the room.

Jory coughed, nearly gagged. Not from the smell but from the *idea*. The zombie was absolutely screaming. The handler even had to lean back to counter the pull.

"Henh," the handler said, and Jory cued into the handler's tiny eyes, up there behind its leather mask.

They were watching this white blade go in. The handler's left hand, the nonleash hand, it was at the handler's codpiece of a catheter. Just rubbing in a dull, frenetic way, this handler ceasing to be an *it*, becoming a *him*.

"No," Jory said.

"No?" Mayner hissed back.

The zombie jerked forward again, pulling for the peach smuggler, and the handler was pulled forward, and then—

"The mouth unit," Hillford said across to Jory. No panic at all.

Slowly, Jory swam back to the surface of this moment.

The mouth. The zombie's mouth.

The grate was still on.

"What?" Jory said to Hillford.

"Open it," Hillford said. Just that.

Jory looked to the zombie again.

"Open it. The grate."

"No."

He dragged his eyes up to the handler, to the handler's busy left hand. The grate release was sewed into the back of that glove. Such a simple mechanism. One pull, and done.

But that wasn't going to happen.

"He's going to code us," Jory said to Hillford.

"Jory?" Mayner asked in the helmet. "Gray?"

"Open it," Hillford said again, nodding to the zombie. "Let the process complete itself, come full circle, encompass each of us."

The world came down to this, for Jory—that catch on the side of the zombie's mouth grate. That monstrous, hateful catch.

"I—I can't," Jory said.

"You must," Hillford said back, wrenching back farther on the rib. Letting more scent out.

The handler was still rubbing himself with the ball of his thumb. Deeper now, with Hillford putting his weight against that blade in the peach smuggler's dead heart.

Jory laughed to himself, a sick little laugh, and stepped forward, turned his torch around, and slammed the butt of it into the zombie's face, a bright gout of flame slashing up beside his head, lighting what was left of the ceiling.

"Jory, Jory!" Mayner was yelling in response to this, but that was in a place far removed from here. Another lifetime.

When the grate didn't come loose, Jory stepped in, did it again, the flame shooting up through the ceiling now, into the sky, a fountain of metallic orange and red and blue.

And, just when Jory thought it wasn't going to, the grate flopped away, altering the blue current coursing up the chain. Waking the handler up. Reminding him where he was. That he wasn't a *he* at all anymore.

The handler stepped forward, letting the zombie at the peach smuggler.

The zombie pulled to within inches of the peach smuggler's open side, tasting the wound from all angles, Hillford right there beside it, not at all concerned.

And then it turned away. Wasn't straining forward for that first bite. It turned instead to get a fix on Jory, the next-best meal in the room.

"What—what's this, what's it mean?" Jory heard himself saying.

"Another victim," Hillford said, taking a clean step back. Positioning himself between two urinals. "Another child of God."

This, more than anything, told Jory what his next move was.

He stepped back, set his feet, angled the torch down, and pulled the trigger.

On nothing.

That last blast through the ceiling, the impact on the butt— the torch thought it had been dropped. It had cycled down.

Hillford angled his face down to the peach smuggler.

"Jory Gray," he said, Jory's eyes following the priest's down to the peach smuggler. To the fingers, spasming now, unsticking themselves from the tile floor one by one, prob- ably in response to the tremors in the ground the virus had detected. The tremors that meant food. "This would be an honor for me," Hillford said, calmly. "You, however, have yet to be anoint—"

"*Shut up!*" Jory screamed, the stock against his thigh, his index finger feeling in the dark for the ignition button, just forward of the trigger guard.

There.

The flame caught, held.

In it, the peach smuggler was sitting up, his eyes milky, mouth open, leaking blackness.

Jory opened up the torch, went for more like a twenty count, until the back side of the restroom caved out, what was left of the roof creaking down a foot or two farther.

"Enough, enough!" Mayner was yelling in Jory's ears, and it was only then that Jory realized he'd been screaming the whole time.

The torch cycled down. Pure silence now. Just the zombie, cowered back from the heat, but pulling against its chain again now. For Jory.

"Don't do it," Mayner whispered into Jory's helmet. Because, through the helmet's feed, he could see what Jory was looking at.

But it was already happening.

Jory stepped forward, his flame bubbling right on the zombie's mouth grate. Trying to lift it back into place.

But it wouldn't go.

Again, Jory tried, and again the zombie wouldn't stay still. And then the handler took a step forward, leaning over to see where the peach smuggler had gone, maybe. What kind of magic this was. It gave the zombie enough slack in the chain to surge ahead, for Jory, and that zombie jumping like that— Jory was back in the hallway of his house again. Nearly ten years ago.

He brought the butt of the torch down on the zombie's head. Right on the crown, driving it straight down into the concrete floor, his flame blasting up beside him again and then cutting itself off.

And Jory kept going, couldn't stop, until the zombie's head was black paste, its legs and arms twitching, Jory's left sleeve smoking from the barrel of the torch.

Hillford reached in, guided the torch away from the mess the zombie was. Watching Jory's eyes the whole time. His hands not flinching away from the heat of the barrel even once.

"Henh," the handler said, tugging on the chain, suddenly life-less. Propping the zombie up on all fours only for the zombie to fall back down on itself.

"Ehhh," it said then, some alternate programming kicking in, and lowered itself to the zombie's side. The handler pulled the straps built into the zombie's leathers and zipped the zippers that he could, making the zombie into a body-shaped duffel bag, the head—what was left of it—pulled down, chin to chest.

The handler stood with his zombie carry-on, looked around for the door.

And then Jory realized that Mayner had been talking to him for what felt like minutes now.

"What's—?" Jory said, looking up through the gone-roof, and saw the three white contrails from the missiles that had been mounted on the roll bar of the jeep. That he'd pretended weren't right over his head the whole drive here.

Coded. They'd been coded. Standard procedure if you go this long without talking. If the thermals on the jeep's dash were dancing like they had to be.

That whistling sound they made too. Voss had been right. It was just like a cartoon from the old days. Something Jory could just let happen, if he wanted. Something that was going to happen anyway, maybe. That had been in the making for years now.

But then he flashed on Fishnet, strutting out into the middle of J Barracks, his head moving with the music. He flashed on the wiry dude, leaned down between his own knees to light his cigarette. On Linse, turned into a moth, flitting up to the light at the top of the Hill.

Her ID card.

Jory looked down for it, his hand coming up to the mic auto-matically, his voice coming through with a calmness he didn't know he had anymore, "We're good, man. We're good."

In that same instant, almost, the three tiny missiles detonated, maybe two stories above the restroom. Meaning Mayner had already had all but the last number of that kill sequence entered, had been hovering over it, shaking his head no.

Black feathers drifted down around Jory and the priest, the handler already leaving, undisturbed by all this human drama.

"We're good," Jory said again, and fell to his knees, the torch clattering to the side, falling away. He sifted through the rubble for the ID card but it was lost, probably burned to nothing. Along with the rest of the world.

At some point after that, Jory wasn't sure just when, Mayner was standing him up. Hillford was using some sacred little whisk broom to collect the ashes of the peach smuggler, funnel them into an aluminum urn, or amphora. It was about up to Jory's knee, maybe, and narrow like a churn, ornate like a ceremony.

Hillford set it down a safe distance from Jory and Mayner.

"What?" Jory said, looking to Mayner.

"You can kind of melt the lid shut for them. Makes it better for transport. Keeps the virus contained, so they don't need an escort from us."

"Serious?"

"It's nothing," Mayner said.

Jory nodded, couldn't find his ignition button now. Mayner reached down, punched it, the torch starting again.

"Like this?" Jory said, and opened the line of flame onto the metal jar, only stopped when Mayner pulled him away.

"Just a burst," Mayner was saying, trying not to smile where Hillford could see. "It's *aluminum*, man."

Jory turned back to what he'd just done. The smoke still rising from the ground.

When it cleared, there was a perfect black egg there.

Hillford looked from it to Jory. From Jory to it.

"Your general chose well," Hillford finally said, and stepped forward, collected that black egg, Mayner reaching out to stop him—

"*It's hot!*" But apparently not. Or, not to Brother Hillford.

Hillford cradled the egg against his robe, looked up to Jory again, and nodded a sincere *thank you.*

Jory nodded back. *You're welcome.* And then he collapsed against Mayner.

"You're alive," Mayner said to Jory, hugging Jory's head to his chest. "You made it, man."

Jory laughed into Mayner's shirt, then cried, and held on, wouldn't let go, even when Mayner's radio started asking for them.

Mayner stroked Jory's hair down.

"Biology teacher," Jory said, at last.

"You should know better than to smoke, then," Mayner said.

"I killed it," Jory said back. "I killed her, I mean. My own, my—I, with my hammer, I—I . . ."

"I know," Mayner said. "I know. We all did."

DAY FIVE

CHAPTER SIXTEEN

The names, they wouldn't stop. They'd been going for two hours already, since well after midnight.

It was Commando, in his bunk right by the wall, his wide back turned to Jory so that he was cupping the green light from his radio. Like he was nursing it.

It was one of those broadcasts where volunteers would just read through names of the found, those lists passed from operator to operator across thousands of miles, the names by now garbled and half made up. Fairy tales.

Jory was standing in the doorway to the bathroom. Maybe the sixth time he'd risen to splash water on his face. His right hand trembling again.

Over the sinks, just above the tin mirror, scratched with names from before the plague, was an eleven-watt bulb. It was just enough to see the shadow your eyes were. Just enough, if you held it close enough, to study a face in a snapshot.

"So what's her name?" he said to Commando, his voice hushed because everybody else was sleeping.

"Present tense," somebody said—the reprobate?

"Good, good."

One of the sleepers rolled over, winding himself tighter in his standard-issue blanket.

"Juliet," Commando said.

"No, really," Jory said, trying to get some fake smile into his voice.

Commando heard it. "That's really," he said.

"Burger Dude's on in twenty," Jory said.

No response. Just the names.

On the bulletin board was the pink slip, Jory's summons. Going to the principal's office again first thing. First he'd killed a handler, now a zombie. What next, right? The world?

Three bunks were empty now.

Jory sat on one of them, Fishnet's maybe, and lowered his head, woke in that position, he didn't know how long later. An hour, two, more. No pink in the sky yet. Nobody else stirring.

But something.

Someone.

Jory stood, not sure what was wrong. He crossed to Commando's radio to turn it off, Commando sleeping, but then stopped. Because of the names—*Jennifer Winkleman, Jennifer George, Jessica Turner.*

"Juliet," Jory said to himself, his hand to the volume dial.

Julianne Watkins, the volunteer read on, *July, like the month, July Jones, Katy Matheson to start the K's, Katrina—*

Jory rolled the broadcast off.

"Quiet, yeah?" somebody whispered.

Jory spun to the voice. To the shape sitting on his bed.

"Who—?" he said, still whispering.

The shape on the bed flipped its flashlight on, beamed it across the room at Jory's summons on the bulletin board.

"I believe it said first thing," the shape said, reangling the light under his own chin.

A guard, a soldier. Another glorified hall monitor of the postapocalypse.

"You can sleep sitting up like that?" he asked. "That some special thing you learn, teaching high school?"

"Can I at least get dressed?" Jory said, and the shape on the bed lumbered up, didn't say no, just turned his high beam on Glasses, wide awake in his bunk. Watching.

Glasses shut his eyes, kept them that way.

Jory understood.

Ten minutes later, still no sun to speak of, they were at the snake's mouth.

At night, evidently, they left the doors cracked open.

The stench was nearly visible.

Jory covered his nose and mouth with the back of his right hand.

His escort smiled, had already been holding his breath.

"What is this place?" Jory said, stepping down.

"End of the line," the escort said, the jeep already starting to move.

"And the beginning," a guard standing in the shadows said.

Jory tried to make the guard out, couldn't quite do it. Just the blunt suggestion of his gun. Not pointing anywhere in particular, for now.

"I know where to go," Jory said, stepping away from the smell, trying to duck around to Scanlon's portable office, but then another guard was standing in front of him. This one grim, humorless, his face melted, where it wasn't plain scorched.

Jory had heard about this. If you lived through a code somehow, or a torch malfunction, or any of the other hundred fire hazards available these days, you got assigned night duty. To keep you out of the sun.

But that was supposed to just be a rumor too. A warning.

"This way," the other guard said, standing by the cocked-open doors, each maybe thirty feet tall, heavy as a truck.

His eyes on the burned guard until the last instant, Jory stepped in, the snake's breath syrupy now, grainy against his throat.

He coughed, gagged.

The guard waited for him to come back up.

"Gonna do it?" he said. "Spew?"

Jory hadn't been going to, but that word pushed him over.

"Done?" the guard said a few splashes later.

Jory focused on the ground before him. There were hash marks drawn on it Evidently it was something to bet on—how many steps visitors took before losing the contents of their stomach.

Jory'd made it two.

He looked past the guard, down the sloping corridor.

"This the brig?" he said, wiping his mouth and nose.

"Not for you," the soldier said back, and led the way, Jory seeing after a few steps that they were supposed to stay within a taped-off walkway.

After the first switchback, the floor sloping more perilously, he saw why—this was a holding facility. When there weren't supposed to be holding facilities anymore. When there had been assurances that there would never be holding facilities again.

The dead, in cell after cell. Reaching through their bars to just short of the taped walkway.

"Just pick whichever one you want," the guard called back over his shoulder. "We'll have it sent up to your room."

"We still *keep* them?" Jory asked.

"Only the good ones," the guard said, then, "Whoah, whoah," making room for the handler juggernauting up their walkway, oblivious to anything in its path.

Taking the guard's lead, Jory backed to the edge of the tape, trying to find that middle ground between the monster in front of him and the monster just behind, reaching.

And then they were moving again. The guard still talking. "Less we feed them, more acute their sense of smell gets."

"These are—*those* ones?" Jory said, trying to clock the zombie's fingers. "For Preburial?"

"Where'd you think we get 'em?" the guard laughed. "The zombie fairy?"

"I don't want to be here," Jory said, eyeing a zombie with especially long arms.

"One step either way, your worries'll be over," the guard said, and then Jory staggered forward, into him.

The guard turned, ready to push back, but it was another handler that had rammed Jory, bearing down on them from behind.

The guard pulled Jory to the side, let the handler hulk past.

"Guess you picked a busy morning to see the wizard," the guard said, then leaned forward hard, away from the long-armed zombie hooking an uncut finger into the guard's shirt. The shirt ripped away from shoulder to sleeve. "Oh you—" the guard hissed, stepping forward with what looked to Jory like a thick baton, but it had some kind of jolt in it when he slammed it into the zombie.

The zombie arced back into his cell, lay there twitching, steaming from the eyes.

"Don't you just love technology?" the guard said, pulling Jory along.

How could the plague ever be over if the military was keeping it in pens, right?

But how could the military burn the infected dead without the infected to sniff them out, Jory knew. And hated. Without some way to test the corpses that were always turning up, the

Church would rally support, insist on burying *every* body. And that had to be worse. Z Day all over again, on its own tenth anniversary.

No thanks.

Jory followed the guard around another switchback, and another, down to either the third or fourth level of he-had-no-idea-how-many. All the way to hell probably.

The guard deposited him in another waiting room, what felt like a recommissioned cell of sorts. A make-do execution chamber.

At first Jory resisted, but the guard gave him a hard knee, half threw him in.

Jory stumbled to the table, took one of the two chairs.

At which point Scanlon leaned up from the wall he'd taken. Where he'd been waiting, tilting a cup of coffee up to his mouth.

Jory breathed in, out, then let a calmness seep over him. A slackness.

"Jory Gray," Scanlon said, taking the opposite chair. Flipping it around to straddle it, lean across its back.

"Don't you sleep?" Jory said, no real eye contact.

For maybe twenty seconds, Scanlon studied Jory. Then, finally, he nodded to himself. Finished his coffee off. Reached back into a corner for the gun that wasn't a gun, but a torch, a flamethrower.

He rattled it down onto the table between himself and Jory, Jory trying not to flinch, trying so hard not to look at this instrument. Of his own death probably. You don't go this far underground to do things you could do just the same up top.

"You know what this is, right?" Scanlon asked.

"It's a torch," Jory said, swallowing.

"Good, good," Scanlon said. "Torch, torch. Say it to yourself. Torch, torch. Hammer? No, no, not a hammer, Gray. *Torch.*"

Jory had no defense, no excuse.

"But no worries, son," Scanlon said, sliding the torch away. Holding his hand out to the corridor behind Jory. The holding cells. "*These* we've got more of, right? More than we ever asked for. And, your instinct, I'm not faulting that. Some people hesitate. You didn't, Gray. I give you that."

Jory didn't know whether to apologize or say thank you.

"But your handler, it *was* malfunctioning," Scanlon added, leaning back what little he could, backwards in the chair. "We've got the feed from the incident, so you're in the clear there."

"Then . . . this is about the peach smuggler?" Jory said, lost.

"He's not exactly the one we're interested in here."

Jory looked up to try to gauge Scanlon's face.

"I *told* him to call off the code," Jory said. "The driver. He was following proto—protocol."

"Grant Mayner," Scanlon said, like the name left a bad taste. "But he's not of concern here either."

Jory counted heads, his eyes unfocusing.

"The priest?" he said at last.

Scanlon chuckled.

"More like their patron saint," he spat, both his meaty hands gripping the backrest of the chair now.

". . . Hillford," Jory dredged up.

"As near as we can tell," Scanlon said, "and, trust me, that's pretty damn near, Brother Hillford has never been on even *one* of these pissant calls. They just send the expendables, right? Midlevel management. Shit, I would, with this kind of rate." He shrugged an insincere shrug then. "No offense."

"Saint?" Jory said, his eyes flicking to the back corner of the room, where he thought he'd seen a twitch, a flicker. Something.

Scanlon set his hands on the table, pulling Jory back.

"That little trespass a few years back, in the old pens?" Scanlon asked. "Home movie heard 'round the world?"

"Parting the Dead Sea," Jory recited. That recording of the three priests walking through the ocean of zombies.

Scanlon grudged a nod.

"That was him?" Jory said.

"Officially, no," Scanlon said. "Their order, or whatever—they can't take credit for individual shit. Unofficially, though, yeah, it was Hillford. Big boss man, in the flesh."

"You, over there," Jory said.

"He wishes."

"I mean—"

Scanlon slammed his palm down onto the table.

"And if Hillford's out in the field," Scanlon said. "Then—then I don't fucking know, Gray. End of Days? Something to do with this ten-year anniversary coming up? But, do you know what I *do* know? Do you know what I'm absolutely certain of, what I know as well as that I have two balls? That, when their holiest-of-holy boneface waltzes out into the restricted zone, that you don't—can you guess this last part? Help me now."

Jory shook his head no.

Scanlon slid three stills from the jeep's feed down into the part of the tabletop Jory was fixed on.

It was Hillford, cradling a black egg the size of a football. Infected ash swirling in it like yolk, its shell as smooth and shiny as obsidian.

Scanlon pushed the slick prints into Jory's chest.

"I know that you don't give him any more artifacts for his damn reliquary," he said. "They're up there jacking off on this right now. Fucking circle-jerk on the mount."

Jory swallowed, the sound crashing in his ears.

Then Scanlon laughed. It was an evil sound. "And, just so

you know, our best reports are that this, this whatever-the-hell religion they claim to be, they think that the plague—that the desiccants out there eating their way through the world?—that they're *larvae.* That that's why they're so hungry. You following, son? Biology, right?"

"Instars," Jory said. Licking his lips just after.

He'd heard this before, on late-night.

"In-what?" Scanlon said.

"Stages of . . . molting," Jory said, flashing his eyes up to Scanlon. "Insect life cycle. Egg, larva, pupa, adult."

"And, so what do you give them, Gray? What do you give their fucking *he*ro? A black egg. A sign from above. Now we don't have even part of a clue what they're going to—"

"What's the adult stage supposed to be, then?" Jory asked. "After the chrysalis?" Scanlon steepled his fingers burrowed his eyes into Jory's.

"Angels," he said. "Fucking zombie moths, I don't know."

"Angels," Jory repeated.

Had Linse heard this too? Had he fallen asleep one night and let it play? *That* why she left?

"Angels or some bullshit, yeah," Scanlon said, dismissing it with his craggy hand. "And, know what else your little gift out there means? To us?"

"The army?"

"It means we can't leave you out in the *field,*" Scanlon said. "Much as you might be asking for it, even if your dumb-ass driver *requests* it, even if you're the only torch to live in I don't know how long, you're sacred now. Their holy egg giver, I don't know. Their big black chicken." Scanlon liked this. "Or red, brown, whatever the hell color you are. It doesn't matter. We can use you, somewhere down the line."

"I'm not a hostage."

"You're whatever the hell we say you are, Gray. We clear on that?"

"He was only there because you sent me," Jory said.

"Excuse me, soldier?"

"Hillford. Brother Hillford. He said he just came to see why you'd picked me, yourself."

"We've got the feed, Gray. It's got audio. And he knew that feed was rolling."

"I didn't."

"You didn't need to," Scanlon said. "What you *do* need to know is that, because of your unauthorized theatrics out there yesterday, I can't even discipline you properly. I can't have you looking like a prisoner of war, if we have to trade you or something."

"We're at war with the bonefaces?"

"They want what we've got, Gray. People. Influence. Don't think for a second they don't have their eyes on that prize. The future's either theirs or it's ours."

"But they're just a—a—" Jory started.

"We protect the body," Scanlon said. "They shepherd the soul. A new world's shaping up all around us. Who's going to be its beating heart, you think? Keep the monsters at bay?"

"You," Jory said, and, then, because he was a walking suicide, "as long as there's, you know. Monsters."

Scanlon shook his head. More in pity than in appreciation now.

He unholstered his service revolver. It was big, silver, important.

He rolled the cylinder, looked across it at Jory.

"I was never in favor of conscripting civilians," he said. "No discipline, don't really have that gut-level understanding of the chain of command. But desperate times, desperate saviors of the human race. That doesn't mean you can't be part of the disciplinary process, though."

Like he'd probably been planning the whole time, he emptied the revolver's cylinder into his hand, thumbed a cartridge from his shirt pocket back in.

"You said you can't kill me," Jory tried.

Scanlon held the revolver out to him, butt first.

"Like I said," Scanlon started, standing, urging Jory to as well, "we know the handler was malfunctioning. That it needs to be decommissioned."

Jory still hadn't taken the revolver.

Scanlon pawed his big hand up to Jory's shoulder, his neck. Pulled him around the side of the table. Led him to the empty part of the room.

Jory flicked his eyes up, just reflex, and fell back against the wall just as fast.

A handler was standing there, just out of sight. *The* handler, with the outsized codpiece. At his leg, on its chain, a zombie.

Scanlon chuckled, thrust the pistol into Jory's hand. Said, "Want it now, son?"

Jory took it, held it out against the zombie, but then—then.

The zombie wasn't moving. The handler either.

A thin line of blood was dripping down the leash chain, link by link. *From* the handler. From some chip that had been scavenged from its forearm, maybe. The veins there absolutely rigid with effort, the handler doing everything it could to just move one muscle.

He'd been locked, though. Jory'd seen it in the demonstrations—forced rigor, the last fail-safe.

And this zombie, it was wrong too, wasn't pulling against the chain, was—it was under *glass.* The zombie had had molten glass poured on it while it was alive. Or, while it was dead and walking. This was a trophy, one that couldn't infect. The sterilized dead.

"One shot between the eyes," Scanlon said, patting Jory's shoulder, and Jory raised the pistol. "We're going to decommission it anyway," Scanlon added. "Doesn't matter if it's us or you, really, does it?"

"I—I—"

"Show me what you're made of, son. I want to believe in you too, just like Brother Hillford. Pretend—pretend it's not even a gun. It's a hammer, Gray. It's a *hammer,* and this bitch, she's, she's—"

Jory turned his eyes to Scanlon. As if waking up.

And then he did what maybe nobody else in the postapocalypse had ever done, yet—took a step to the side and settled the pistol on Scanlon. Between *his* eyes. To drive a train right through his thick head.

At the other end of the room, the guard stepped back in, immediately pawed at his belt for something to stop Jory with.

Scanlon held a hand up that that wouldn't be necessary, then stepped in so the barrel of Jory's pistol pressed into his white eyebrow. "That's the spirit, son. Think I've never stared death in the eye, that it? Think I'm afraid here? Not for myself, son. No. The rest of humanity, though, you bet. I was wrong about you, I guess. You're not a suicide at all. You want to take the whole world with you, don't you? Is that it, Gray? Come on, then, neither one of us'll be around to see it, come on—"

Jory's hand was shaking now, but it was different.

Scanlon reached up, guided the barrel down between his own eyes.

Jory pulled the pistol away so he could do it himself, then felt the trigger going, going, and, at the last instant, he flicked the barrel over. Away.

His arm was clenched against the recoil, his eyes probably closed—he *wasn't* field-rated, wasn't trained for firearms—but firing Scanlon's pistol wasn't at all like the one he'd shot out on Disposal. The *bang* wasn't a bang at all. More a muted *pop.* A whimper, almost.

Jory turned the pistol to the side, didn't understand this.

Scanlon pointed with his eyes at what Jory'd done.

Missed?

The glass shell around the zombie he'd been aiming at, it wasn't even cracked.

But. There was *more* blood on the leash now. Coming in rivulets down the chain.

Jory tracked it up to the handler.

The blood was coming from his ears, his eyes, his nose and his mouth.

Jory stepped back, fell into the wall. Tried to paw the cylinder of the pistol open, finally lucked on the release.

The cartridge, it was a detonator, *shaped* like a cartridge. The firing pin had just tapped the plunger, sent a radio signal, sent it to—

To the fail-safe planted in the handler's brain stem.

"No," Jory said, the handler slumping forward, catching itself—*him*self—on his massive arms somehow, but it was over.

"That's two handlers you've decommissioned now," Scanlon said, palming the pistol back to himself. "Might have found your calling, here."

"Don't you just love technology?" the guard hissed right into Jory's ear, and led him from the room, dragged him up the long corridor, handed him off to the burn-faced guard. The burn-faced guard deposited Jory outside then stepped back through those fairy-tale doors, grinding some big wheel around to clang them shut. To keep the day out.

CHAPTER SEVENTEEN

That mannequin dad, pacing in his basement. Running his fingers through his wispy hair. Sitting on an old weight bench down there now, too short for him so his knees are up like a grasshopper. An old photo album balanced in his lap, the box it was dug out from still open.

"Dear?" his wife's voice calls down.

He looks up to it.

She doesn't call again.

Back to the computer monitor. Page after page of kitten pictures. He saves them, saves them.

"Daddy?" his daughter says, halfway down the stairs, her hand light on the handrail.

"Yes?" the dad says.

She doesn't have the next part of the question though.

The calendar flips to the next day, a Saturday.

There's a new trampoline in the backyard, its boxes and straps and various tools still on top of the grass, like they're going to get picked up later. Mannequin children bouncing up into the sky, their silky hair following them back down. Screams of delight. The sun beating down. A tall wooden fence as backdrop.

The dad turns away from it all.

The cell phone in his hand still has the image his brother texted him. That slip of bulletin-board paper.

The dad pulls a pen from his shirt pocket, looks to the house to be sure his wife doesn't have him in her sights, then uses a felt-tip marker to crib the number from that strip of paper onto his forearm. Small, tight letters smearing on beige plastic.

And then he breathes.

"Watch me! Watch me!" his daughter screams.

The dad creases his face into an empty smile. He tracks his daughter up into the air and leaves her there, turns around, cupping his hollow torso around the cell phone so that he's shaped like a question mark.

He punches that number into the keypad. Gets a front desk of some kind.

"Yes, yeah, I'm, um. About the offer on the bulletin board. Six weeks, right?"

His call's passed back, up the chain of command. No apology, an efficient feel to it all.

Government?

"Yes, I'm just calling about—" he starts, the one time there's a presence on the other end, but then it's back to the hold sound.

Behind him, the kids are staying in the air longer and longer. "Daddy! I'm taller than you! Daddy!"

He nods, closes his eyes. Can't turn around yet, because his face would be a giveaway.

Finally, "Yes?"

A gruff voice. One with no time for this.

"Um, yeah," the dad says, the cell phone held to the side of his head with both hands now, so not even one word will get away. "I just wanted to know. You're doing a study, right? I just, we have, my family. Certain allergies. A history. I just wanted to be sure—"

Listening, listening.

Nodding.

"No, no, not for me. This is—I think I know somebody in your, for those six weeks. Okay, four left, yeah, four."

Behind him now, his son goes rocketing off the trampoline at a bad angle.

"Daddy!" his daughter shrieks.

The dad switches the phone to the other ear. Takes a step away from the commotion.

"But, but. Is there any way I could, you know. See him? Or even just—I understand he can't take phone calls, is that correct? No, no, of course I haven't been in contact—It's just—he's my . . . I haven't—"

At which point his wife brushes past him, all business.

He turns, vaguely aware.

She returns with their son on her hip. His plastic arm flopping against his side, the angle all wrong.

"I don't mean to interrupt, dear," she says.

The dad holds the phone out like a shield, like proof. "I was just—I was . . ."

"Yes?" she says.

The dad opens his mouth once, can't trust it, then opens it again, and all that comes out is that long shrill beep. "XXXXX."

Then, not looking down to do it, he ends the call.

A very real unmannequin dog explodes against the backside of their fence, slobbering to get through.

The rest of the neighborhood dogs hear it, join in.

The dad's mouth still open. "XXXXX."

The album in the basement is still open too, to a snapshot of two lanky kids at a pool. One of them running for the edge, to jump in, the other already in the air, pulling himself into a cannonball.

It could have been any one of us.

CHAPTER EIGHTEEN

"How can you not know about *kill* shots, dude?"

Timothy. It was Timothy asking. Like everything was starting all over again. Like Scanlon was giving Jory a chance to do it right, maybe.

Not that Cleanup was any kind of gravy assignment.

Jory sank his shovel into the ash of this torched house, came up with a trampoline spring.

"What do they call that?" Timothy went on, leaning on his shovel, his aviator goggles cocked on his head like always, "Like, 'selective stupidity,' or just the normal kind?"

"It was just a gun," Jory said, letting the rusted spring slide back into the ash, one more thing the world wasn't going to be needing anymore.

"A gun with invisible bullets," Timothy said, studying their horizon. "I think I'm kind of offended to even know you, man."

"You and me both," Jory said, and sank his shovel into the ash again.

This was a safe zone, just recently cleared. Meaning, no dead walking around, complicating things.

Still, between the four of them on this detail, there was only one pistol. Jory didn't have it—he was sworn off them now, not that anybody'd asked—and Timothy didn't have it, and neither did Wallace. Not that Wallace could be trusted with much more than a toothpick. Somewhere on the balding side of fifty, shambling around in a suit, a look on his face like he'd just stepped out of the past, had no idea what kind of bad dream he was in here. 'Mental zombie' had been Timothy's whispered term. Jory didn't disagree. Wallace had been staring at them the whole time.

The one of them *with* the pistol strapped to her leg was Sheryl. Because, individually, maybe Jory and Timothy and Wallace weren't rapists, but, in a group? All the way out here? No supervision?

The gun wasn't to protect Sheryl from zombies, it was to protect her from her own crew.

At least that's how Timothy had explained it on the ride off base. Sheryl had been listening to this as well. Shrugging her so-what shrug. Jory kind of liked her for that.

"They're still there," Timothy was saying now.

Jory didn't look up. The two priests, just standing down the block. Barely within view, but never not there.

Timothy pointed to them with his chin, said, "Dalton used to say that if we ever really wanted to know where the plague started, track its spread, find its point of origin, that their data banks could—"

"Used to?" Jory interrupted. "He *used* to say?"

Timothy came back to him. Made a cursory swipe at the dirt with his shovel.

"Dude, where you been? Dalton's been dark now for like forty-eight hours. Think we're the only ones tune in? I think the right wrong people heard what he was saying."

"He was the burger dude, right?" Jory said, angling his shovel under a sliver of white, like glass.

"What you got there?" Timothy asked, peering over.

Jory choked up on his shovel to pull the white sliver closer. A blade? It was what they were supposed to be looking for. Yesterday this site had been coded. The ash was still warm, the houses to either side spray-painted with big green *Xs,* for Disposal to take care of.

Supposedly, a priest had gone down here, along with a novitiate, out on training. More important, that priest, of course, had a knife, to perform the ceremony, start the taste test. Now, the Church, like always, they wanted that knife back. It was one of a set or something, Timothy hadn't known exactly. Just that they'd have a chaperone for the duration of their dig, to make sure they didn't mess with the thing. Which he translated at volume for Jory as 'mess up with their dirty, sinful hands.'

If they found it, they were under strict orders not to touch it, get it all unblessed.

Jory just pulled the shovel with the white sliver in it, Timothy nodding a *maybe* to it, limbering up the scanner dangling from his belt. Directing its invisible beam down.

Two seconds later, the light on the readout went red, non-organic—the blades were supposed to light up green, from the leather handle's carbon afterprint or something.

"Toilet bowl," Timothy said, packing the scanner back down.

"Somebody's wedding china," Jory tried, picking the shard up now that he could.

"Saber-tooth tiger," Timothy said, miming it with his gloved finger.

"That'd register green," Jory said, flinging the shard out past the edges of what had been the house. Aiming vaguely for one of those green *Xs,* like, if he hit it just right he could bring the whole house down, save Disposal a trip.

"Ewww," Timothy said then, pulling up a boot with his shovel. The foot was still inside, coated in ants. "Could have been you, right?" he said to Jory.

Jory watched Timothy walk the booted foot over to the wheelbarrow, tump it in. Use his *own* boot to kick the lever over, the teeth in the wheelbarrow chewing the bone to dust, sterilizing it with heat. Because infected bone, as of today and counting, was supposed to be able to infect indefinitely. So far, that meant nine years and twenty-nine days out. Not that whoever's boot that had been had definitely been infected. But still.

"Break!" Timothy called out then, Sheryl just looking up at him then leaning down on her shovel again. Wallace, watching Timothy stand his own shovel up, walk away from it.

"It is just—" Jory said, angling his wrist up for the watch he didn't wear.

"We call our own breaks out here," Timothy said, waggling his eyebrows. "So, save any of that menthol?"

Jory planted his shovel as well. Shook a normal cigarette up for Timothy.

They sat on what had been the brick edge of a garden-bed, smoked. The priests were still out there, white sentries. The sun not even touching them probably.

"I find it, I'll whistle all secret like this"—doing it—"so you can come over, yeah?"

"The knife?"

Timothy breathed in, blew it out in a straight line. "It's a golden ticket, man. You take that up to the doors of the Church, they just might let you see her."

"Linse."

Timothy ashed onto the toe of his boot.

"Doesn't matter," Jory said.

Timothy turned, waited for the explanation of that.

"They're changing," Jory said. "The dead. They're—I don't know. Used to, you had to get bit to get infected, right? Like, chewed on but not quite enough? Now. That peach smuggler. He was just killed by some other peach smuggler. It's airborne, or dirtborne. Or, I don't know. A curse. Humanity's expiration date."

"The end of our alphabet."

"The beginning of theirs."

Timothy held his cigarette sideways, scried into his cherry like he did each time. Like he was reading the tendrils.

"Wish he'd been a black-eyed pea smuggler," he said. "I didn't used to like them. Now I'd cut my pinky off for half a spoonful. Just to smell them cooking in my grandma's kitchen."

"With bacon," Jory added, "or ham, whatever."

"Use my pinky," Timothy said, leaning over to nudge Jory off-balance.

"I—I saw him, man," Jory said, moving his fingers on their brick's edge, in echo of the peach smuggler's. Drawing Timothy to look there, watch. "He sat up. Alive, but, you know. Not."

"Maybe it's like the Venus radiation from the old movies. Just soaking through everything. So that anything that dies, it comes back meaner. Hungry."

"Or it's second generation," Jory said, pinching his cigarette to his lips. It was stale and brown, in comparison to the menthol. "It used to transmit by contact. Now that there's less of us, though, less contact, it's found some other way."

"You saying that as a survivor, or as a biology teacher?"

Jory squinted at the priests in what he thought of as a gunfighter way. A particularly western way.

"You heard that bullshit on the radio, didn't you?" Timothy said, like finally getting a punch line.

"Doesn't matter," Jory said back. "They're changing, man, serious. It's probably best she went up the Hill. They'll last longer, with the bonefaces to . . . to keep them out. Away. And this—this torch bullshit, with the handlers. It's not going to last. We don't have enough bodies to make it last. They don't have enough knives."

"You hear they carry two?" Timothy added, eyeballing the priests now as well.

"Urban legend," Jory said.

"You never kept the good tequila back when your in-laws were over?" Timothy said. "Just showed them the cheap stuff?"

Jory smiled, almost even laughed. "Least we're out in the sun," he said, holding a hand out to the beautiful day.

"You're right," Timothy said, standing, his arms out while he spun, soaking it all in. "This is grade A *great,* man. Good honest work in the honest-to-goodness outdoors? *Hell* yeah. Hey, you want to camp here tonight, with me? We can steal a couple of smokes from my dad's emergency pack, he'll never know. Then, man, then just listen to the zombies at the fence moan. Yeah. Hey, your brother still got that magazine. . . ?"

Jory tossed his cigarette at Timothy. Timothy recoiled like it was more, stumbled back, over some exposed rebar from the driveway. He came up from that holding . . . the other leg? From the knee down. Part of a leg.

He pushed it away, backed off from it.

Then he cocked his head, came back. Jory edged over.

"Hunh," Timothy said. Then, about the priests neither of them were looking back to, "They still there?"

Jory faked a cough, sneaked a look.

Timothy squatted down anyway, poked the leg.

It rolled over, the toes pointing at the sky now. Fused together, not from heat, but from the factory.

A prosthetic. For a giant.

"Hey hey," Timothy said, coming up with it like a prize.

Wallace looked over. Sheryl shook her head, wasn't amused. "It's not real!" Timothy called across to them, then, "Screw 'em," rolling the leg over in his hands. Two nubs of leather strap were still at the top, like garters. "What do you think they'd give me for this?" he said, hooking his head to the idea of the priests.

"Ten Hail Marys," Jory said, stepping back to his shovel.

"Isn't it Holy Marys or something?" Timothy said, following at a half hop, trying to hook the prosthetic leg's leather strap to his belt. "Whoa, whoa, incoming," he hissed to Jory.

They each claimed their shovels.

"Boneface?" Jory said, not looking yet.

Timothy was.

"Where you think they recruit from?" he asked, fingers laced on top of his shovel, a pad for his chin.

"What?"

"I mean, see any basketball players around these days?"

"Shut up," Jory said, sinking his shovel deep. Praying not to thunk into whatever the priests were looking for.

Except he knew already it was going to be him.

"Jory Gray?" the first one called ahead, his voice not at all muffled by the mask. It didn't make any sense.

They should be cooking out here too. Boiling in those robes.

"What'd I do this time?" Timothy said, pushing his shovel to the side, holding his arms to the side, offering himself. "I forget to say grace before breakfast this morning? Shit, you *seen* what they're feeding us over there? Don't think you'd be praying eith—"

"Jory Gray," the second priest said again. Right to Jory Gray.

Jory swallowed. Looked up, and up, to that bone-white face.

"We need you to verify something for us," the priest said. "Your commanding officers have already released you from duty, and asked that we deliver you back to your next site."

"I always graduate last," Timothy said, picking his shovel up again just to lean on it some more.

"I just got here," Jory said, trailing off, a white helicopter—they have *that* kind of fuel on the Hill?—thumping down in what used to be the street. Everybody turned to watch it, except Jory, scratching the tip of his shovel through the ash. What he was uncovering was a flash of skin, the wind from the blades dusting the rest off—a forearm. A series of *Z* tattoos snaking up it.

Jory covered it back up.

"This new world asks much of each of us, yes," the priest said back to Jory.

"That'll take me?" Jory said, nodding to the copter.

"Up the Hill," Timothy added. "Who knows *who* you might run in to up there, right?"

Jory got it already.

"Let me pee," he said, and leaned his shovel against a shower pipe, caught it when it fell, tried to balance it again—his hand shaking, shaking, Timothy finally grabbing the shovel for him.

"Of course, urinate," the first priest said. "Deny the body and the spirit—"

"It turns yellow, right?" Timothy said, stepping in as if to block Jory from view, giving him some privacy. Leaving Jory to ease into what had been the backyard, a plague or two ago.

"So, you guys hoop it up, up there?" he heard Timothy asking, and let go, splashing down into some more ash. Cleaning that ash off something . . . white? Glistening?

"More toilet bowl," Jory mumbled, zipping shut, but pulled a cigarette out anyway, still hadn't turned around. "Fuck it," he finally said, and opened his fingers, let that cigarette fall. Had no choice but to go down after it. Thread that white shard—definitely the blade of one of their knives—into his boot, then lace that boot tighter. Peer around by his arm to see Timothy, his right leg folded up to his butt so he could gimp around on the prosthetic, holding it in place by the two strap nubs.

Both priests were watching, disgusted. They turned as one with Jory's scuffling approach.

"Jory Gray," the first one said, stepping aside for Jory to have the straightest line to the helicopter.

"See you never," Jory said to Timothy, and Timothy nodded back, his teeth too set with effort for him to say anything. Just crutch-hop, crutch-hop, *crash.*

Jory didn't look back, even from the air.

CHAPTER NINETEEN

Jory had been expecting any numbers of things inside the walls of the Church—the compound, really—human sacrifice, ritual cannibalism, gory statues, bodies on display, hymns gone wild, something strange and disturbing with the three crosses, but what he hadn't even considered was armadillos.

Walking from the landing pad to the main courtyard, he thought at first that the helicopter ride—being airborne for the first time since being plucked from that water tower—that that kind of altitude had left inky spots in his peripheral vision. Spots that scurried away, into oversized mouseholes in the interiors walls. Spots that scurried in, then pulled a flip turn, kept their hairy noses just there at the edge of that line of darkness.

Armadillos.

When there were no dogs anymore, hardly any cats. Just undulating lines of coyotes (too fast), Pharaoh vultures with their mossy shadows (too high). The occasional black rat, fat with corpse meat (too deep).

And armadillos.

Jory licked his lips, followed his assigned priest, the pilot who'd taken a vow of not-talking-to-Jory, evidently. The priest he was handed off to, though, he walked beside Jory, instead of in front.

"So what'd this place used to be?" Jory asked, unable *not* to see the deep scratch marks in the tall white wall. The *inside* of the tall white wall. "One of the old holding facilities?"

"The Church has always been here, Jory Gray," the priest answered, his voice not betraying even a tinge of insult. "Perhaps it's simply that you haven't recognized its relevance until these pressing times."

"You talking *church* in the big sense, or this particular . . ." Jory trailed off, zeroing in on a slight female novitiate, crossing in front of them. Looking up, then back down to the ground just as fast. "Linse," Jory said to himself, and jogged forward, his eyes already hot with this dream coming so true, so fast. "Linse, Linse, hey," but, then, when he got there, pulled her to face him, combed the hood back off her bald head . . . not her.

"Sorry, sorry," Jory said, still holding the novitiate by the shoulders. "Have you seen her, though, like at mass or whatever? One blue eye, one brown, pretty, real—yeah, probably bald. Like all of you . . ."

"Please don't mistake her silence for unwillingness to help, Jory Gray," Jory's escort said, standing there. Not trying to stop this at all. "Novitiates don't have the Word yet. It's nothing personal."

"She can't speak," Jory said, letting go. Still staring at this girl, her eyes so kind, so apologetic.

She scurried on, out of his hands.

"Just in here, if you will," Jory's escort said, holding his arm out as if opening the door beside them, but it was just a doorway. Maybe that was part of their religion—everything open, no secrets, all places connected.

A *tall* doorway of course.

Jory nodded thanks, stepped through, into a room completely bare, save the one simple table a few steps in. A chair on either side.

STEPHEN GRAHAM JONES

"Not again," Jory said, flashing back to Scanlon's recommissioned cell, then he flinched to the side, away from the white
shape stepping out from the far wall.

Brother Hillford. Perfectly camouflaged, except for his eyes.
Like he was taking shape, stepping through from some holier
plane.

Saint indeed.

"Jory Gray," Hillford said, indicating the table.

Jory took a seat, the chair tall enough that the soles of his
boots just brushed the floor.

Hillford took the chair opposite him. He just watched Jory,
until Jory had to look away. To the giant mouseholes all along
the wall. That one golden, scaled face watching him.

"Ah, yes," Hillford said, about the fascinating, fascinating
armadillo. Jory came back to him. "They were never on your
dissection tray in lab, were they?" Hillford asked. "Because
what would your classes have learned from them, right? All
the lessons about them apply only to the order Cingulata. As in
singular, Jory Gray. Dasypodidae, as the order used to be called,
they're like the Church, you could say. A singular survivor."

"Nine—nine-banded, right?" Jory asked, having to cock his
head to shake the old information down into his throat.

"Of course, yes. This is, or used to be, North America, after all.
Do you know what it means in Spanish, I wonder? *Armadillo?*
Little armored one."

"It help them?" Jory said.

"Pardon?"

"Against the conquistadors. Who named them."

"Oh, well," Hillford said, looking to no spot in particular. "I
suppose their armor was no real defense against halberds and
pikes and shod horses, no. Though of course your Western
culture's predilection for conflating *little* and *cute* might have

154

been . . . interesting. As I'm sure you know, aside from their shell, Dasypopidea, as they used to be classed, are known to be carriers of certain diseases, easily contractable were any of these explorers, *their* armor allowing, to have reached down, attempted to cuddle, pet, or transport any of these little ones home."

To show what he was talking about, Hillford lowered a hand to the armadillo nuzzled up against his leg now. Jory looked around his own chair, to make sure he wasn't surrounded.

"Good thing you aren't a conquistador then, right?" Jory said. "Nothing imperialistic about religion, of course."

Hillford laughed a tolerant laugh.

"Don't be alarmed, Jory Gray," Hillford said. "The only way one of these little ones could hurt us would be to itself die, thus denying us the reassurance of its timid company."

"So, you said 'used to be' dasypopidea," Jory said, scooching his chair in closer to the table, no mean feat when you can't touch the ground so well.

"Yes, yes, good. It rather fills the modern mouth, no? Blame Linnaeus for that. He thought the original Aztec term for them, that it wasn't descriptive enough. So he fell back on his Greek. *Dasypopidae* is the compound term he came up with. It means *turtle rabbit*. Colorful, yes? Remember, in his time there were no photographs, only words and crude sketches drawn from memory. But of course a biologist needs neither history nor taxonomy lessons from me. I apologize. Nerves, I suppose. Does that surprise you, Jory Gray? That we can be just as weak as you under these?"

Tapping the cheek of his mask to show.

"I want to see her," Jory said.

Hillford processed this, came back with, "The one you had the, um, identification card for."

"Linse. She has one brown eye, one blue. Real easy to spot."

"They leave their old names behind, of course," Hillford said, producing an apple from some pocket. A crusted-black blade from his left sleeve.

"Hunh," Jory said, seeing that second blade.

"Excuse me?"

"That's—that's a real apple," Jory lied.

Hillford began cutting the skin from it. One long spiral, around and around, so careful, the red skin partially transparent.

"You've got a mature tree up here," Jory went on, pushing it too far, he knew.

"We're blessed in many ways, yes," Hillford said, offering a slice to Jory, balanced on the edge of that blade. "The fruit you get on your base is in sauce form, is it not?"

Jory watched that apple slice.

"I just want to talk to her," he went on. "Make sure she's—that she's all right. Happy with her decision, all that. And, and I understand if she can't speak yet or whatever. Her vows."

Hillford cut another slice.

"I want to say goodbye," Jory added, quieter.

Hillford nodded, let the slice fall over, rock back and forth.

"What's meant to be always happens, Jory Gray," he finally said. "Whether we intend it to or not. Once we learn to submit, to 'let slip the mortal coil,' as the poets say, then the road to perfection, to grace . . . This means nothing to you, does it?"

"I'm sure it's good stuff," Jory said.

"No, no, no apologies, please," Hillford said, "please. This, it's—it's so fascinating. The basic principles and tenets, they elude you. No, not *elude*. You're not so much as looking for them, even. Yet, of all of us, Jory Gray, of all our centuries of combined perseverance, it's you who intuited the truth, and presented it in the least encumbered manner."

To show what he was talking about, Hillford produced the black egg Jory had made.

"Whether you were aware or not," Hillford said, his voice taking on a reverent tone now. "Your *hands,* they knew. Your flame that day, it was divine. Your spirit, pure."

"I just wanted to live," Jory said.

"Exactly. Yes, perfect, Jory Gray. That we could all winnow our desires down to such basic concerns. Glean that focus."

"And now I just want to see her. That's my focus."

Hillford moved his head back and forth, unsurprised, maybe a little regret mixed in.

"The one you rescued from her basement sixteen months ago," he said.

"It wasn't the basement."

"Where she'd been living for . . . for how long?"

"'This world asks much of each of us,'" Jory cited.

"'And what it takes away it gives back, sevenfold,'" Hillford cited back. "Her years of darkness are over, Jory Gray. Now let her years in the light commence. Be satisfied that you were instrumental to her—"

Jory shuffled his feet, an armadillo squealing away from that contact. Had it been licking his *boot?* The *side* of his boot? Hillford lowered a hand to console the animal.

"Listen," Jory said, reaching down to touch where the armadillo tongue had been. Feeling the foreign object in there now. The white blade. "I mean," he stumbled on, pretending now that he had an itch, making a production of scratching it, "I know it's better for her up here and all, and I'm happy for her, really, I just—I need to *see,* can you understand that? I'm not like you, with faith. I wish I was, that I could, but if I could just . . . I don't even know for sure she made it all the way *up* here. She might have gotten jumped between here and the gate, for all I know."

Hillford processed this too. Choosing his words now. "However, you are sure that she made it as far as the Weeping Poles, yes?" he asked. So polite, so casual.

It was a trap.

If Jory, technically a soldier, had burned the poles, then the Church could have legitimate grievance with the military. More than just all the first-time torches coding themselves out, taking the Church's newly minted clergy with them.

"I woke up and she was—she was gone," Jory said, pretty sure Hillford was grinning under that mask now.

What Jory really wanted was to watch him navigate an apple slice past that mask.

Hillford accepted Jory's version. He didn't press it anyway. Just shifted gears.

"For nearly a decade now we've believed that the—the *plague,* as you call it, that if there was a purpose for it all, the violence, the bloodshed, then it was to punish us, to cleanse us. But there rose within us a faction, no, a minority, a group of doubters, of long-seers, who suspected there might be more to it than that. Much more. And, this, Jory Gray"—the egg—"it's all clear now. The message we've been praying for, that can heal what threatens to become a schism. The reason I went into the field that day, as it turned out."

"It was an accident. I didn't know to turn the flame off sooner."

"To those without eyes to see," Hillford said, "everything is accident and coincidence. But—what this represents, Jory Gray. The changing sleep is coming, after the feast. We know that now, can share it. That decades-long slumber wherein these quickened dead, as you call them, dream of the men they once were, and never will be again, only to rise as angels, of which our former selves will have been only the inconsequential shell, and then will begin the true afterlife . . ."

Jory breathed in, breathed out. Watched an armadillo watch him.

"If all that's so," he said at last, "then why don't you infect yourself, be part of it?"

Hillford nodded, his knife at the apple again. Quartering, eighth-ing.

"Your education serves you well, Jory Gray," he said, a mournful slant to his words now. "But some are shepherds, some are the chosen flock. I could no more change that than I could—"

"You stepped around that place in the floor the other day," Jory said, looking as deep into Hillford's eyes as he could. "Out there with the peach smuggler."

"'Peach smuggler'?" Hillford repeated, still cutting, his eyes not giving anything away.

"How could you have known to step around it?"

"You're looking for an article of faith, just as I was that day, aren't you?" Hillford said—cut, cut. As punctuation, he swept the minced apple over the side of the table, golden armor flashing to it from all around. More than Jory would have guessed. "And it was your first time in the field as well, I believe?" Hillford added.

"I saw what I saw."

"And interpreted it as you will, yes. Maybe next time—"

"It was my *last* call too."

"Just as well, just as well," Hillford said, watching the armadillos eat. "We only needed the one . . . call, yes? More would only mean we were blind to the first, undeserving of it, not ready."

Jory pushed back from the table, reached for the floor with his boots.

"You needed me to verify something?" he said.

"And you have," Hillford said, standing as well, opening his fingers to show that Jory was here, being Jory.

When he did, though, the tip of the ring finger of his left glove—did it flap? Like he'd *cut* it when destroying the apple? And not even noticed?

Not just the fabric of the glove either. There was enough fingertip in it that it swung a bit.

"Wha—?" Jory said, but Hillford swept his hands behind himself and leaned forward, so that there was only that face. That mask.

One armadillo darted around behind those floor-sweeping white robes.

To nibble up a fingertip?

"What did I verify?" Jory corrected.

"That the most holy can come from the most base," Hillford said, stepping around the table as if he hadn't just insulted Jory. "From the least devout, the most divine. A lesson we should keep in mind."

Hillford guided Jory to the doorway. His cold hand on Jory's shoulder. *Down* on Jory's shoulder.

"She's not tall enough to be one of you, you know," Jory said, half shrugging away from that contact.

"There are many stations in the house of the true Lord," Hillford said, letting Jory walk on. "But, in recompense for your gift to us, I'll attempt to look in on her myself, just as you were given special attention by your commanding officer."

"Is that a threat?" Jory asked, not walking now either. The hungry armadillos were rushing his feet. Jory raised one leg, the one with the knife.

"Don't mind them," Hillford said. "They're just doing what they do, being themselves, as it were. Welcoming you, or attempting to. Carrying all they own on their backs. Surviving unchanged, while the world around them falls away. It's a trait the Church might envy, if we allowed ourselves to indulge in that kind of behavior."

"'If,'" Jory spat back, high-stepping out of the pool of golden scales, reaching for the doorway with his fingertips, for balance.

"Yes, of course," Hillford went on, so demure. "And, I never answered your question, did I? Sincerest apologies. Excitement. About their current classification? Yes. It's *Xenarthra,* a term synonymous with *Edentata* in the older textbooks, which you may have seen in your introductory—that's *without teeth*—but you, of course, should never make that mistake, Jory Gray. They do indeed, as you say, *have teeth.*"

Behind Jory, his escort chuckled.

Jory started to say something, but bit it off, turned around. Walked where he was shown to walk, let the helicopter—different pilot—tilt him up into the sky again, the poles underneath them smoldering now.

"Thought they just burned a couple of days ago?" Jory asked through the racket.

The pilot steadied them up, pushed forward on the yoke, spinning for traction in the sky, some of the smoke from the poles swirling up into their blades like string.

"No one would ever intentionally vandalize Church property," the pilot said, not looking across to Jory.

Jory nodded, cupped his hands around a cigarette to light it against all this wind, and mumbled an "amen" to that.

CHAPTER TWENTY

The driver kicked back in his jeep didn't even look around when the helicopter touched down behind him, in the hug-n-go lane. He just cocked an arm up, clamped his nonreg hat down, the hurricane from the blades hard enough that it slapped his windshield frontwards on its hinges, looked from Jory's angle like a sheet of water that had fallen onto the hood, exploded.

Jory stepped down, just one holy rail touching the ground, his cigarette whipping away from his lips, spiraling into hyperspace.

The Cleanup truck was here already, one tire cocked on the curb like it didn't really have to be here, and wanted everybody to know that.

"Yep," Jory said, then turned to wave to the pilot that he was good, that that was definitely his friend's parking job, but the pilot was already stepping off the broken asphalt with that one rail, pulling his rig back into the sky. Out of the secular, into the blue.

Jory eyeballed the driver of the jeep, pebbled glass cascading down into his lap.

Jory eased up alongside, half studied the flag threads still flapping at the top of the flagpole after all these years, their rust-proof grommets slapping aluminum in no particular rhythm. There hadn't even been time for half masts.

"What room?" he asked the driver, tilting his head at the school.

"Follow the smell, Einstein," the driver said, sweeping the glass off his thighs. Looking at his hand to see if he'd scraped it or not.

Jory picked his way across to the twin sets of double doors, once bright blue probably, team colors, now faded and gouged, their wire-embedded safety glass crashed through nearly a decade ago.

Everybody thought schools were the safest places. Punk had said that. Real name . . . what? Blaine? Blake?

Alive now? Not?

Inside maybe. Where there's a driver, there's a torch, right?

Jory grabbed the extra shovel leaning up by the door, backed his way through, the curve of his back making him feel like a scuba diver, rolling out of one world, into another.

That was about right.

The entryway was full of all the grinning skulls and trophy rubble and general havoc typical of last-stand places. First wave, probably, going by the naked ribs underfoot, no longer carti-laged to anything.

"I'm ho-ome," Jory called ahead, again too quiet for anybody to hear. It was his first time back in a school since that last good Thursday. Like he'd taken a ten-year unpaid leave and the place had gone to hell in his absence.

He tried to muster a grin in response to that, but—this place.

The layout, it could be exactly the school from Glasses's video.

Jory stepped around a line of vertebrae, followed the lights already set up at intervals. Places like these, like this, they still had that film-set feel to him. Some movie about the weeks and months after the nuclear holocaust, the asteroid collision, the gamma burst, the bad solar flare, all the other ways we thought we were going to buy it.

But it wasn't the leftovers from a soundstage at all, Jory told himself, stepping carefully, to keep those breaths of dry marrow from puffing up. It was more—it was like you'd stood too still by accident, your feet deep in the moment, instead of stepping ahead with the clock, so that now you were stuck in a faded, decaying past.

Stuck here with a lot of dead people who don't get that they're dead.

"Don't be melodramatic," Jory told himself, in his gruff estimation of Scanlon's voice, and tried to slit his eyes like he had before, gunslinger-style.

Somewhere there was a basketball bouncing. On a wooden gym floor.

Timothy.

Jory nodded with each bounce.

Everything else in the postapocalypse could change, but, for better or for worse, Timothy never would.

Using his shovel like a staff, Jory pulled forward through the hall, waiting for the stench the driver had promised. Instead, a torch stumbled from a classroom, his hand covering his mouth, vomit spilling through anyway.

Glasses.

Jory stood there until he was done.

"Hey," Glasses said when he could, hitching his torch around. Cleaning his glasses with the tail of his shirt. "Thought you were, you know. Empty bed."

"They call them bunks," Jory said, in his recruiter voice. "This is the army, son."

Glasses laughed, vomit still spattered on his chin and chest.

"In there?" Jory asked, leaning to the side to see into the room Glasses had just left.

Glasses shook his head *no, no no no.*

"It's their—their, what do you call it?" Glasses said. "*Latrine,* yeah."

"You followed the smell," Jory said.

"Don't—don't say it—" Glasses said back, coughing some more.

Down the hall, Sheryl stepped out of a room. She lifted her chin to Jory. Jory lifted a hand back.

"Got some pears down here," she called.

"Shhh," Glasses laughed, trying to palm his headset's mic.

"Here," Jory said, and reached to the dial under the right ear of Glasses's helmet. Twisted it off.

Glasses was impressed. He stood taller, now that he was more alone.

"Your driver show you that?" he asked.

"I used to have a Walkman," Jory said back, distracted—one of the lights behind them was flickering, looking like it might be going to fail. Leave a dark part to walk through, on faith.

"You used to work in a place like this, right?" Glasses said, swinging his torch around so they could walk down to the black-market pears.

Jory looked behind them again.

"Priest coming or what?" he said.

"False alarm," Glasses shrugged, the strap on his torch still not right enough for him. "A can house, somebody left the door open. Coyotes were sniffing around."

Jory nodded. Using wild animals as detectors, there would have to be false alarms.

"So no handler either," he said.

"No zombie," Glasses finished.

"Good," Jory said, leaning to the side to try to see deeper down the hall ahead of them. Where Sheryl might have gone.

Nowhere.

Just the sound of that basketball, slapping the hardwood.

"So your crew's cued on torch units?" Glasses said. "Wherever we go, you show up?"

"Ghoul crew," Jory nodded. "We follow the grave robbers, yeah. What you still here for, though?"

Glasses shrugged, didn't answer.

Step, step.

"They do carry two knives," Jory said then.

"Bonefaces?"

"One black," Jory said, miming pulling it from his left sleeve, "one white," drawing the other. Angling them to catch the light.

"You saw?"

"I think the black one's, like, utility."

"White for ceremonial," Glasses added, liking the neatness of it, then looked behind them as well, finally answered Jory's question with a question. "Know what he calls me?"

Jory stole a glance over, saw Glasses was kind of serious here. "Your driver?"

"Nothing," Glasses answered. "Says it's not worth learning my name."

Jory had no answer for this.

The next room they passed was some sort of central office. Converted now, to—?

"Pirate radio booth," Glasses decided out loud, angling his head over to study the equipment. "Don't need that much, really." And then he walked on, leaving Jory to catalog—microphone, car battery. Some wires bundling towards some kind of make-do transmitter, maybe, or desktop CB. Wires trailing from that, up into the tile ceiling, to the idea of an antenna.

"Pears," Glasses called back. "Maybe even in syrup. . . ."

Jory nodded, moved on.

"Here?" Glasses asked back, stepping into the approximate classroom Sheryl had been at.

Jory looked behind them one more time and eased in, very aware that all he had was a shovel.

He didn't need more.

At each desk was a child. The body of a child, its grey skin paper thin. Heads down on folded arm bones.

Glasses just standing there, his helmet in his hand, slipping away.

Jory stepped forward to catch it, but was too late.

The crash of metal on the desiccated carpet was thunder. Followed by static, that On dial jogged over.

Glasses was past words.

The teacher, she was still at her desk, the instrument she'd opened her own wrists with still in her hands—a compass. For geometry.

But what she'd done with it—the story was all there.

And on the chalkboard, undisturbed for all this time.

HEADS-UP 7-UP!

Her handwriting, it had been so good.

And then, her class all hiding their faces, she'd circulated through the room one last time, up one row, down another, pushing that sharp point up under the base of the skull, into the brain stem, and angling it sharply one way or the other, to be sure.

The backs of the children's shirts were still black with it.

Jory felt something collapse in him. Felt himself holding on to Glasses's shoulder, Glasses holding on to Jory's arm.

They gulped their way back into the hall, their eyes hot, lungs, both empty and full at the same time.

"You have any kids?" Glasses asked, and Jory closed his eyes.

"Hey," Sheryl said, stepping out into the hall from the door just eight inches down from this one, an opened can of pears tilted up to her mouth like a coke, her face a question now. "What?"

Jory shook his head *no, nothing,* and shut the door on the dead children. None of their parents would be coming.

He still couldn't talk, quite. Was back in the upstairs hallway of his own house again, not completely aware yet of the hammer in his hand. Just the small shape lunging for him.

"No," he creaked out.

"You all right?" Sheryl asked, wiping pear syrup from her lips, her free hand dropping instinctively for the butt of her pistol.

"It's nothing," Glasses said, and limped Jory past her. "We'll walk it off, cool?"

Jory nodded, tried to, and when he looked back, Sheryl was just watching them. Then looking back to the classroom with the closed door.

"Sorry, man," Jory said, Glasses still propping him up.

"Know why I'm really still in here?" Glasses said, kind of laughing through his nose. At himself.

Jory looked over.

"This," Glasses said, and angled his torch up. "Fucking can't get it going. I mean, I can hear the shit sloshing around in there, I think the nozzle's just clogged, or the igniter, and, and it's not the autocool, I haven't even . . ."

Jory stood on his own, took the torch. Studied it.

"Ignition," he said, clicking the button just forward of the trigger guard, the two of them still walking deeper into the school, then, when it didn't light, he pushed it harder, faster, like trying to surprise it. *"Ignition,"* he said again, the magic word.

"See?"

"Maybe you just have to—" Jory said, and stepped over, tapped the butt on a locker, once, twice, holding the ignition button the whole time.

On the third tap, Glasses already shying away, the flame bobbled on.

Jory passed the torch back.

"A natural," Glasses said to him.

"Yeah," Jory said, looking up to wherever they were—the double doors of the auditorium. Two old lines of white tape forming a cross in front of it. A sideways *X*, the vertical line sealing the crack between the doors like a biohazard.

"They can do that?" Jory said. "The Church?"

"I'm guessing there's more than pears in there," Glasses said, looking to Jory for confirmation.

"They can't mark stuff off . . ." Jory was still saying. Trying to figure it out. "Can they?"

"Exactly," Glasses said back, and nudged the white tape with his flame, the tape flaring up and dying in an instant. Just a column of ash, falling.

Way down the hall—that basketball, still dribbling.

A sound they were walking away from now. Into the auditorium.

It was so black, and still. The air stale.

"I don't think—" Jory said, and then the door slammed shut behind them, and it was too late for thinking.

CHAPTER TWENTY-ONE

"Hit it," Jory said, his hand finding Glasses's forearm.

"The—?"

"Now!" Jory hissed.

The flame from Glasses's torch arced out, stylized in the high, empty space of the auditorium.

Underneath that chemical flame, aisle after aisle of neck stumps. Headless shoulders.

"Holy shit," Glasses said, his hold wavering, the doors rattling behind him when he backed into them, couldn't back up anymore.

Two hundred decapitated people, or whatever capacity was here. A congregation of bottleneckers, bottlenecked.

And recently.

The flame sucked back up into the torch, dropping them into a deeper kind of darkness.

"I meant the flashlight," Jory said, his voice seeming to float away from him.

"Oh yeah," Glasses said, and found that slider, clicked his headlight on, autocool sucking the burble of flame back in.

The dead people were still there.

And they hadn't been for long either.

Not long enough.

The smell was an oily wall.

Of course this door had been sealed.

"Heads-up, seven-up . . ." Glasses said, his voice lilty, falling apart. Every place his headlight found, it was worse. Fingers still digging into armrests. Faces looking up from the aisle. Burger wrappers skidding across the carpet, from the air Jory and Glasses had disturbed.

"Thought they were all gone," Jory said at last.

"Burgers?"

"Bottleneckers."

"They are now," Glasses said, reaching behind them for the push handle of the door. "We should, um, you know."

But Jory wasn't. In spite of the thick air, making him blink faster than he wanted.

Moving slow, he took the warm barrel of Glasses's torch, swept the headlight systematically across the auditorium.

Dull silver collars, snugged up to neck vertebrae. Collars the people had lived with for years. Deaths they'd always known were coming. Some of the heads just folded back like Pez dispensers. Some of the bodies fallen out into the walkway, chickens who'd run blind for a last few steps.

"Why would they. . . ?" Jory said. "They know their signals can be jacked, all together like this."

"It wasn't the army, was it?" Glasses said, slinging his beam over to some scuffling.

Rat, probably. This being rat heaven and all.

"The Church," Jory said.

"Survival of the meanest," Glasses said, then, his headlight settled on the facedown corpse up behind the podium, "preacher man knows."

"What were you before?" Jory said, taking an almost involuntary step forward. To that stage. Like he was being called. Like it was a revival, not a necropolis.

"I never knew it was practice," Glasses said back, following.

"Practice?" Jory asked.

"Video games, man," Glasses said, "this"—then, when he reached up to pat his naked head—"shit, my helmet!"

Jory stepped around a headless man. One who'd been reaching for his head too, it looked like.

"Why kill this many at once?" Jory said. "They weren't infected. They wouldn't have been sitting down if they were . . ."

"Wrong denomination," Glasses said, stepping around the reaching man now. His boot catching the man's head, sending it bowling down the slight incline.

They stood still until the head stopped. Until Glasses found it with the headlight, just to make sure a hand hadn't stabbed down to stop its roll.

"We weren't supposed to find this," Glasses said. "You know that, right? What do you think happened to the smugglers, I mean? They just moved on to the next perfect warehouse?" Step, step. "You know how many of these places there could *be*, then?"

"Disposal'd find them," Jory said, almost to the stage now, his arms up and ready, like when he was a kid, in the neighborhood haunted house.

"Did you?" Glasses asked.

Jory shook his head no.

"We're not supposed to," Glasses said again, more sure now.

Jory reached forward for the leading edge of the stage. He clambered up easily, Glasses passing the torch up, Jory lighting his way, then spilling the beam out across the congregation, still in their seats. Waiting for the Word.

"Dude," Glasses said, calling for the light.

Jory aimed it down to the preacher.

"Not a bottlenecker, anyway," Glasses said, half-impressed— the head *still* attached, the neck bare—and, using his hands like he wished he had gloves, he rolled the body faceup, the chest matted with blood.

"Knife or gun?" Jory asked.

"What do I look like?" Glasses said back, angling his face to be on the same plane with the corpse's, then jerking away. Coming back to be sure. *"No,"* he said, and looked up at Jory for confirmation.

Jory shrugged, had no clue.

"It's Dalton," Glasses said.

Jory wasn't looking down, was holding on the shadow shapes of all the headless people, watching them up here.

"They weren't even infected," he said again, trying to crack the code of this room.

"Maybe they were," Glasses said, finding something long and cylindrical on Dalton's inner thigh and slitting the sweatpants over it, praying out loud for it not to be a dead man's distended penis. It was a scroll. A sheaf of papers tied together, rolled into a tube, a condom pulled over them at each end, tied off with twine at the middle.

"What?" Jory said, shining the light better.

"They were getting infected with *this*," Glasses went on, completely forgetting what kind of room he was in. Sitting like a child with his blocks. Shuffling through these papers. "Can't be," he said. "No no no."

"This is why he went off the air?" Jory said, still playing catch-up.

"Shit shit shit shit!" Glasses said, looking up to Jory, his eyes brimming over now.

Jory turned to the door, held his light there.

"Shhh," he said at last. "Timothy'll hear, bring everybody."

"They need to . . . Do you know what this is?" Glasses said, a real actual tear rolling down his face now. "I never—never thought it was really real," Glasses loud-whispered. "The . . . the Lazarus Complex, man. The whole story right here. The one that ends with us, get it? The one that starts with who we used to be."

Jory looked from the papers to Glasses, then back to the papers.

"Lab wars?" he asked.

"Genesis," Glasses said.

"Like all the rest?" Jory said. "President's up in space, waiting all this out. If you go to a port, the old Disney ships'll come pick you up. All you have to do to cure the plague is shoot up for three days straight."

"No, no, there's pieces of it, I've heard of *them,* but—this is the real, true, actual thing. Before the Net went down, this, it was just starting to leak out, people were just . . . *shit!* Did you know that the servers all went down three days before the power did? A *week* before the last of the phones? Think that was any accident? So, so, this one guy on battery backup, he, he screencapped it from his history, page after page, or transcribed it, I don't know—"

"And then he's dead," Jory finished, still not buying it.

"King Tut's curse," Glasses said. "Just spelled with a Z. But—but nobody thought that any copies had survived, but Dalton, he *was* the fucking Buddha, man. He *found* it. And they, they killed him for it. And"—nodding out to the congregation—"everybody else too. Everybody who heard it. Or might have."

They were dead, Glasses was right about that anyway.

"So?" Jory said, Glasses laying all thirty-odd pages out like tiles.

"This is where it starts," Glasses was saying, rolling his standard-issue backpack around to the front, reaching in for a—a *video* camera? With *batteries?*

"Over here, here," Glasses said, directing the torch's headlight, and Jory did as he was told, showing each page in order, Glasses's camera in sync, its red light blinking.

"This is where what starts?" Jory said.

"There being more than one copy," Glasses mumbled. "That's what Dalton was doing. They took the one he was reading from. But they didn't pat him down for another, and would have—would have just thought—"

"Rigor priapism," Jory completed.

"Exactly, mandrake kind of bullshit," Glasses said, making sure the recording had taken. "But this was, it was too *close,* man. We can't have it—it can't be all in one place again, get it? Like, with Dalton? Everybody has to know. This is going to change the world. It's going to give it back to us."

"It's not magic."

"Information *is* magic."

"You haven't even read it."

"I've *heard,* man."

"What is it?"

Glasses looked up at Jory. Not like Jory was being difficult, but like it was too much to explain. "Read it later," Glasses said. "You'll see. This is a house of cards we're living in right now. This, this can knock the whole thing down though."

"And that's good?"

"If you don't know your own history . . ." Glasses led off.

"You're doomed to have somebody tell it to you?" Jory finished, still studying the congregation, then coming back to Glasses, tubing the papers up again, sliding them into his inside chest pocket. The camera was already in his pack. Jory smiled. "Oh, not have them all in one place again like *that*, you mean?" he said.

"You're right," Glasses said, and took the tube and the camera out as if weighing them, finally handed the camera across to Jory. It was the less sacred version. The furthest from the original.

"Hey, I don't—" Jory said, trying not to take it, but not wanting to drop it either. Not for what was on it, but because of what it was. A *camera*. With *batteries*.

"Just until we get back to base," Glasses said, hurried now. Looking all around. "C'mon, let's—We don't want to," Glasses went on, climbing down off the stage, walking backwards, waiting for Jory to follow.

Jory looked down to the torch, still burbling its flame, and slid the camera into his pack, lit their way back to the door.

CHAPTER TWENTY-TWO

Back in the main hallway of the school, Glasses was leading, Jory following, the torch held across his hips like Voss had taught them.

A couple of classrooms ahead was Wallace, at the right-side locker bank. Just opening each one, looking in, then closing it.

"He for real?" Glasses said.

"Wallace!" Jory called down, smiling just to be seeing another person, one with their Pez-dispenser head in the proper position, and Wallace looked up, fixed them in his sights. Lifted his unsteady hand in greeting, that light behind him flickering again, going dark now.

Jory's hand kind of froze midwave.

It was the moment he would remember, later.

Wallace smiled a little, maybe, his old-man version of a secret grin, and shut the locker he was looking in, opened the next, shut it too, and by the time he got to the next one, Glasses and Jory were almost to him.

"What you looking—?" Jory started to ask, but then Glasses's spread hand was in Jory's stomach, stopping him.

"The camera, the camera," Glasses was saying, snapping for. "This is classic, man."

It took Jory a moment to process—Sheryl stepped out of the pear room—and then that was all that was left: moments, frames.

The first was in the locker—a ragged, dead cheerleader, hair forever long, skin sick, teeth broken.

The next was her lips, thinning.

Then it was her springing from the locker all at once, tearing into Glasses, Glasses falling back, her nails and teeth all into his face, his glasses skidding away into Wallace's right shoe. Wallace pinching his suit slacks up in order to bend down, lift the glasses up by their bridge, so as not to print the lenses.

Sheryl was screaming important words. They were just sounds to Jory.

Her hand motions, though. She was waving him out of the way with her pistol. Trying to get Jory out of her line of fire.

Jory's mind, though, his thoughts, they were syrup, wouldn't process.

All he knew was that he had a torch in his hands. A lit torch.

Slowly, he raised it, Sheryl's eyes going wide, the rest of her falling away, scrambling back a classroom, diving into that door.

This meant Jory was doing the right thing.

By now, the cheerleader had most of Glasses's cheek pulled away with her teeth, was into his throat with her fingers.

"No," Jory said, and then did it anyway. Opened the torch. Stood on it for a ten count, a twenty count, until the autocool shut the flame off.

Finally it was Wallace, the mental zombie, who guided his arm down.

"There, there," Wallace said, patting Jory's forearm.

His voice was grandfatherly. It was a voice he'd had all along, apparently.

Together they edged around the scorched crater in the floor. The bubbling meat, the smoldering bone.

"She wasn't infected, was she?" Jory said. "Just scared, right?"

Wallace didn't say anything.

In the doorway of dead-children classroom, Sheryl was just standing there, the pistol slack by her leg.

"Sh-Sheryl?" Wallace said after her, but he and Jory didn't stop. They might never move again if they did.

Crossing the pool of darkness thirty seconds later, Jory closed his eyes fast when he heard the shot. Just one.

Sheryl.

All the children's names, they were written on the board, first name and last name, in five even columns, for the five rows of desks.

In case anybody wanted to know. In case anybody wanted to count.

It's not that the world had never had heroes, it's just, these ten years later, we needed another.

CHAPTER TWENTY-THREE

Outside, the jeep was still there, but at a different angle now. The windshield whole.

Mayner?

"I know him," Jory said to Wallace, and Wallace shuffled off, to the truck.

Jory watched him to make sure he made it. Before the plague he'd been an executive of some sort. Now he was like a toy—push him in the right direction, wait for him to eventually get there.

The grommets were still slamming into the flagpole in their random, meaningful way.

"Thought you retired," Mayner said when Jory got there, hauled himself up into the passenger seat. Jory ditched the torch and his pack behind the seat, then sat there studying Glasses's glasses. He polished a lens where he'd smudged it.

"What are you doing here?" he asked Mayner.

"Till death do us part," Mayner said, "right?"

Jory cracked a smile, his eyes tearing up at the same time.

"Live one in there?" Mayner asked.

Jory shut his eyes.

Should he torch Sheryl as well? Would that be saving her? If it was airborne now, then he owed it to her. Because he should have warned her. He should have melted that door shut, sealed that classroom shut forever.

"She was—sixteen?" Jory said, trying to answer better. "She'd been living in the walls or something. Since the first wave probably. Stealing peaches and pears. Opening them with her teeth. Going fe—going feral . . ."

Jory made a fist that crushed Glasses's glasses.

Mayner reached over, extracted the breakage from Jory's hand.

"Your buddy's helmet's still live," Mayner said then, tapping the fold-up display on the console.

Jory peered down, looked through the helmet's camera. Upside down, black-and-white children's feet were in the background, Sheryl's legs in the foreground, a pool of blood spreading. Then, close to the camera, the sound of a basketball dribbling, and the helmet, obviously picked up, put on. Walking down the hall now, stopping to tap the dead light, get a flicker but nothing else. A hummed tune coming through the speakers.

Jory stood in the jeep, waited for that tune to sashay out the blue doors, restore his faith in the world, and living, and life.

Maybe twenty seconds later, the jeep appeared on the viewscreen.

Jory looked up to . . . not Timothy.

"What?" Jory said, looking to Mayner for an answer, but Mayner didn't even know what was wrong here, much less how it had happened.

Jory intercepted the dribbler, who held the ball in both hands, unsure of Jory.

"Who are you?" Jory demanded.

"You the torch?" the dribbler said back. "Thought he had"— and did his upside-down *okay* fingers to mean *glasses*.

"No, where's—where's the other guy?" Jory said, looking behind this imposter, like this was a joke, a big misunderstanding.

The dribbler shrugged, studied the jeep, the helmet exaggerating his movement.

"I saw that chick Sheryl," he said, holding his pistoled hand up under his own jaw.

"*Timothy*, his name was Timothy," Jory said, stepping into the dribbler's face.

The dribbler shook his head like he'd had enough here, pushed the ball into Jory's gut, for some distance.

"All I want to know is what happened to the guy you replaced!" Jory said, turning around, slinging the ball a disappointing distance away.

The dribbler just stared at Jory. He peeled the helmet off, set it down very properly. Nudged it away with his boot.

"Listen," he said, "my orders were that this crew was a man short, I should catch a ride—"

"That was me who made the crew a minus-one," Jory said, stepping in, taking as much of the dribbler's shirt in his fists as he could. "I'm asking about the *other* guy—tall, wore these old-timey flying goggles—"

At which point the dribbler broke Jory's weak hold, slammed his own hands into Jory's chest, driving him to his knees.

"Exactly," Jory said, launching from there, only stopping because Mayner had him by the scruff. And about thirty pounds.

"Sorry," Mayner grunted to the dribbler. "Probably best if you, you know—"

The dribbler stood there a breath or two more, then waved this whole stupid scene away. He walked to the truck, climbed in with Wallace.

"Ten years tomorrow, you know that?" Mayner said to Jory, letting him go now.

Jory shook the rest of the way out of Mayner's hold. He stepped off, breathing hard, then just squatted down, his back to the jeep, his face in his hands, his shoulders shuddering.

"Happy birthday, world," Jory said, laughing a nonlaugh, and stood. "I just want to see her, you know?" he said then, picking up Glasses's helmet delicately, on both sides, like Glasses was still in there. "That's all. Just—I just want to see her one last time."

"See who?"

"She went up the Hill," Jory said, lifting his hand in that general direction.

Mayner looked that way.

"Listen, man," he said. "Something I want to show you, yeah?"

"No thanks. Seen enough today."

Mayner shrugged one shoulder, said, "Could be worth another menthol, I suppose."

Jory looked over to be sure Mayner wasn't lying.

On the way up the hug-n-go lane, Mayner leaned down, slowed the jeep enough to scoop up the basketball.

Where Mayner took them was a barren place way at the edge of a safe zone, almost right up against the chain-link fence.

"There, yeah," he said, Jory's menthol down to a nub. "Told you."

Jory studied his menthol butt, looked up, his eyes guarded.

A malformed goat was hobbling up to the jeep, its radio collar heavy.

"Hey, a goat," Jory said, unimpressed.

"No, look at it," Mayner said, draping himself over the steering wheel.

"So it's messed up," Jory said. "Welcome to paradise, right?"

Mayner popped the cooler between them, ferreted a candy bar out. "They like chocolate," he explained, handing the icy bar to Jory.

Jory peeled it, looked at it from all angles, then to Mayner.

"Like this?" he said, holding the chocolate out the doorless door.

The goat edged in, shy like a dog that's been beat, and took it. It chewed, and chewed.

"Its eyes," Jory said. They were watching him. And they were wrong in some way. "What is this?"

Mayner chewed his cheek, satisfied.

"You know about General Scanlon, right?" he said.

"War hero, crimes against humanity, saved us all. Breath smells like pimento."

"Serious?"

"What does he have to do with this?"

"When he wants to clear a zone like this," Mayner said, shrugging like it was common knowledge, "this is how he does it."

"With radioactive mutant *goats*?"

"I wouldn't go that far. But, he does make them in the lab, yeah. Or has them made, I don't know." Mayner breathed in, started over. "You know how he's supposed to have used kids for the first wave? Because they smelled the best, were the best bait?" Mayner did the tic-tac-toe in the air. "Yeah, well, these guys—you know baby goats are named 'kids'?—he figured out how to cross genes, I guess. Or something. How to get that same sweet smell. Something about the glands."

Jory looked back to the goat, still chewing. Licking its lips clean.

"You mean," he said, "you mean these are . . . that they're part *human*?"

"They can understand words some, I think," Mayner added.

"So, so, what? If their collars are still blinking green or whatever—?"

"Then the zone's clean," Mayner completed. "Bad thing is, it works. The dead can't resist these guys. They're the ice cream truck to the zombie's inner child, like. They'll come in from miles around."

Jory was studying the goat again. Those eyes that weren't looking away. Like the goat was confirming Mayner's story.

It made Jory's skin feel cold.

"All the lucky people died early on, didn't they?" he finally said. "Why are you showing me this?"

"That girl you torched back there," Mayner said, sliding Glasses's helmet into Jory's lap. "We can make up for it here."

"Make up for the cheerleader?"

"Far as brass knows, this helmet, it went up back at that school, right?"

"So?"

"So. Put it on that goat. Make the world right."

"This isn't funny," Jory said. "I don't want to—"

"I think he'd see your torch coming," Mayner said. "But this"—his keypad on the dash—"it's more humane. Has to be, right?"

Jory processed this. Watched the goat.

"You're saying the code missiles," Jory said, looking up to them, bracketed just above his head, "they key on the *helmet*?"

"Kill the head and the body will die," Mayner said.

"A little torch humor," Jory said.

"Get it where you can."

Jory considered, considered, then, "Got another candy bar?"

Three minutes later, the goat was wobbling around, lips chocolatey, the helmet strapped over its head. Jory was petting it, then pressing the side of his face to the side of its face—it was human, in there somewhere. He finally had to push away from it.

"It won't hurt," he told it. Then, to Mayner, "Will it?"

Instead of starting the jeep, Mayner let the goat wander off on its own, front-heavy and stumbling now, sugar racing through its veins.

"It's happy," Jory said.

"It's a he," Mayner answered back, the goat maybe thirty yards off now, like it was waiting, the sun sinking behind it so that it was just a bulbous-headed, wobbly silhouette of a goat. "Cover your ears if you want. It won't matter."

Jory did, Mayner's fingertips natural on the keypad, and, like that, the missiles were whistling off the roll bar. They dove into the sky as three then came plunging back down as one, furious, nipping at each other to be first.

"All the lucky people died," Jory said, just before. "Left the rest of us here in hell."

Then the sound, the slam, the wave of pressure rocking the jeep. Slabs of charred goat slapped down on the hood.

"It doesn't have to be hell," Mayner said, and backed the jeep up, turned them around.

"Think I want to go to church now," Jory said, looking over to Mayner. "Catch a ride?"

Mayner stopped the jeep, stared straight ahead, his arms folded over the thin steering wheel.

"They're not going to let you see her, man."

Jory leaned down to his boot, came up with the slick white blade.

"Never know," he said, his voice slack in a way that made Mayner look over.

CHAPTER TWENTY-FOUR

Late night in the mannequin household. The wife at her side of the double–sink vanity, a night-cap keeping her hair up, her nightgown floor-length, very proper.

The husband is sitting on the bed in rumpled slacks, his shirtsleeves rolled up to his smooth elbows. His elbows that will never callous, would just rub away into powder and dust, if it came to that.

The wife sneaks glances at him in the mirror.

What he's doing is holding his tiny phone in his basketball-player hands. Reading the last text over and over, then looking away, out their second-story window. Maybe trying to pretend he hasn't seen whatever the message is.

But he keeps coming back to it.

On the computer, in its fold-out armoire across the room, is a black page with grey words. And kitten pictures.

The husband breathes in, breathes out.

"Mommy?" the son says from the door, his voice weak in a fake way. The wife rolls her eyes, but by the time she's turned around, her face is pleasant.

"Yes?" she says.

"It itches," the son says, holding his cast up.

The husband rises, reaches for the straightened coat hanger already on the nightstand, and goes to one knee before his son.

"There?" he says, manipulating the hanger in, then bending it, turning it like a slim jim, like he knows this car door well.

The son moves his shoulder, changing the angle of the hanger, then nods.

"Not too much," the wife says from her mirror.

"Your mom's right," the husband says, reeling the hanger in. "Now, think you can sleep, big guy?"

The son shrugs, looks to the mom for help, but her plastic back is turned.

"Can't find X-Ray," he says into his own chest.

"His action figure," the wife calls, her voice even more pleasant now than her face. "With the glasses, dear?"

"X-Ray," the husband says, like it's the pressure release valve for the night. For this week. "We'll find him tomorrow, will that work? We'll look everywhere, promise. Then go fight crime."

"He's an explorer," the son says.

"Probably in the car," the wife slips in.

"Then we'll explore," the husband says to his son, the cheer in his voice less sincere now.

The son shrugs, but isn't committing to anything. He slumps back down the hall.

"It didn't itch," the husband says, putting the hanger back in its place.

"He's scared," the wife says, not needing to explain why.

The husband sits down on the very edge of the bed again. Like sitting too fully would be a betrayal.

"Simmons at work checked it out," the husband says into the floor. "It's legit this time."

The wife is tending to her eyebrows.

"It's always legitimate," she says, closing her eyes now. "It was legitimate last time, remember? Fifteen hundred dollars of legitimate? *Surefire,* was that the word he used? What word is it this time?"

"This is different," the husband says, looking up to her back. "He's not even asking for anything. That's why I'm scared, see?"

The wife sighs. "I'm not going to be the bad guy here," she says.

"It's just," the husband says, leaning back like he's going to stand, but staying on the bed, his mouth too full of words, "he's in some *study,* I mean. For cash. An experiment. Taking who knows what, mixing it with whatever else he's already taken."

"Or caught."

"He was in Jakarta. Do you know what they've still *got* in Jakarta?"

"Monkeys?"

"Everything. God. You know him as well as I do."

"Well."

"I mean, he wouldn't have told them about our medical history. I know he wouldn't. Do you think he would have? They don't even let us donate blood. It's, it's—"

"If he messes their study up, so what, right? If they've got money to run a hush-hush experiment like this, don't you think they've got enough to run it again? And, maybe he's in the control group anyway, right?"

"He's not even supposed to have his cell phone though. What does that tell you? Does that sound aboveboard? Like people who aren't going to get seriously pissed when his blood, when they—?"

"Rodge looked it up, this study?"

The husband finally stands. Pacing now.

"Not directly. Watchdog groups, whatever they're called. They were protesting at first, I guess. Trying to get it in the media. The people involved, the doctors, but then it all went dark. One of them was working on a project called the . . . It was the Lazarus Complex. Does that sound good?"

"Was that that movie?" the wife asks, angling her head over to take an earring out.

"You don't," the husband says, "XXXXX. They've got him locked up, he signed away his—and he doesn't even know what it's going to do . . . and, and he's in there and I'm—"

"Still the brother," the wife finishes for him. Sweeping in from behind, hugging him around the middle, her face sideways to his back again, accentuating their height difference again. "Go," she says, just loud enough. Maybe just moving her injection-molded lips in that very particular shape against his back.

Two feet above her, the husband's face changes, as much as it can. His hands come down to cover hers, on his stomach.

"I'll tell them it's a family emergency," he says.

"Emergency?" their daughter says, suddenly in the doorway.

"No, no, dear," the wife says, then, to her husband. "Do you know where it is? Where you're going?"

"Listen," the husband says, already moving, "this won't be like, I won't let it"—leaning down to kiss his wife's fore-head, then, on the way out, cupping his daughter's head in his hand to keep her standing so he can swivel around, his long fingers the last thing to whip around the edge of the doorway, disappear.

He's been leaving for two weeks already. Since that first call. It's all right there on the wife's face.

"Hurry back," she says, a hopeful smile ghosting up at the corners of her mouth.

"Where's Daddy going?" the daughter asks, going to sit on the edge of the bed too, the mom settling at the computer now. Shaking her head at the endless kittens. She clicks them away, one by one. Behind them are pages and pages about Jakarta. Instead of x'ing them all, she powers the monitor down. Leans over so she and her daughter can see each other in a surprise angle of the bathroom mirror.

"You know how sometimes you help Trey when it's his own fault, but he's your brother, so you do it anyway?" she says.

The daughter lifts a *maybe* shoulder.

"Well, your Uncle XXXXX is *Daddy's* brother, see?"

"Is he really maybe married now?" the daughter asks, hopeful.

"He's really maybe something." The wife smiles back. "We'll ask your father when he gets back, how about that?"

The daughter nods a prim nod, then her hand comes up with something.

"Shouldn't Daddy have his phone?" she says, holding it out across the bed, instead of towards the mirror.

The wife takes the cell phone, trying not to ring any alarms in the girl's head.

"I'm sure he—" She starts navigating his screen with her thumb. Scrolling to the last text message, the one her husband's been coming back to all night, that kept him from dinner—*Ima kill Oppnhimer.*

She clicks it away from the daughter, brings up the attached image—a plastic utensil handle, rubbed to a sharp point.

"Who's Oppen—Openhammer?" the daughter asks.

"*Oppen*heimer," the wife corrects, and presses the phone to her chest. Blinks away tears. She looks to the window, out into the night.

The husband already driving through it, his windshield wipers slashing the rain away, a phone book on the passenger seat, open. Both his hands are tight on the wheel, his face hovering just over them, trying to see through wall after wall of water.

Because this mission's taking all his attention, he doesn't notice the small body curled sideways around an action figure in the backseat, asleep.

All around them, the world is starting to end.

CHAPTER TWENTY-FIVE

Downtown was ready to explode. There were more people in the streets than Jory'd seen since the last wave. And not all of them had been people then.

"Z Day," Mayner tour-guided needlessly, tiptoeing the jeep through the rubble.

Jory watched the clumps of bodies smear by, some of them wearing dug-up Halloween masks. Skeletons, ghouls. The hungry dead.

"Ten years," he said at last, then turned to Mayner. "Ever think we'd make it this far?"

"We haven't yet," Mayner said, braking hard for a kid in a cape, scuttling from curb to curb. He was running from a ghoul-faced reaper, the reaper the kid's mom or dad, just trying to catch the kid. But when that mom or dad leaned down to pick the kid up, they had to lean down on their scythe. The kid ran screaming away again.

There were soldiers too, AWOL from base, bottles in one hand, guns in the other.

By tomorrow, it would be a parade. Fires, drinking, accidental deaths.

We'd made it, yeah. We were back.

Jory shook his head, kept his hand clamped to the fold-down windshield frame.

The Church was just coming into view, still these holy flashes of white through the broken buildings. But they had to slow for more soldiers first. Ones who had started earlier, come farther. A mass of civilians was circling them, cheering them on. Flames gouting up into the sky.

"That's a torch," Jory said, holding his hand out for Mayner to stop. Both of them stood in their seats to see, but didn't really want to see.

It was a female zombie. She was chained at the neck, the last ten feet of the four chains running through pipe, to maintain a no-bite zone. Four soldiers were manning those chains, keeping her in the middle for the other soldiers, darting in with heated-up crowbars and crackling Hot Shots. Going by the chant seeping in, they were trying to get her to dance, to take it off.

"Friends of yours?" Mayner said.

"She's not even alive," Jory said back.

"'She,'" Mayner repeated, then sat back down, harder than he needed to.

A soldier with a liberated shovel came down hard on the zombie's right knee, folding it in. The crowd screamed with joy when she tried to stand up on it again, and again.

A few steps farther back, with the torch, was the punk, his mohawk pink now, and straight up. No—*erect.*

"Blaine," Jory remembered, seeing him now.

A few steps over from him, watching all this, proctoring it, was Voss.

He looked up, past all this, to the antibody Jory was, and touched his own forehead, anointing it, telling Jory he remembered. That he wasn't going to forget. Then he nodded to the zombie, for Jory to join the festivities.

"In or out, man," Mayner called up.

Jory didn't answer.

One of the soldiers had a gaff, it looked like. This far inland. He was hooking it into the zombie's stomach, already oozing who knew what.

"No," Jory said, but the soldier got a loop of black intestine all the same, started working it out until it spilled at the zombie's feet.

When she tried to come up the gaff and grab him, her feet tangled in the guts and she fell, as much as she could on the chains. She slashed ahead with her hands. Snarling, snapping, screaming.

Jory sat back down, closed his eyes. Mayner started to let the clutch out, but Jory shook his head, held his hand out for the brake again.

"What?" Mayner asked.

Jory stood back up. *With* the torch, the one he'd gotten from Glasses.

"Gimme a sec here," he said, stepping down, his first footfall into the street thunderous, at least to him. What he was doing here was deciding to be one person, not another. It wasn't an easy thing. And there was no going back.

He wanted to be human though.

Not a monster, like the world wanted him to be.

The crowd parted for his bubbling flame, and then he was ringside.

"Good, good," Voss said, his arms crossed, and Jory nodded, looked over to the punk, his face rabid with this fun. And then he studied this zombie.

Her black intestines were still spilling. She didn't even know, not in any real way.

"Cauterize that wound for her, son?" Voss said.

"Yes, sir," Jory said, and opened the throat of his torch as wide as it would go, the soldiers all cheering at first, the ones in the back shielding their eyes from the heat. The cheering trailed down to nothing. Just the *pop* and the *sizzle* of dry meat burning.

Jory held the trigger until the soldiers holding the chains had to drop them.

Towards the end of it, before autocool, Voss was just staring through that wavering air at Jory. Jory just stared back.

"Shit, man . . ." the punk whined, letting the tip of his barrel fall.

The crowd was murmuring. Looking around. Blinking from the oily residue in the air.

"Feel better?" Voss said into that new silence.

"Not even a little," Jory said, and shrugged out of his torch, left it there. Didn't look back.

One day short of ten years was how long it had been since Black Friday then.

Every hour of that had been a miracle.

Maybe two blocks from the Hill, the crowds thin enough to chug along at twenty. Mayner stood on the jeep's brakes, slid them to a stop.

Jory caught himself on the dash, rocked back in his seat.

"Dude, I can just, you know, walk," he cobbled together, from awkwardness and apology, then tracked over to what had Mayner's fascination—the green *X* spray-painted on the side of a burned-out apartment building. One of Scanlon's crematoriums probably. A historic battlefield.

Jory'd walked by it on the way to the parking garage, twice in the last five days.

"You used to work Disposal, right?" Mayner said, still not looking away.

Jory shrugged *sure*. It was what the green *X* meant—this building was ready, was going to fall on some other, still-good building if something wasn't done. "They never get to these though," he said. "Heavy equipment, squatters, collateral damage."

"They're going to tear it down," Mayner said in something like wonder, making his fist into a tube to breathe through.

"You know this place?" Jory said, looking up to the building again.

Mayner straightened his right leg against the floorboard, pushed hard enough to work his wallet out. Thumb his license up onto the dash.

—*3315 Delany.*

Exactly what the big brass letters by the bright green *X* read.

"Shit," Jory said. "Sorry, man."

Mayner nodded like it was no big thing, but then said, "You really anxious to get up there?"—the Hill.

Jory leaned back farther, cocking his knees against the dash. "Go," he said.

He didn't have to say it twice.

Mayner slid a sidearm out from under the dash and set it on the console for Jory, then climbed down and crossed in front of the jeep, running his hand along the grill guard, like still holding on to now. But when he stepped up onto the sidewalk, looking both ways before moving on, Jory knew he was gone. Into the past.

And, this pistol.

Jory took it up. Sighted along its spine.

Another reason Disposal had been created was population control. Not the old kind, trying to get people to quit birthing more mouths to feed, but the new kind, where you kept people from killing themselves. Kept them from, once a zone was cleared, sneaking back into their old bedroom, hanging themselves.

Jory understood, kind of.

His old neighborhood had burned, but still. He'd gone back and stood there, let the old days rise around him.

He slid the pistol under the seat, and, when it would only go halfway, reached under to make room. He came up from that with his small pack.

Jory poured the video camera out, had to study it from every angle to find the Power button. Even then, holding it the right way in his hands, he just looked through it, autofocusing in on a narrow strip of white between two buildings. The Church.

He lowered the camera, fiddled with the buttons. Hit Playback. Had to pop the small screen out, then look around, see if there was anybody to eavesdrop.

Nobody.

He raised the screen, angled it away from the glare.

The recording was hip level, from training. Voss in black and white, the veins in his neck tight with anger. The wiry dude, Williamson, a close-up of his Z tats, recorded during a break probably. Before they all got a turn with their first real torch.

Jory lowered the camera, looked up to Mayner's building.

When he came back to the camera, he advanced past that first day, hit Play at Commando out by the parking lot of J Barracks. His armor right there at the curb already. Feet unable to stop pacing.

Jory tilted his head back, jabbed the Fast-Forward, stopped at some overexposed frames, all flashed white.

But—no—it was those papers. From the auditorium. Whatever Burger Dude had recovered from some old server. The papers that had gotten him killed.

"Hunh," Jory said, and figured the Zoom Out—it was the tracking slider—came in close enough to read the blurry letters, having to hold the screen sideways to make the lines be straight across.

It was in sections, and was formatted like an old—*blog*? Was that the word?

Jory smiled, hadn't even thought of one of those for years. People alone in their houses, making their diaries public. Sculpting the version of themselves they wanted to be true, then going back, editing some more.

Now, everybody packed together over small fires in the middle of what used to be lobbies and restaurants, you didn't show yourself to anybody. It would be like scratching a wound open.

But it was definitely that format—entry, entry, entry.

No—*post.* Jory smiled, to be remembering all this.

And the headings for each post, they were all—he paged through fast to be sure—*Z MINUS 53 DAYS, Z MINUS 48 DAYS,* and closer and closer. Meaning Glasses had been right— this wasn't first generation, but compiled, because how could that original blogger have known what was coming, turned his blog upside down, so it read first to last, not last to first? That wasn't how they'd worked, was it?

This had been cribbed from a series of screencaps, though, reentered, character by character, so it would never be lost. Because the Play button was the same as the Pause button, Jory could page through with just the tip of his index finger, each freeze-frame taking him one day closer to where he already was. Where everybody was.

Z minus 44 days

'Telemorse.'

He typed it in wrong, probably couldn't look at the keypad of his cell except in stolen glances, taking mental pictures of the clusters of letters, then having to type by feel, with one thumb. And he was never a spelling champion.

Telomerase is an enzyme that steadies chromosomes, aids in their continual repair. Age researchers believe in telomerase. The geneti-chemical key to eternal youth.

Three of the top telomerase researchers are currently stationed at ███████.

Today I bought masking software for my home computer. Both of them. There's freeware all over, but I wanted to pay cash.

If they search his first name now, '███████,' he won't be one of the 179,000,000 million hits anymore.

I can't change my cell, though. It's the only number he has. So now, this, what I'm doing to all instances of his name, it's my shield, the beep I say instead of ██████.

If there are ever two days of me not posting, then my absence here will be proof of my suspicions.

And apologies for all the sudden kitten photos. If this were the jungle, I'd wear camouflage. If it were the arctic, I'd duck into a white blanket.

Not that I have anything against cats.

Jory looked up again, was still alone. No Mayner, no Punk, no Voss, no bonefaces.

Just him. And this.

He leaned back farther, his knees ratcheting closer to his face, and pulled the screen in tight, started at the beginning instead of the middle. Opened on a cell phone ringing during dinner, then went post by post, finally stopping on another kind of table altogether, the same man sitting at it, his face in one of his large hands, the old world crumbling away around him.

Jory's scalp was crawling, his breath deeper than he meant.

This *was* it. How it started. The beginning of the postapocalypse, in seed form.

And the last scroll had burned up with Glasses. Under Jory's flame.

"What?" Mayner said, leaning in to see.

Jory snapped the screen shut.

Mayner had an improvised bag of mementos. Keepsakes. In spite of all the public service posters to the contrary. All the propaganda about not holding on to the past, but looking to the future.

"I'm ready," Jory said, sitting back up, leaning over to tuck the camera under the seat, get Mayner his pistol back.

Mayner cranked the jeep over, nodded down to the idea of the camera, said, like he'd never believe it, "You mean that's still got juice?"

Yes, Jory nodded.

Juice.

CHAPTER TWENTY-SIX

Because it was custom—feet, not tires—Mayner killed the jeep just this side of the Weeping Poles.

"So's this goodbye?" he said, both of them just watching those white walls of the Church.

"If it's airborne," Jory said, "then that means we've all already got it, right?" He looked over to Mayner for confirmation. "That means the only way to finally, really kill it, it's to kill ourselves."

"It wins, then," Mayner said. "Thirty-seven seconds later."

"I just want to see her one last time," Jory said.

"And you're, like, *sure* about that?" Mayner said. "I mean—I mean, *shit,* man. Is she *asking* to see you?"

"What were you, before?" Jory asked.

"Tell you when you get back," Mayner said. Then, like he was just remembering, "Hey."

He rolled the top of his keepsake bag back. Inside it was all menthols. Pack after pack, green stripes forever.

Jory stared at them, his mind swirling.

"How?" he said, picking a sacred pack up, threading a single menthol out.

Mayner pushed the jeep's lighter in and they stared at the Church some more.

"She used to quit every week," Mayner finally said, swallowing hard after saying it. "But, they were all over the apartment, man. It was like it was made of cigarettes she'd hidden. Like it was made of promises she knew she'd never be able to keep."

"They didn't even burn," Jory said, studying the one he had. "How long've they been there?" he asked then.

"You worried they're stale?"

"Them, I mean," Jory said, pointing with his chin up the Hill. "The Church. Was it ever even a holding facility?"

"Those were all west of town," Mayner said. "The wind. Think this was a, like a military museum or something. Yeah. Since Korea or so anyway."

"Military?"

"Used to be the army base, or station, fort, mission, garrison, I don't know. But they needed places for the planes to land, places to blow stuff up for fun, room to salute, all that. Maybe it was before my dad, even . . . Why?"

"Guess I'm getting interested in history," Jory said, laughing at himself. "You don't need to wait, cool?" he said then, holding a single pack of menthols up in thanks, then setting them down on the passenger seat. "If they make me do confession . . . Man, hope they can stay awake that long."

"You wish," Mayner said, holding his hand out for a drag.

It caught Jory off guard, but Mayner snapped, was committed to this gesture.

Jory flipped the menthol around, passed it over.

Mayner coughed, coughed some more, his eyes full of water, getting fuller.

Jory looked away, understood. It wasn't about the menthol. It was about who had hidden them.

You can honor a dead person in so many secret little ways.

"I'll pick you up tomorrow," Mayner said, coughing some more, hooking his head back to the idea of base. "J Barracks."

"I'm not a torch anymore," Jory told him, blowing a clean line of smoke out.

Mayner chuckled, let it turn into a smile. Said, "Shit. You might be the *only* torch," then dropped the jeep into reverse but kept it clutched.

Jory stepped away, the camera safe in its pack, and Mayner coughed his way back.

The Weeping Pole beside him was already blowing with left-behind marriage licenses, with song lyrics scavenged from liner notes, with a fast food receipt, its date circled with a heart. An old, curled address sticker peeled from a magazine, two names above that street number, printed side-by-side once upon a time. Somebody's only proof, all they had left.

Behind him, the jeep crunched away.

Jory stared down at the cherry of his menthol.

It was his firing-line smoke.

He studied the cherry, brought it to his lips, breathed in so deep it hurt, wonderfully.

Z minus 33 days

I'm sorry, I'm sorry. I'm still here. Really me. Here's another kitten picture, if that proves it. Or, for those here since the early posts, my brother's name, it's got the same number of letters as the word 'brain,' okay? Or 'bingo.' 'Baste.'

Apologies.

Nothing new, either. Well, I did sit in the car in the garage until I got dizzy, but the air doesn't get grey and hazy like a bar, and you can't see anybody through it, or explain anything to them.

How old I am is 37. ███████ was a senior the year I was a freshman.

I spilled so many glasses of tea on my brother, on purpose, because he asked. So he could act mad enough to blast off into the night. So many times.

███████. I've had a glass of tea on the table all day. Waiting.

I'm sorry.

Or something like that, all the way down to *Z minus 1 Day.* Nothing posted after that. Just a blank, white page. The pitted surface of an eggshell, each one of us inside, the plague yolking around us, a dab of blood in there already.

Jory blinked all of it back, held it in.

"I'm sorry too," he said aloud, to the Kitten Man, and breathed the menthol hotter, deeper, then leaned up the Hill, his cigarette wedged under the staple behind him, not even catching the fast food receipt—two double-meats with cheese—until he'd knocked on those tall doors, ducked inside.

CHAPTER TWENTY-SEVEN

Coming across the main courtyard of the Church was completely different than being led along the winding passage from the landing pad. It was expansive, huge, designed to make the sky feel like an upturned bowl.

At the lip of that bowl, on the ramparts of the walls, were novitiates. Looking down on the city. Not sentries, just watchers. Students. All of us ants down there to them, throwing bottles, shooting flames. Being so human.

Did they miss it?

Or maybe the novitiates were looking down on the poles, wisping smoke up by now, days before the next scheduled burn.

Jory lowered his head to hide his grin and pushed on, his upper arm in the firm grip of his new escort. He looked just like the last escort.

In his boot, still hidden, was the white blade.

It was curved like a human rib, he thought.

Like the outer edge of a toilet bowl.

A walrus tooth. Penis bone from a juvenile whale—*baculum.*

Jory nodded to himself, thought that word would have been long gone by now.

He was ready.

The line they were taking—a path of packed dirt—would spit them up at the same door he'd been through last time. Doorway, Jory corrected, giving the rest of them a casual eye, all of them the same—rounded at the top, doorless—except one off in the corner. It was shackled in iron, a real-true railroad-tie-looking crossbar cocked up beside it that would take three priests to engage.

So, there were *some* secrets. Some places the rest couldn't go. Holiest of the holies, the best prayer chamber, the secret library. Where they kept the apples, maybe, or the ketchup.

Jory swallowed his grin, hated this world.

All along the walls, just like last time, were the deep gouges, just slightly higher than a person could scratch. About exactly as high as an infected person could reach, especially with a city on the other side.

Maybe the plague *had* passed through here, but they'd— they'd starved it down, given it holy water. Stood in their open doorways and told the children to behave, to "settle down now."

Or maybe it didn't matter.

Standing in the only doorway that mattered to Jory was Brother Hillford, his hands holding each other over his stomach, the perfect groomsman.

No, Jory told himself. Not groomsman. More like the Fourth *Horse*man, dismounted. The whole world before him, his for the taking.

"Jory Gray," Hillford said, nodding to the escort, that grip fading from Jory's arm, but the escort hovering close.

"Decided I want to look in on her myself," Jory said.

"Again you surprise us all," Hillford said. "I trust you've received no lasting injury?"

"Physical or psychological?"

Hillford chuckled behind his mask. Said, "The *instrument,* Jory Gray."

"You mean did I cut myself with it?"

"You didn't," Hillford said, playing some eye-footsie with the escort. The escort bowed away, taking a long, scraping step back.

"I already told them at the gate," Jory said up to Hillford. "I'll tell you where it is. I don't even want it. Just let me see her."

"Don't even want it . . ." Hillford said, as if to himself. "Do you know how many there were originally?"

"How many *zombies*?" Jory answered, squinting around for the escort. Creeped out again about how they could just be so gone, so fast. "One, right?" he said, coming back to Hillford now. "Typhoid Z, Suspect Zero, the Lone Zebra Hypothes—"

"How many *instruments*," Hillford said, pointing his words now, like the knives he was talking about. "What you claim to have in your possession?"

"They already checked my pockets," Jory said, holding his arms out for another search.

"Of course you wouldn't have it with you," Hillford said, like he was having to work to keep his voice civil here. Priestly. "The *story* of it is what you have to offer, not the artifact itself. I regret to tell you that this isn't the first such . . . *offer* we've been presented with."

"I'm guessing it's the first one you've dealt with personally, though," Jory said back.

Hillford looked down to him, his scarred-up eyelids blinking slowly.

"You've already given us one artifact," Hillford said, drawing his long knife from his sleeve, studying the graceful sweep of its blade. "Perhaps I wanted to see what you might have brought this time. Unknowingly, of course."

"And?"

"Yourself, it would seem. On this not unmomentous day. The

end of a brief but intense epoch, as it were. The beginning of another, not so brief. A new world being born from the ruins of the old."

"Myself?"

"Twenty-four," Hillford said, looking past the blade to Jory now. "In the beginning, to use an exhausted phrase, there were two dozen of the first class, like this one. Do you know how many remain, for us to do our work with? Do you know the sacrifice we've made, in our—what you would I suppose call 'midwife' capacity?"

"You're the ones who wanted to start coming on the calls," Jory said. "Things were going great until you made us invent handlers."

"*Four*," Hillford said, cradling the sharpened edge of the white blade in his right palm. He made a fist around it, pulled the knife out hard.

"What?" Jory asked, turning half away, unable not to watch as Hillford let his right hand bloom open, trailing fingers like petals. No blood.

Jory stepped back, into the white wall.

Hillford laughed behind his white mask.

All the novitiates on the ramparts were staring down at this.

They're gathered for a ritual, Jory registered.

"Now," Hillford said, his stump-fingered hand fatherly and kind on Jory's shoulder, the blade already up that sleeve, "I believe you intended a trade, yes?"

Jory looked up to Hillford, and then to where Hillford was indicating, through the doorway.

A female novitiate sat at the table, her feet not touching the floor either, the chair making her into a child again.

Her face was hidden in the hood, mostly. The white blindfold on tight.

"As you know," Hillford said, "names are left behind, in the other world. But—you said she was the one with the . . . one blue eye, one brown, correct?"

"Linse," Jory called through, leaning in, not wanting to scare her.

Hillford kept his stump-fingered hand tight on Jory's shoulder.

"At the stage of development she's at," Hillford said, "it's strictly prohibited for her to look on any faces from the past, especially ones she might have . . . lingering emotional ties with, or seeming obligations to. You understand."

"But I can talk to her," Jory said.

"Two chairs are at the table," Hillford finally said, "yes. Though, you know of her vows, do you not?"

"No speaking."

"Exactly. But, to show our undying gratitude, Jory Gray, she won't have to wear the scarf—not across those wondrous eyes."

Jory looked up at Hillford.

"Of course, in recompense, you'll need to present a face she's accustomed to, that won't jar her from her current state of enlightenment," Hillford added, bringing the fingertips of his left hand up to his own face, his own mask, and dislodging it, the sound wet, sucking.

When he pulled it away, down, Jory understood—Hillford's face, his whole head, it was raw, a festering wound. Down to the cheekbones almost, his eyes so naked in there, his nose just two slits in a skull.

Jory dry-heaved as politely as he could.

And now Hillford was holding the mask out to Jory. Like a plate. Like a saucer of maggots.

Jory tracked up to that wasted face, what was left of it, and past, to the novitiates, all of them kneeling now as best they could on their ramparts. Faces averted, lips mumbling prayers.

Evidently a priest taking his mask off was an event.

"What happened to you?" Jory managed to get out.

Hillford just stared back at him, then, looking down to the mask, produced a rag with his stump-fingered hand, began to scoop out the rot, let it plop to the packed dirt, an armadillo already there to nibble it up, its hairy ears laid back in pleasure.

"You call it a 'code,' I believe," Hillford said at last, the backside of the mask cleaner now. An oversized ChapStick tube—*glue* stick—in his good hand, coating the area he'd just wiped down.

"You mean—you lived *through* a code?" Jory said. "Nobody lives through a code."

"The flesh matters not," Hillford said, offering the mask again. "Does it matter yet to you?"

"But Scanlon said you'd never been in the field."

"And his information is of course unimpeachable," Hillford said.

Jory took the mask, his own fingertips hooking through the eyeholes, his heart pounding in his throat.

A saint, Scanlon had called him.

More like a living martyr.

Jory looked through the doorway again. To Linse.

"I'm sorry," he said.

"Don't be," Hillford told him.

Jory still couldn't look at that face.

"It's—that knife you want. The white one, the one I found. It's where you killed all those bottleneckers," he said, keeping his eyes fixed on Linse, like she might just blip away. Get dragged headfirst into an armadillo hole. "Seat 13J. It's on the left, kind of the middle."

"Bottleneckers?" Hillford asked, the shadow of his head on the white wall cocking over.

"I pushed it into the fabric of the seat," Jory said—*Linse Linse Linse*. His PIN for the gate at the plant coming to him so easily now—*54673. 54673*. "School auditorium," he recited, with the leftover parts of his attention. "Blue fabric. Don't pretend you don't know."

Jory looked up to Hillford now, Hillford for once speechless. *Sermonless.* "Now?" Jory asked. "That good enough?"

Hillford nodded as if admitting defeat, motioned down to the mask, and Jory turned it over, looked at the expressionless face.

"She'll still know it's me," he said, and pressed it up, the medicinal-smelling smears of adhesive keeping it there. His world reduced now to two eyeholes.

Linse was in both of them.

He pushed past Hillford, crossed the room in three desperate steps, not sitting down at all, just grabbing for her hands, taking them in his own, pulling her face to his chest and holding it there, his breath coming in hitches, in sobs. Saying her name over and over, patting the back of her head. Apologizing, saying, "I'll never, I'll never," not even sure what it was he wouldn't do, just that he was promising not to, that he had to make that promise, had to promise her something, had to make everything better.

Then he held her out at arm's length, pushing the hood off the back of her shaved head, and reached around to undo the blindfold, see her eyes, both of them narrowed, afraid.

And brown. *Matching* brown.

Jory turned to the doorway, the silhouette of Hillford just standing there, same pose, same serenity. Same satisfaction.

"You lied," Jory said in something like wonder—bonefaces can do that?—his voice cracking somewhere in the middle, the rest of him stumbling unaccountably when he tried to take a step. Falling forward. Because of the mask, the mask, that medicinal taste. Sleeping something—gas, fumes, vapor, paste.

No. No no no.

Jory pawed at the mask, couldn't find the edge, his fingers numb, already somebody else's fingers.

Hillford cradled him down to the ground, saying through some long tube into Jory's ear that he'd never had a blade at all, had he? That that particular auditorium, with the blue seats, the rows were an educational exercise for the students, weren't they? Not letters, but states—J should be the *tenth* row, Kansas the eleventh. Right in front of Kentucky, Louisiana, Maine, all the other places that weren't places anymore.

Jory's eyelashes were raspy against the back of the ceramic mask, the lights in this room in rows now too, for Jory, banks of lights going black, section by section, so that Jory closed his eyes before the darkness could get to him, on the chance it would pass him by, leave him alone.

CHAPTER TWENTY-EIGHT

The past, the old world. When mannequins roamed the earth, completely unaware that their age was almost over.

That night the husband drives through all the rain to save his brother.

He's in a building now, a reception area, the chairs and lamps from decades before. Everything is miniature, up against his lankiness, his face even more gaunt than usual. His long-fingered hands on the reception counter are pale spiders, the palms not touching the Formica at all.

He's begging.

"I don't care, okay? You're not—I'm sorry, I'm sorry. Okay, okay. It's not you, I know. I want to see whoever's in charge then. You can't hold him against his will. I don't care who—"

The night receptionist stands up to *her* full height, has maybe played some ball herself, back when the hoops were orange baskets. Like, for fruit.

The husband—*brother,* now—leans up off her counter, still has her by about four inches.

"Sir," she says, her tone telling him exactly how interested she is in his case, "if you'll just sit down, I'm sure we can straighten this misunderstanding—" then she stops, the entry doors behind them swishing open.

It's two MPs. Military police, helmets, armbands, posture.

Their presence ramps the husband up. "No, no, you can't, I insist on seeing the project coordinator. Don't make me"—the MPs each taking one of his arms—"*Lazarus Complex! Lazarus Complex*!" he starts screaming, casting about for a camera to scream it into.

They're alone though. It's after hours.

He tries to whip an arm free can't.

"Listen," he says, slumping down to their height, "I just . . . he's my—"

"That'll be enough, gentlemen," a female voice cuts in. With authority.

The husband looks up.

It's a doctor. White lab coat, sensible shoes, severe bun, or the display-window estimation of a bun. Clipboard. About his age.

"You've got a sister, don't you?" the husband says to her. "A brother?"

"'Lazarus Complex,'" she repeats when he's done. "This is inflammatory enough that merely shouting it in an abandoned waiting area is supposed to compel us to abandon our research? Am I following correctly, Mr. XXXXX?"

The husband doesn't answer.

"Do you feel compelled, Maddy?" the doctor asks the night receptionist, leaning around the husband to ask it.

"He's my brother," the husband says.

"Not according to his entry interview," the doctor says—*that's* what's on the clipboard. She runs her eyes up it, down it. Flips it over like there might be more.

The husband laughs. Kind of blubbers.

The MPs let him go, but stay close.

"You know my name," the husband tells her.

"Not that I'm disregarding the family resemblance," the doctor says, holding the clipboard to her chest now. "The pronounced height. The tendency towards theatrics."

The husband closes his eyes. Is not going to lose control here.

"He didn't put me on there," the husband says, nodding to the clipboard, "he didn't put me on there"—not even slightly in control of his lower lip anymore—"because last time I, because, when he left, I told him, I told him . . ."

"I know, I know," the doctor says. "I do have a sister, Mr. XXXXX. We say things we wish we hadn't. It's part of this human race, I'm afraid."

"Then you understand?"

Stare, stare.

"I just want to *see* him," the husband adds, taking a step closer, to implore at close range, but the MPs step in with him.

"The project coordinator, you mean," the doctor fills in, deep in her clipboard again.

"What?" the husband says. "No, no—"

"Then you were—Is it your *habit* to always be saying things you don't in actuality mean, Mr. XXXXX?"

The husband just studies the floor here. For an answer.

"Oppenheimer," he says at last, his eyes coming back up to the doctor. "Sure, okay, whatever."

The doctor steps in now, interested. "*Robert* J. Oppenheimer, Mr. XXXXX?" she asks, trying to catch his eyes. "I'm sorry, but I believe you have us confused with another project. In another decade."

The husband looks past her. To the door she must have come through.

"What are you doing to him, that I can't see him?" he finally says.

The doctor smiles, says, "It's strictly dietary," then nods the MPs away, one of them slipping her a manila envelope first.

"Dietary?" the husband asks, watching the MPs make their exit, when what he should have been looking at, using his height to see, is the grainy black-and-white photograph the doctor was keeping angled away from him, slightly—his broken-armed son in the backseat of the car, as seen past the orange-and-white-striped dropbar of a guard booth.

"This way," the doctor says then, all business again, nodding once to the night receptionist, then turning on her sensible heel, the manila envelope closed now, tucked at the back of her clipboard.

The husband swallows, his Adam's apple more supple than it would appear to be, and follows, ducking his head to get through the door, back into the bowels of this Lazarus project.

CHAPTER TWENTY-NINE

The humming was what finally brought Jory up from inside himself. It was like being trapped in a dial tone. If there were still phones.

Opening his eyes was no better.

Standing within arm's reach, miles taller because Jory was lying down, was Hillford. *All* the novitiates shuffling past glancing at him then away.

Jory raised his hand to peel the mask off, but it was already gone, was—it was back on Hillford. And Jory's hand wouldn't reach his face anyway.

He tracked down to it, from it to the thin white sheet knotted around his wrists. He was tied to a smooth pole in the center of the courtyard. And his back, the skin on his back, it was wrong, too stiff, too painful, like he'd scraped it.

From dragging him on the ground?

There was no time though.

"It's only fitting," Hillford was already saying, his voice so even, just stating a fact, "only fitting that you would deliver yourself to us, Jory Gray, to be the messenger. Perhaps for a while you even believed you actually *had* one of the instruments—"

"No!" Jory said then, trying to stand—boots still on, pants

too, but . . . wearing one of their stupid white robes over it all? Was *that* what was wrong with his back?—"I *do*, I have one!"

"Of course you do," Hillford said, turning to address the congregation. "Now, is there anyone here willing to speak on behalf of the messenger?"

"'Messenger'?" Jory said, pulling against his tether.

No response from the novitiates. Just another hum, building. And Hillford, stepping into Jory's line of sight, his white blade suddenly in his left hand, his right hand . . . *whole?*

Hillford saw him looking, raised that hand for inspection. Moved the fingers against the thumb, as if dislodging wet sand, or rolling a tiny marble.

"There are many mysteries, Jory Gray, yes," Hillford said, holding the knife out to Jory, as if offering it. "Of which you are now an intimate part."

The humming swelled at that.

Instead of looking at the knife, Jory turned his head to the rest of the courtyard, and each doorway was still doorless, but there was a boneface in them all now. A real priest, not just a novitiate.

So, not a door that would keep *Jory* from passing, not if he really wanted to get through, but one that would—that would keep the *dead* from coming through?

Jory studied the novitiates, one by one, only stopping at the one female who turned her face away at the last instant. Just the slightest readjustment of her face, but he couldn't see her eyes now.

"Linse?" he said, but Hillford was blocking his sight line again. *"Linse!"* he screamed then, fighting to see around Hillford's robes. The pole creaked, the sheet straining.

"You can chew through it," Hillford said quietly to Jory then, like it was a kindness he was offering here, and held the knife out again, for Jory to take it. But the only part Jory could touch would be the blade, and then he'd be a short-finger in everything but virus.

"No, no no no," Jory said, looking up to Hillford.

Hillford stepped in closer, with the knife.

"It's not—you can't," Jory said, cringing back, looking up again to the deep gouges in the wall. The scratch marks.

Chew through it.

It's why the soldiers in the street had been using chain and pipe. Because the dead used their mouths like dogs did—the first tool.

And then Jory's face went cold. His head shaking *no.*

"You're going to infect me," Jory said. "That's what this is all about."

"*Anoint* you," Hillford corrected, so calm, and now Jory was pulling the other way, his feet against the pole, the sheet a guitar string.

Those gouges *were* from the dead. But from one at a time. All the novitiates would be up on the ramparts by the time it had chewed through its bindings. Allowing them to see the dead's true nature, up close, and accept it.

But who would *make* a zombie? If you needed one, if you were the *military* and you needed one, you'd just go out into a restricted zone, set a trap.

"I'm not your messenger," Jory said, up to Hillford. "Just let me—they're already, my friends, my unit, my driver, they know where I am, they're coming to look for me."

"Yes, the soldiers on their violent parade," Hillford said, keeping his distance. "I expect them to come asking after you at any moment now. But—there's a shortcut, as it were. As it *is,* I should say."

Jory pulled harder, his left boot slipping off the pole, his right still there, all his attention on it, on pushing, straining.

"Yes, yes," Hillford said, watching, impressed. "Maybe you'll be the one, Jory Gray. Maybe you'll—"

Hillford was still talking, but Jory couldn't hear anymore.

The knife, the stupid fucking white blade.

It was still in his right boot.

Jory faked a slip, collapsed, his new robes billowing all over him. Giving him room.

He stood with the white blade, cut through the knotted sheet like nothing.

All the novitiates stepped back, eyes large.

But not the priests. Not Hillford.

"Jory Gray," Hillford said, impressed again, not intimidated at all.

Jory edged around. Keeping the pole between himself and Hillford, he crabbed over to the novitiates, pulling their hoods off as he went. Bald head after bald head. All with eyes that matched each other.

"*What did you do with her*?" Jory said then, coming around to face Hillford again.

"Her place is with us, Jory Gray," Hillford said back, his hands holding each other again. Not even close to slipping up his sleeve. "As, I would offer, is yours. As you reestablish so elegantly each time we meet. A truly amazing specimen, yes. Let your anointing take place, Jory Gray, and you can be the first of a race of angels. In your pupa dreams, you can be with her again, as before, and never have to, have to use a-a . . . what was it?" he asked, knowing full well. "A hammer?"

Jory looked down to his hand, the curved white blade flickering into something more blunt. Something more matted with blood and hair. Jory's fingers started to let it slip, but then, his mind accelerating enough to slow the courtyard down, he came back up to Hillford's satisfied mask of a face. His patience.

And he tried to cut it away.

He came up fast with the knife, slashing across, trying to go from hip to opposite shoulder, spill Hillford out of himself like a piñata, but Hillford's arm was already in the way, the blade burying itself there, Jory's hand continuing the motion without it, the rest of him backing away, falling down, using the smooth pole to stand again.

"Ah, yes," Hillford said, rotating his arm around to study the blade, "one of the originals," then centering his rotting eyes back on Jory. "Have you suffered any injury?" he asked then, nodding down to Jory's hands, but Jory was coming at his midsection now.

Hillford sidestepped easily, guided Jory past, into the dirt.

Three times this happened, Hillford careful with his left arm. Careful for the blade, not the flesh.

"Children," another of the priests intoned somewhere in there, the novitiates hearing, lowering their heads. They lined up for the unfurling rampart ladders and climbed up into the sky, then rolled those ladders up behind them, tying them off, their eyes on Jory the whole time.

They were waiting for it to happen, Jory knew. Waiting for Hillford to cut him, for Jory to bleed out, die his first death, breathe his last breath, then rise again after they poured the infection in.

"If you knew only the singularity of purpose that awaits," Hillford said, "if you only knew, then you wouldn't insist upon this charade, Jory Gray. This flailing after a thing already gone."

"What'd you do to my back?" Jory said.

"You're the messenger."

"No, no I'm . . . Why *me*, then?" Jory said, standing now, gasping for breath, his face streaked with dirt.

"Because you don't want it, Jory Gray," Hillford said, no

hesitation at all. "Only those without the desire to live actually get to live forever, yes?"

"Amen to that," Jory said, casting around now. Seeing only doorways with priests, doorways with priests.

Except for one.

The wooden door they usually kept shut, it was yawning open now, forgotten.

Jory looked back to Hillford.

"That passage is not for the meek," Hillford said, no levity in his voice now.

"Tell me where she is," Jory said back.

"Look inside yourself," Hillford said.

"Bullshit," Jory said, and backed over to the black doorway, only stopping to study the ramparts again. The novitiates.

And then, as if it had been foretold, he stepped through, pulled the door shut behind him as hard as he could.

Hillford stared at it until Jory was gone, then calmly removed the blade lodged in his arm, turning to scan the ramparts as well. Turning to zero in on the female novitiate with her hood still up, her different-colored eyes wet, terrified, the smoke from the Weeping Poles rolling over the walls in waves now. The whole city burning, maybe.

Z Day.

CHAPTER THIRTY

A match flares in a dark room, doesn't light anything.

Another.

What the mannequin dad can see in the flare, in the glow, is another plastic face, another approximation of a human. He's military, of course, a corporal, a major, some kind of decorated war horse or another, though without Scanlon's scarred-up neck. Almost old enough to be the mannequin dad's father, though not nearly tall enough. Just another upper-level grunt.

"'Lazarus,' you say," this corporal says, shaking the match gone.

"Oppenheimer," the mannequin dad says back, like an indictment.

The corporal laughs this away. A very fake, congratulatory laugh. "And here we thought communications had been tamped down."

"I don't mean—"

"I know what you mean, Mr. XXXXX. But—do you even know who Lazarus was?"

"John," the mannequin dad says, like he doesn't want to. "Eleven-ten, I think."

"A religious man, good, good. Then you know Lazarus, that he rose from the dead after three days in the tomb. Nary an ill effect."

The mannequin dad shuffles his feet. Swallows. "I just want to see my brother," he says. "Please?"

The corporal leans back, cradling the back of his head in his laced fingers. Studying the ceiling maybe. Not even acknowledging what the mannequin dad is pretty sure is a two-way mirror beside them. Their only light's coming from it, side glow from what looks to be a dashboard pressed up against the glass.

Nobody's behind that dashboard.

The corporal doesn't even look down to explain, just says it straight up, already bored by it. "We turn the overheads on, the cameras start rolling, the tapes start reeling, and then, then we can't have a private chat like this, now, can we? Man to man, I mean. Just the two of us."

Chuckle chuckle.

A lone bead of sweat rolls down the mannequin dad's plastic face, from temple to jawline.

"Crops all over the world are dying, you know that?" the corporal says then. "Rain forest's going all belly up. Too many mouths, not enough wars. But what if—what if we could dream up, say, a revolutionary strain of cattle. Just spitballing out loud here, if that's okay. But, a breed of cattle that you could carve steaks from all *week?* Nary an ill effect."

"You said that already," the mannequin dad says. "And we don't have that kind of technology."

"You don't know what we have," the corporal snaps back.

"My brother, for one."

The corporal shakes his head. "If you're so worried about him, he's fine. Trust me. Little cabin fever, nothing else. Part of an FDA approval. Eating hamburgers three times a—"

"He didn't tell you everything," the mannequin dad says. Just loud enough.

"About you, for one."

"No, his, our—"

"Little genetic peculiarity, yeah, yeah. So? Think we don't screen blood six ways from Sunday, an approval like this? Your brother, Mr. XXXXX, your pain-in-the-ass brother, he's the future. Maybe of the whole damn species."

"I think he's got something else too. Not the Creutzfeldt." Eyes closed, words in order, in order, please. "I think he might have *caught* something. I called his . . . the girl he was with. His wife. And she was at a—"

"*Wife?*"

"I don't know. But she's sick now. Sir."

"'Sir.'"

"I called the number he gave me before. For her."

"Of course."

"I found her. And they told me she'd been, um, what do you say? Committed?"

"Head case," the corporal shrugs. "More like she caught it from him. I know I almost have."

"No, she's in a—"

"Hospital for the relationship challenged, I get it."

"Leper colony. Sir."

The corporal looks over to the glass wall.

"So, let me keep this straight," he says, "you think we can test for mad cow disease—"

"He doesn't have that."

"We can test for the *propensity* for bovine spongiform encephalopathy then. You think we can test for that and miss something from the Middle *Ages*?"

The mannequin dad looks to the glass wall as well. Each of their reflections are transparent. Like they're not even really here. "I'm just saying," he says. "Variants like that, you can't— He'll mess up your study."

"No, I think what you're failing to understand here, Mr., Mr. XXXXX, is that those variants, they're like, they're manna from heaven, you get it? Your brother, he just walked right off the street, see? Right into history. Without him, I don't know where we'd be."

"This can't be legal."

"I say what's legal, son. Get it? What was that? Oh, oh. I'll do it"—tilting his face up to the dead microphones, the dead cameras—"Lazarus Complex! Lazarus Complex!"

It ends with him laughing. Rubbing his chin with his thick fingers.

"Why are you telling me all this?" the mannequin dad says then. "Unless—unless you're not letting me go." His big hands contract into balls. "I've got a family, sir."

"Kind of thought so, yeah," the corporal says, hauling something up from the floor, setting it on the tabletop between them. "But what I really want to know, see, it's . . . do you have a brother?"

The mannequin dad doesn't follow, narrows his eyes down to the object on the table.

The cast. His son's arm cast.

"Well?" the corporal says then, leaning back, flicking another match off his thumbnail. Watching that wavering flame. Speaking through it. "You, your kind. You don't have any idea what it's like, trying to save the world, do you? Caring about it enough that you'd pay whatever cost?"

"No," the mannequin dad says, hugging the cast to him.

"No what?" the corporal says, holding the flame up to his eye, to study the mannequin dad through it like a microscope.

"No, I don't have a brother," the mannequin dad says, covering his eyes with one of his hands, his shoulders hitching up, once, twice.

CHAPTER THIRTY-ONE

Jory felt more than heard the crossbar slam down, once and forever.

He was sitting knees-up, his back to the thick door.

Blackness all around. Dank, cloying.

Except?

The robe.

He lowered his hands, ran his hands along the fabric.

It *did* glow. It glowed *more* wherever he touched it. Light by friction, amplified body heat, reclaimed static, magnetism, the power of prayer—he didn't know which. But it worked.

"Hunh," he said, and stood, found he could see in a dim, sepia-toned way. Maybe three feet in each direction. Like he was in an old, old movie, where the frame was a blurry circle, not a neat rectangle.

To his left, beside the door, was a cinder block wall, sloping up to a rounded ceiling. To his right, another cinder block wall, coming up to the same ceiling, the wood there spongy, ancient, part of the earth now. The ground under his feet had been the same wood once, but it had seen more traffic, more contact, was mostly dirt now.

An old bomb shelter? Some kind of bunker?

Jory wished he had the knife back. Or his torch. Even just a stick.

He rubbed the right arm of his robe brighter, studied the backside of this door.

Same as the front, except no ring to pull it open.

It made sense, kind of.

And the gouges clawed into the wood, they were the same gouges on the inner walls of the courtyard.

It meant this was where he was supposed to have gone. After Hillford cut his fingers off or whatever, let him bleed out for however many hours, then tipped some ceremonial black vial into his open mouth. Thirty-seven seconds after *that,* Jory was supposed to have woken up all at once, chewed through the sheet at his wrists, then shambled to each doorway—priest, priest—then tried the walls, the novitiates probably trained not to flinch, then, at last, gone the only place left—here.

Only he wasn't dead. He didn't have the virus.

For all the good it would do him.

And—if the zombies were supposed to finally settle on this room, if this room was where they were supposed to end up, then wouldn't they still *be* here?

Jory made himself breathe, breathe.

No, he told himself. If they'd already been here, then he wouldn't be. If they'd already been in here, then the door wouldn't have been open. The novitiates wouldn't have been idling around the courtyard, anyway.

Unless it took X amount of time for the dead to find the door again.

Maybe *that* was how Jory was supposed to have gotten the virus. Not a black vial of infection at all, but one of the dead flashing through the door, catching his unclerical scent. Passing all the priests by, going straight for the new meat.

That would mean this wasn't a room at all, but a hall. A tunnel.

Keeping his right hand to the cinder block, Jory felt along it, away from the door. Deeper, deeper, the floor grading down under him, making each step so easy, like falling.

There was no corner, no back wall. At least not yet. Not this far.

Jory rushed back to the door he knew, slammed the side of his fist into it. Finally collapsed in front of it, sobbing.

"You have to let me see her!" he screamed into the wood. "I brought you the knife!"

No response.

The door wouldn't so much as shake, no matter how hard he rammed into it. His voice just slipped away behind him, echoing down the walls. Calling up whatever was down there, surely.

"Okay, okay," he said, his hands in his hair.

Okay.

If—if this *was* the pit or tunnel or cell or whatever where they kept their pet zombies, their dead altar boys, then that meant the next time the crossbar came up, that he'd have company, right? Dead company. Hungry company.

Jory bounced up and down with nerves.

That was the only answer though.

The next time that door opened, he was food.

"Breathe, breathe," he said out loud, trying to use his nose for in, his mouth for out.

After a few cycles of that he could stand.

Moving slow, he found the right wall with his whole hand, then just with the fingertips of his index and middle fingers.

"Linse," he said, looking down the slope he could only feel with his feet, "I'm coming, baby," and started walking. Slow at first, then faster, until the ground leveled out under him and he could run without jamming his knees, his fingertips crumbling old cinder block from the wall. At least until he tripped on a root or something, went spinning into the middle space, what he'd been thinking of as the dead space.

Totally lost now. No direction whatsoever.

He kept to his knees and hands, unsure if the ceiling was even tall enough here.

What he'd tripped on, it was a pelvis. Human. Gnaw marks on the thicker parts, where the muscle had tried to hold on.

Jory pushed it away, stood to run, ran flat into the wall, spun back to the ground again.

This time he stayed there.

More breathing. In, out; in, out.

Finally he stood again, found the wall with his raw finger-tips again, and started walking, walking for what felt like hours, until the ground sloped up like it was taking him somewhere, delivering him from this cursed place.

He stepped faster, faster, running now, and it was pure luck his free arm felt the wood door, giving him just enough time and space to roll into it with his shoulder, the fabric there spiking brighter, so that, from the ground, he could see the same gouges, the same iron shackles. The same door he'd shut on himself.

The wrong wall.

He'd stood from the pelvis, found the wrong wall.

Jory folded over on himself, stayed that way until his back was stiff, the scratches or whatever there dried into the fabric of the robe.

Three hours. It had been three hours, no more than four. Maybe less.

And he'd gone exactly nowhere.

He stood again, his hand to the door, and pushed off, pressing his whole palm hard into the wall, and started to move along it for the second time, more cinder block crumbling off behind him now.

This time he wouldn't run, wouldn't break contact, no matter what. He couldn't circle back again, not if he wanted to live. And he did want to live. He laughed, realizing it—he didn't just want out, he wanted to go *back*. To the world. To the stupid-ass postapocalypse. He wanted more of those stale cigarettes, he wanted more apple sauce in the top left corner of his scarred-up cafeteria tray, he wanted a shovel in his hand, a job to do, a part to play, a radio to tune in late at night, a fence to look through.

But mostly it was the cigarettes.

Some X amount of time and footsteps later, Jory found himself mumbling. About the curve of the roof of this tunnel he was walking through. How it was exactly the curve of an armadillo's shell. One from the Miocene period, when size mattered.

Jory stumbled deeper, deeper, his throat dry, the palm of his hand blistering already, probably leaving a bloody smear.

Some amount of time and footsteps ago, he'd kicked through what he was pretty sure was the pelvis that had tripped him before, and had stepped down into the flat part of the hall or tunnel or never-ending long room. The flat part that felt like it was never going to end. And then he walked right into an open metal door. It creaked away from him, its hinges mostly seized. The porthole window built into it was barred, crusted with rust.

Keeping his hand to the right wall, Jory broke a dirt clod off the ceiling, tossed it through the door.

If it hit a wall, he couldn't hear it.

Was this a branch, a fork, or a cell, a guard booth?

Jory shut his eyes, tried to imagine a lighter in his hand, the flame telling him which way the wind was sucking.

Straight, he decided. This *was* a cell, a guard booth. A way station, a distraction, trouble for sailors, or whatever they said. The main tunnel was the one he was in. If this door was shut, it would become *part* of that right hand wall, making it a tributary, a feeder, not the main course. Not the right way.

It was the only thing to think.

Jory slid his hand over the top of the door, never breaking contact with the wall he'd come to love, and kept going, shying around the slow curves, stopping once to pee onehanded. Wondering what would be sniffing that damp earth later.

And then, coming around a gentle turn, he caught a glint ahead.

"Hello?" he called, his voice a boom, after so long silent.

Nothing.

A trick of darkness, he told himself. A twitch in his eye, a shard of mica in the wall—he could never find it again.

But ten, twenty minutes later, a thousand steps deeper into this darkness, there it was again.

The glint, flashing. Catching the glow of his robe.

"What?" Jory said, and stepped closer, stopped again.

It was a hair clip thing, a barrette. The metal kind, like a paper clip for the hair.

That's what he used to call it, what he used to tell his daughter it was.

A paper clip for the hair. For *her* hair.

No.

But, unable not to, he stepped closer, and the glint of clip had a head of hair to hold it. The dim outline of a girl's body below it. His worst nightmare. His best dream.

Jory fell to his knees, lost the wall.

He promised not to tell anybody, if this could just be real, please.

Except.

He'd—he'd *aimed* for that barrette, hadn't he? Used it to guide the head of his hammer. Driven it down, in, through. And then lost it.

Until now. It was surfacing. After ten years, it was coming back.

He pulled his right hand to him, saw how bloody it was and fell down some more though he was already on his knees.

His daughter still standing there. Waiting. The glint of her barrette anyway.

"Come on, Daddy," she said from the darkness then, *obviously,* that tone she had like he was being silly, and Jory rose, had forgotten the wall altogether.

"I'm here," he said, and stepped closer, only to have her step back.

And then he ran, her small, shadowy form flitting before him, hardly even touching the ground.

For miles, hours? Minutes, feet?

X. For X hours, X feet. Because that's two letters before Z. It's somewhere you can stay, somewhere you can hide.

Jory stumbled on faster, more headlong, his shoulder flashing brighter each time he brushed the wall, only stopping when she did.

She wasn't looking at him, but to the tunnel *behind* him.

Jory turned without thinking, looked too. Listened.

A zombie.

Hillford had made another, from his own flock probably. He'd made another then lifted the great bar of that great door, set the zombie loose after him, to clean up, finish the ritual, close the circle. Make the blood sacrifice Z Day was going to need.

The zombie wasn't close yet, but was close enough. Such a distinct sound—snuffling, the pads of its feet and hands hardly even touching the ground—and Jory nodded, knew then that he should have stayed in that halfway cell, screeched that door shut, but it was too late, and it didn't matter anyway.

His daughter, he was with her again.

It was best this way.

But when he turned, her face, either the one he was seeing or the one he was remembering, it was so urgent, so pleading, and he almost said her name again, was about to, except she was already turning, running, her middle and ring fingers pressed into her palms like she did when concentrating.

Jory followed, his legs stiff now, uncoordinated, using the wall for balance when he had to. Pushing off to go faster. The snuffling closer and closer yet.

Jory smiled, was ready, was going to turn this time, stand between the plague and his family, like he should have, like he'd give anything to have gotten the chance to do, but, coming around a sharper corner than there'd been so far, his daughter was just standing there.

Another door.

No, half a door. A door that was just her height.

Jory smiled, understood.

Everybody died differently, right?

For him, it was a game with his daughter. One leading finally to where she lived now. To a playhouse with a short door, low windows, so that, walking through it, he was going to get to feel like a giant. Or a dad.

"Okay," he said out loud, the snuffling closer behind him now, too close, if that mattered anymore, and he followed her, ducked down, stepped through, was blinded by the light that was over on this side, dim as it probably was, and, because his daughter was already in this perfect afterlife with him, he pulled the door shut behind them.

An instant later, the zombie slammed into it, hard enough to sift dirt down all around the frame.

"Hunh," Jory said.

If that way was death, if the dead were on the other side of that door, then this, here, it must be life, right? Or, anywhere with his daughter, *that* was life.

And then there was a breathing behind him. More raspy than an eleven-year-old girl in her forever playhouse.

Something licked his raw palm.

Jory closed his eyes, didn't take his hand back, and finally looked down.

A goat. One of Scanlon's goats, its child eyes looking up, and up, waiting.

Jory looped his arm over this goat's neck, pulled it to him, and looked over its thick coat to the bars that walled this room. This *cell.* Twin lines of white reflective tape telling you where to walk.

The pens.

Base.

He was in the snake's belly.

DAY SIX

CHAPTER THIRTY-TWO

Jory woke to screaming. Right in his ear, against the side of his head.

It was the goat.

The guard who loved technology had his Hot Shot pushed through the bars, was cooking her.

"Careful now," he said to Jory, when Jory reached over to pull the goat away.

One of the goat's eyeballs leaked down its face, leaving a very human socket, wisps of smoke trailing up from it.

The guard couldn't stop laughing.

Jory pushed away, up against the wall, his chest spasming.

"You're right," the burn-faced guard said, stepping up from the darkness. "He does have one of them."

One of them, one of them, Jory repeated in his head, looking both ways, for a way out, please.

On either side, though, and on either side of that, and probably across too, it was all goats. This deep, it was livestock only. Scanlon's private tribe of perfect victims.

One of them cooking in its own skin now.

"Doesn't just *have* one, he *is* one," the tech-loving guard said.

The burn-faced guard was shaking his head *no*, though. Stepping closer, guiding the guard's Hot Shot away like it was nothing.

"Know how long the army's been wanting to get its hands on one of those?" he said through the bars to Jory.

"Your vestments, *brother*," the tech-loving guard said, when Jory wasn't following.

Jory pulled it over his head, tearing it loose from his back like a scab. He threw it at the bars.

The burn-faced guard pulled it through, rubbed a bright spot in it. He smiled in his melted way.

"Lab boys'll like this," he said, handing it across to the other guard. "Blast-resistant silk?" He laughed, took some in his hand again. "You know it's supposed to kind of all melt together when the air pressure changes, like from a shock wave? Make a shield or cocoon or some bullshit. What do you think?"—modeling the profile of his face—"It could have saved me?"

"You were a torch?" Jory said.

The burn-faced guard didn't dignify the question.

"They like chocolate," Jory said then, about the dying goat.

"More like they're *like* chocolate," the burn-faced guard said. "Their sweet scent brings all the kids to the door"—nodding to the half door Jory'd come through.

Jory looked to the door, stared at the ground, and understood—the goats were what brought the zombies down the tunnel. What kept them from just scratching at the big wooden door at the Church.

This was a delivery chute. A system. The Church was feeding the dead across to the military. For Preburial. Which the Church was insisting upon.

The tech-loving guard snapped, the sound loud, close, bringing Jory back.

"What'd you see down there?" he asked.

Jory framed his lips to answer, but threw up instead.

Both the guards stepped back.

"He is infected," one of them said, hardly concerned. "Late bloomer, that's all."

Jory shook his head *no*, threw up some more, trying to cup it in his hands, like maybe he was going to need it later.

"Better get this topside," the burn-faced guard said, about the robe.

"Messenger's here," the tech-loving guard recited in a singsong voice, impressed. "Don't go to sleep now, think you can handle that? Be back in two shakes of a . . ."

Instead of finishing, he reached through with his Hot Shot, wagged the goat's tail a couple of times.

Jory gagged again.

When their footsteps were all the way gone, Jory breathed in, the air grainy, particulate. Like he was tasting the light. It didn't taste good.

His neck was in poor control of his head, and his eyes, they were lying to him. They had to be. If not, then there really was a zombie watching him from the black recesses of the cell directly across from him. A zombie rotted half away, sores on its face, hair gone in clumps, eyes scooped out then sewed over with crude thread. So, not watching him at all. But seeing him all the same, its broken-fingered hands hanging in front of it, forearms on its knees.

It was breathing in and out, in and out. Not crashing into the bars like it should be, to get to Jory.

But still.

Jory felt behind him for the door he'd come through, that there was for *sure* another zombie behind. A hungry one.

The door had caught, was locked. For now.

It was just him and this calm zombie then. And the terrible, delicious smell of cooked goat. And the soft brays of the rest of the goats, mourning this one. And there was also the promise of Scanlon getting roused a half mile above, giving him about a thousand steps to work up a proper head of steam. It was the kind of walk you guarantee you're going to make worth it. And Jory wasn't just weak, he was wasted. Done, over, finished with all of this already.

Except all of this wasn't finished with him yet.

"Mess-en-ger," the dead man croaked out, its vocal cords parched, the word breaking into parts.

Jory pretended not to hear. Because zombies don't talk. He patted the goat, slicking down what hair he could.

"Tic, tic, tic," the dead man said then, its throat clearing. And, the closer Jory looked, he wasn't a zombie at all. He was worse, somehow. Worse because he wasn't dead yet, had skipped that part, gone straight to the long decay, the slow rotting away, an ambling state of decomp.

Jory stopped patting the goat.

"You're not dead," Jory said across the walkway.

The man who wasn't dead shrugged, like the argument could go either way here.

It was the single most human gesture Jory had ever seen.

"What did you do?" he asked. "To be . . . to be here."

The dead man laughed through his torn nose a bit, said it again, "Tic tic tic," then mimed an explosion with his hands. He pointed a spindly finger at Jory to show where that explosion was going to take place.

Jory stood, felt all over himself. He was just himself, nothing strapped on.

Across from him, the dead man scraped something from his

scalp, worked it into his mouth. The teeth there were all broken off and black, the tongue a blind eel, stabbing around.

"You're saying I'm infected," Jory said. "That they infected me. That I'm going to turn."

The dead man just stared with his gone eyes.

"What happened to you?" Jory asked.

"History," the dead man said, his voice clearer than Jory would have guessed possible. "The world."

"You can't see, can you?"

"With my ears."

"There's something on my . . . they did something to my back, I think. Something you can't hear, I guess."

The dead man used two of his crooked fingers to drag a shaky cross in the air before him. Or a plus. Like he was blessing Jory.

"You're a *priest*?" Jory said. Because of how tall he was, even sitting down. Because of the rotted, pitted face. Because the other end of this tunnel was a doorway to the Hill. Maybe one of them had come here on a spy mission, got himself nabbed.

The dead man's mouth cracked into a smile about this idea of him being a priest. It made a seep of blood spill from his lip. He tried to finger it back in, didn't look to have enough to waste.

"Kind of the"—cough, cough—"kind of the opposite of a priest," he said, "according to them."

"Them?"

"GI Joe," he said, tilting his head up the passageway.

Jory looked that way, and came back. Then, moving slowly and deliberately, he held his own two fingers out before him, like the dead man had, but, instead of dragging a plus sign in the air, he spread the fingers like the dead man couldn't, so that what he traced through the air, it wasn't a cross, but—"Tic-tic . . . tic-tac-toe," he said.

It was what Hillford had carved into Jory's back.

"His move now," the dead man creaked, pointing with his chin up the passageway again. To Scanlon.

"I'm not infected," Jory said. "I'm not going to die, come back."

"You're just going to die, then?"

"Probably."

"They like to make me watch, make me"—cough—"atone."

"Watch?"

"Listen. See it worse in my head. What are they calling themselves these days?" the dead man asked.

Jory stared into the dirt at his feet. He looked back to the half door.

"The Church?" he said, not tracking the question so well.

The dead man nodded, his face slack.

Jory shrugged, said, "The Church, I guess, I don't know. I was just visiting, didn't mean to check in."

The dead man rubbed at the blood seeping down his chin, got enough on his index finger to rub it against his right tear duct, pushing in past the stitches a bit where he could, like he could touch his brain.

"*The* Church," he repeated. "Like, the only one, right? The last one."

"I guess."

"Then they won," he said, looking at whatever he'd snagged with his fingertip. Looking at it with eyes sewn over.

"Who are you?" Jory asked.

"There used to be more churches, at first," the dead man said, looking off, into some past.

"Bottleneckers?"

"Other"—cough, cough—"other one."

"Church of Z?"

"Z," the dead man repeated, spitting afterward. "Glorified suicide cult."

"Infected their own, from what I hear."

"Sound familiar now?"

"I'm not a priest. Or a novitiate. Not even the janitor. I was just wearing one of their . . ."

The dead man nodded when Jory trailed off. Point made—the Church *does* infect its own, apparently.

"So?" Jory said.

"So," the dead man went on, redistributing his gaunt weight, his shoulders creaking into a different, less crooked angle, "so they *found* it one fine day, this Z Church. By accident, on purpose, who knows. But they found it."

"Found what?"

"Maybe some suicide walked in with it in his pocket," the dead man went on, his gone eyes looking deep into the past. "Left it on the altar. In the collection plate."

"Left what?"

"What really *happened*," the dead man whispered, reverently, "the truth, the gospel. It changed everything. Gave them power, made them grow up all at once. Tend their flock more carefully—one a month, instead of everybody at once. And"—more coughing, worse coughing—"and they called in their saints from across the sea, who walked on water the whole way here, set up shop in the old garrison, just to be close to, close to where it—"

"The Hill, you mean?"

The dead man kind of chuckled. "Historical site," he said. "Big church back before, before cars, then"—more coughing, and from deeper—"underground, underground—" but he lost it in coughing.

"Underground railroad," Jory completed. "The tunnel."

The dead man nodded, collected himself, his head lolling around on his shoulders like it was going to Pez back. When he spoke now, it was more into his chest, "But then, during the war, the army used it for a, for a munitions depot. Armory. After we won, the army had their engineers improve the tunnel, so they could, so they could"—bad coughing—"could move all their hush-hush ordinance out of the heart of the downtown."

"To here."

"And now you're that ordinance." The dead man laughed. "Their agent of mass destruction. Of infection. Like the pipe got clogged, is backing up."

"I told you," Jory said. "I got away before they could do it. I'm not infected."

"Not with the virus," the dead man ceded.

"The—the tic-tac-toe?" Jory filled in, not buying it.

"Monthly reminder," the dead man said, coughing at the end of it. "Round fired across the"—cough, cough—"across the bow. Monthly reminder that they know."

Messenger, Jory heard again. From Hillford.

"A message about Scanlon," he said. "What he did."

"About *Genesis.* That they know it. That they have it. It keeps the brass in line."

Jory stared at this dead man, then stared some more.

"So the army's afraid of the Church?"

"Long as there's dead people walking, there's somebody to blame," the dead man said. "But it'd be suicide for them to let that document leak. That's the stupid part. It'd be a disaster. For both damn houses."

"A pox, you mean," Jory said.

The dead man looked up at him, the question written on his face.

"A pox," Jory explained. "I subbed for English once."

The dead man got it, nodded. "'On this the world depends,'" he recited.

"'This'?" Jory asked.

"The truth," the dead man said, looking to the sound of important boots coming down the passageway at them. "The *gospel* truth."

This time it was just the tech-loving guard and Scanlon.

Before coming to Jory's cell, Scanlon stood at the dead man's, studying him. Goats braying all around.

"Hear that?" the guard said to Jory, about the goats. "Know what they're saying? They think he's their dad. Listen. *'Da-addy, Da-addy.'*"

The guard still had the Hot Shot, of course. Patting it with his other hand, like he was crowd control here. Just waiting.

"So you're this month's special delivery," Scanlon said.

Jory closed his eyes, swallowed. When he came back, the guard was smelling the tip of his Hot Shot.

"I know why you keep them down here," Jory said, his eyes glancing off Scanlon's.

"Know what happens we keep them in open air?" Scanlon said right back. "Ever seen dogs lining the butcher's fence? A desiccate'll come for miles, he smells a stash like this. All of them will. And to get here, they'll have to cross downtown. Have to cross base."

Jory studied the bars of his cell again—solid—said it, "Meaning you're the butcher, here?"

"Don't start," Scanlon said. "Save it for your new spiritual guide."

"Hillford's the one who put me here," Jory said.

"Gave you back, more like," Scanlon said. "Turn around."

"You know what you've done."

"Saved the world, you mean?"

"It's my move."

"Good, good, yes. I could have made something of you, you know? Used all that pissed-offness. That mouth."

"Just get it over with already."

"What?"

"Whatever you did to him"—the dead man across the way—"I don't know. I'm not walking out of here, am I?"

"A suicide to the end."

"I died ten years ago."

"Ten years ago *today.*"

"Anybody ever finish one of those games?" the dead man said from his cell then, his chin still on his chest.

Jory and Scanlon and the guard all turned to study him.

"Xs, Os?" the dead man said, speaking loud enough that it was going to cost him some lung, Jory knew. And then he looked up, his dead eyes right on Scanlon. "Or were they all"—cough, cough, two fingers dragged through a cross again—"were they all—all"—but he lost the rest, had to bend over to try to breathe, the ridge of his vertebrae stark, reptilian.

"Xs," Jory finished.

Scanlon came back to him.

"This is all underground because if one of these short-fingers gets loose, everybody'll know it's true," Jory said. "Not the goats. The kids. No, your *kids.*"

"You're not standing here otherwise."

"I'm just the messenger."

The guard shook his head in something like pity.

"No," Scanlon said. "You're more than that now, son. To those fairies up on the Hill."

The dead man laughed at this, somehow.

Scanlon pretended not to notice.

"But guess what?" Scanlon went on. "Because you're more than that to them, you're more than that to me now too. Last time you went in the field? Your buddy, he showed up too."

"Hillford?"

"Brother Hillford the saint maker. Exactly. I send you out again, I'd put money down he'll be there waiting. See what holy bullshit you pull next."

"He offered me an apple," Jory said. "I didn't take it."

"Well, there's all kinds of apples," Scanlon said. "But that's not why I'm here. Why I'm here is that I think it's time for a regime change." With that, he squatted down to Jory's level. "Know what I'm talking about here, son? Because, know what we think? The plague's over. All that's left's cleanup. But your buddy up the Hill, he knows that if the scary shit's all done with, then people will stop going to Church. So they've been bringing them back somehow, cooking up a new brew—"

"Airborne," Jory said, half on accident.

"Or in the dirt, or some other way, we don't know. But they *can* do it, we've seen them do it right where you're standing, and, what's worse, they've got their finger on the button. And I think they're just bat shit enough to do it."

"Do what?"

"Start the bad old days up all over again. Kick-start another swarm."

"They wouldn't."

"They already are, son. They're just refining the formula, the method of dispersal. Don't you doubt it for one minute. They're waiting for a certain anniversary, think? Gonna make us all into angels, whether we like it or not. Except we got to be devils first, right?"

Scanlon shook his head, studied the far wall.

"Sometimes you've got to be the devil, though, to do good," he said. "That's the part they never understood."

Jory blinked, the cell becoming real around him. The world shifting, somehow. It was the scent of cooked goat all around him. It was the same as the peach smuggler had smelled. The same as Glasses and the cheerleader.

Jory dry-heaved, held it down.

The guard nodded *yes, yes.* That this was just the beginning.

Scanlon was waiting for Jory now.

Jory looked past him, to the dead man across the way.

"So you want me to go another call," he said. "Draw him out—Hillford."

"Cut the head off the snake," Scanlon said, "the body, it dies. Every fucking time."

Jory was just staring at the goat now.

"No," he said.

"I'm not asking," Scanlon told him.

Jory's face was hot now.

"Why me?" he asked.

"Because you're special to them. Because if you do it, if it happens while you're there, then it'll be holy to *them,* that's why. No retaliation. No harm, no foul. And it'll mean something, being on the anniversary."

The guard standing beside him nodded.

"You want me to kill Hillford," Jory said, just to be clear.

"He should have died in the old pens seven years ago," Scanlon said, reaching in to the goat with his own baton.

"You want me to be your next ten-year-old kid," Jory added, quieter. More level. "Your last kid."

Scanlon didn't even stop what he was doing with his baton—pulling the goat closer to the bars—just said, "Thought she was more like eleven?"

Jory had to turn his face away. Lick his lips hard.

Scanlon chuckled his old-man chuckle. "And, if you're asking if I know what's in these?" he said, the goat to him now, the skin on its flank splitting, spitting up smoke. Scanlon dug into that rip with the first two fingers of his right hand, balanced a dollop of meat there, still trailing its sheath of fat. "I know *exactly* what's in here," he said, and set it into his mouth, chewed it down, never flinched once. Even half of once.

Jory's lower lip trembled.

"You know why I know, Gray?" Scanlon said around the dry swallow. "I'll tell you, since you're so special. On this of all days. It's because I'm not going to let humanity fall down, son. Not under my watch, so help me."

"Even if it costs us our humanity," Jory said.

The guard grunted something about this.

Scanlon stood, staring at Jory the whole while.

"If that's the way you want it," he said, drawing his antique revolver, pointing it down to Jory, Jory just looking up to it, waiting.

"Still a suicide?" Scanlon said.

"I'm already dead," Jory said back, and closed his eyes, didn't want to see it coming.

The shot filled the cell.

And Jory had time to think that he'd heard it.

That he was hearing it echo *away* now.

He looked up, cringing.

Beside Scanlon, the guard wavered, blood crying from his eyes, slipping from his ears. A hole in each temple. Or, in one. The other side of his head, it was gone, a red mouth yawning open.

"Way I see it," Scanlon said then, pushing the dead guard away, "you owe me one soldier now," blowing the smoke from the end of his barrel. "Gotta love the tech, though, don't you?"

Jory watched the guard drop to his knees hard enough to jar his hat off, then tump forward, his face cracking into the bars, his top lip dragging on the dry steel, exposing a mouthful of perfect white teeth.

"Why?" Jory said.

"Because the Church has a mole in here somewhere. And I can't take any chances."

"I don't live through this, do I?" Jory said. "Through killing Hillford."

"You live forever is what happens," Scanlon said, amused with himself. "You'll be a hero. But, if it's your life you're suddenly worried about, aren't you already dead? Inside? Melodramatically? Metaphorically?"

"And this," Jory went on, "the cell, the pens, the goats—it'll all stop if Hillford dies?"

"That's all I want, son. Long night's over. Time for the sun to show its big red ass to the world again."

Jory hauled himself up. Hated himself.

"He survived," he said.

Scanlon, wiping his fingers clean on his lower pant leg, stopped, looked up. "'He'?" he asked.

"Hillford," Jory said. "His face is—from fire. He was coded. Like that other guard."

"That what he told you?" Scanlon said, curling his now-clean fingers to somebody waiting in the dark, up the passage, telling them to come on. "I told you, son. Other day with you, that was his first call, ever. And his next, thanks to you, it's going to be his last. I know why they didn't like him though."

"'They' who?"

Scanlon studied Jory again, like he was mishearing. "They, the *dead*, son. The desiccates. Why he was able to walk through them like he did. What did you call it?"

"Parting the Dead Sea."

"Yeah. I like that. Kind of what I do, too."

"Why didn't they attack him?"

"Because he's just like them," Scanlon said, then nodded once to the handler, just suddenly there, hulking in place. His short-fingered zombie pulling at its leash. Neither of them with enough brain to be the Church's mole.

Jory fell back, splatted into the straw floor of his cell.

Scanlon shrugged, said, "You understand, of course, that I can't take your word here."

"My what?"

"About not being infected. Maybe they've found a way to delay re-an, think? Sent you over here like a time bomb? Solar activated, or elevation, air pressure."

"They didn't—"

"Yeah, well," Scanlon said, unlocking the cell, "some things you take on faith, and some things you find out yourself." He swung the door in, directed the handler in. And the zombie.

Jory pushed back into the corner, the zombie straining, pulling against the ground, standing up from it.

"No, no!" Jory was saying.

"I'd recommend playing it cool here," Scanlon said. "Don't want any accidents now, do we?"

Jory tried, but his chest was heaving, his feet still trying to cram him deeper into the corner, and then the zombie was there, its rancid breath blasting into his face, the handler letting it stay, smell, taste.

And then the dog pulled harder.

"It wants me, it wants me, I'm clean!" Jory yelled up to Scanlon.

"Turn around," Scanlon said back, through the din, and Jory did, flattening himself against the wall, hearing the last sound he wanted to hear—the zombie's mouth grate, clacking open.

Jory's tic-tac-toe was crawling on his back now, alive, the blood trying to get back inside, the zombie's mouth right there, inches away, its breath hot and fast, its forelegs pulling at the concrete, spraying straw all up into the handler.

And, finally, though he didn't have any left, Jory peed himself, felt it coat his right leg with warmth, maybe the last warmth. He had his mouth open to the wall now, his teeth to the stone like he could chew through, get flatter.

"Guess you are alive," Scanlon said, and called it off.

The handler yanked the zombie back, let it feed on the cooked goat instead.

"Waste not, want not," Scanlon said, holding his arm out for Jory to cross the cell, step through the door. Jory's legs were hardly even his own anymore. "You still know how to use a torch, right?" Scanlon said when Jory was finally out, trying to get his lungs back under his own control.

Scanlon clanged the door shut, but didn't lock it.

"I want, I want, I want the same driver," Jory told him, the tears coming now. Too much oxygen in his blood. Adrenaline sloshing around in his throat.

"Same driver, check," Scanlon said, turning for Jory to follow, Jory falling in, then flinching back, the dead man in the opposite cell at the bars now. His forever fingers wrapped around the bars three times, it looked like. Because—because he was six-nine, six-ten, it looked like. His chest was caved in, his nipples just craters of burn, his ankles festering in an ancient set of shackles not connected to anything anymore.

But he could still speak.

"*I am become Shiva, destroyer of worlds,*" he hissed, his voice grand and broken, saved up for years, it sounded like, and Jory, directly behind Scanlon, saw Scanlon stiffen, palm his neck, like a rotten fleck of spit had landed there, and in that moment, Scanlon's skin shifted for Jory. It went smooth, plastic, generic.

Shiva, Jory repeated in his head, trying to place it. *Shiva Shiva Shiva,* and then—

Oppenheimer.

J. Robert Oppenheimer.

I am become death, destroyer of worlds.

Scanlon.

Jory turned to the walking dead man, looked all the way up to him, and then knew him, recognized him, had read about him. *God.* Had read what he *wrote,* had read his fucking *blog.* He was the Kitten Man. It was why he was here, having to listen to these new zombies get birthed into the world. Because he'd helped birth the first. Because this world, it was his, he'd made it.

The opposite of a priest, he'd said.

And all because he'd loved his brother. Because he'd loved his son.

"You," Jory said up to him, but the dead man was trying to track Scanlon, was just clutching the bars now, sliding down from the effort of having crossed the cell, and Jory broke away from Scanlon, pulled himself up onto those same bars, his face right to the Kitten Man's, so the Kitten Man would have to hear when Jory said it over and over, as fast as he could, *"Bingo!* Bingo brain baste, bingo brain *baste,* bingo brain"—the Kitten Man angling his dead stare over to Jory now. To those five redacted letters of his brother's name.

"No, Brian," he said simply, pulling his lips away from his broken teeth, a smile maybe, his shattered fingers rolling over to cover Jory's, in thanks, which is when Jory felt it in his back— forty thousand volts.

Because he was just the middle of the circuit, the current hit the Kitten Man as well, arced him across his cell, left him openmouthed against the wall, grey wisps trailing up from his throat, a grimy arm cast there beside him, tied together with string, or hair, or spit.

Jory nodded, remembered that too, and then, the end of the circuit gone, felt the rest of the jolt himself.

CHAPTER THIRTY-THREE

Behind his eyelids, asleep, but not, Jory was where he wanted to be—at a car wash from the past. Chasing his daughter with the soapy wand, no car at all, just a pocketful of surprise quarters, this stall whispering to them as they'd walked by.

But then, stepping across the rusted grate of the drain, Jory saw decomposed fingers wrapping up, folding over the toe of his daughter's shoe, and he lowered the wand to the hungry face down there—

And sat up, grabbing at the blankets. Breathing hard.

Not waking really, he'd been awake for a few minutes, but finally opening his eyes. Coming back to here. Falling back to the present.

"Welcome," a face across from him said. It was just one of many.

He was in the bunkhouse. J Barracks. Scanlon had had him delivered back here as . . . what? An example?

It was all new faces too, except the reprobate, his name still at the bottom of the call list, evidently. He was on his top bunk, dealing himself through a deck of cards, sweating through his shirt.

"Continue," the reprobate said to all, waving an ace of hearts, as if releasing this roomful of baby torches, each of them older than him.

They fell back to whatever they were doing.

"Mr. Biology, right?" the reprobate said, laying down another card.

Jory swung his legs over the side of his bunk, rubbed his eyes and swayed his back in, knew it was blue and green from the electric prongs, and scabbed into a grid from Hillford's black knife. His face was sore on one side, probably from where he'd spasmed into the Kitten Man's cell bars.

Scanlon wouldn't have shouldered him up to daylight himself either. He would have pulled the handler over for that.

Jory could see no sign of that on his arms though. Or his hands. His right palm was still raw, from that long cinder block wall.

"Everything in place there?" the reprobate asked.

Jory didn't answer.

Against the far wall, all the bunks pushed away, the new recruits were making a music video. Make-do scarves doo-ragged over their heads. Their one real guitar was stringless, the lead singer using a large-bore revolver for a microphone. Holding it right up against his top teeth to wail.

Each of them were hamming it up for their devoted cameraman.

"Remember?" the reprobate said about them, what they were trying to do, and Jory did, yes—Fishnet, strutting out onto the floor, trying to dance perfectly enough that it would hold the day back. That it would keep morning from coming. That it would keep all of them alive.

Now the band was huddling around the cameraman, to see the playback. Collapsing with laughter.

Jory almost smiled, watching them, but then it hit him—if they were watching, laughing about their fake instruments, then that camera they were using, it wasn't dead, wasn't just a prop, like the pistol, like the guitar.

Jory looked down, between his feet. At his pack, the flap opened.

"Mayner," Jory said. Mayner had ditched the pack here for him, like that would close the circle, make it where Jory *had* to come back. There had probably even been a pack of the sacred menthols in there, smoked down to nothing long before one of Scanlon's guards walked in, feed-sacked Jory down onto an empty bunk.

Jory stood up fast enough that the room swam. He fought his way through it, over to the playback huddle, parting the recruits harder than he needed to. He ripped the camera away, tried to hunch over it to see the viewscreen, but hands were grabbing at him. Pushing, pulling.

"Who the hell do you think—" the lead singer said, stepping in, leading with the revolver, the reprobate suddenly standing in front of Jory, his knife just casual by his thigh, and not flashing in the light. But just because the reprobate's eyes had that covered.

"Teach?" the reprobate said back to Jory, calling him by name.

The large-sized recruit didn't give ground, but he didn't come any closer to that knife either.

"They—they—" Jory said, cueing through the tape or disc or chip or card or hard drive or *whatever* was in the damn camera.

It was all faces and action. From the bunkhouse. The music video. Zoomy, smeary, loud.

"They recorded over it," he said, looking up at each of them in turn. "It was here . . ."

"What?" the reprobate asked.

Jory could only shake his head.

"It was here," he said again, and let the camera slip from his hand, shatter by his feet, that one large recruit pulling lips away from his teeth about that.

"It was there," he said. "The last copy."

"Everybody's a critic," the lead singer said, cocking that revolver to his head, pulling the trigger on nothing.

"Like he could do better?" the guitar player said, Jory crossing in front of them, the bathroom the only thing in that direction.

"Pay attention," the reprobate said, still standing between the recruits and Jory. "This guy, he's not careful, he's gonna be a legend, you just wait." To Jory, for all, "How many calls you been on?"

The whole room was hanging on his answer. Ready to riot or applaud, depending.

"Sometimes," Jory said, finding his voice, dodging all eye contact, "sometimes you have to, like, kick their mouth grate open."

He mimed it.

Silence. More silence.

"Than what?" one of the baby torches said.

"Never stop talking to your driver," Jory said. "Sing him a song through the, the headset, if you want. If you remember any." The lead singer smiled one side of his mouth about this. "And the smell," Jory added. "Be ready for the smell."

"Because they're dead?"

"Because they're zombies," Jory said, and turned, felt his way into the head.

"Fucking old-timer," he heard one of the recruits saying about him.

"Lifer," another added.

Jory held both sides of the sink, leaned over.

In the tin mirror, scratched deep, was a new Z.

Jory's face was in the middle of it.

"I'm coming," he said to the girl running around the car wash, and closed his eyes.

* * *

Instead of lunch, Jory smoked cigarettes.

He paced around and around J Barracks, looking up at each jeep. None of them was Mayner. All the radio chatter was about the fires downtown. The ten-year blowout. This next End of Days.

It was a joke. We were the punch line.

On his fiftieth or two-hundredth loop around the bunkhouse, Jory stopped, leaned against the wall in the exact same spot he'd watched from six days before, deciding whether to go in to work or not.

The factory was still there, squat and grey, the same exact cinder block as the long tunnel from the Church. He should have known all along. He should have seen it from the very first.

"What is it?" a recruit said, close enough for Jory to look over, but Jory didn't.

"Nothing," he said.

"You're Gray, right?" the recruit said then. "Almost made it through a whole week?"

"Doesn't matter," Jory said, dropping his cigarette before it was done. Grinding it out with his boot.

This recruit kept watching him.

"Like I said, just stay in communication," Jory finally said to him, touching the side of his head, "they won't code you if you're still talking."

"Gray," the recruit said then, again. "*Mr.* Gray, right?"

Jory turned, studied this recruit.

Something about the way he'd said that *Mr.*

Like it wasn't the first time.

"I know you?" Jory asked.

The recruit smiled a shy smile, looked back to some commotion going down in front of the bunkhouse—some baby torches had to be dragged out, Jory had heard a few weeks ago, dragged out and strapped into the jeep—then came back to Jory, and the way he came back, moving his head to allow for the bangs he didn't have anymore, the bangs the postapocalypse wouldn't allow, Jory remembered—he'd sat in the back of the class, was always watching the halls, for who might be walking by. Always watching the halls, then looking back like he'd been "paying attention, sir, really."

"Second period," Jory said.

"Mark Davies," the recruit said, and held his hand out.

Jory pulled him to him, hugged him for too long, too hard.

"Mr. Gray," the recruit said somewhere in there, embarrassed—he was taller than Jory now—and Jory closed his eyes, felt tears on his face but didn't care.

"I just wanted to say, to say thanks," the recruit said when Jory finally let him go.

"Thanks?" Jory said, his fingers nervous, peeling the crackly plastic from another pack. Letting the gold string drift away.

"You gave me a B on the midterm," the recruit said, shrugging. "I couldn't have played in District if you hadn't."

It took Jory two tries to get the cigarette between his lips. "Did you win?" he asked.

The recruit nodded that he had, yeah, and Jory lit up, breathed deep.

"Mind?" the recruit said, his hand out for the pack.

Jory shook a cigarette up, just reflex, even started to angle the pack over for the recruit, but then folded it back into his hand.

"Just one," the recruit said, not quite following.

Jory was laughing to himself now though. Shuddering with it.

"Teachers can't, we can't," he said. "It's against policy to share tobacco with students."

The recruit smiled, reached in again, the joke surely over, but Jory pulled the pack in deeper, tamped the cigarette back.

"Sorry," he said, not looking at the recruit anymore, the recruit staring at him for maybe twenty seconds—Jory could feel it—then backing away. Gone.

One more person, gone.

Jory swallowed and it was loud in his ears. At what felt like a cellular level, he became aware that each time he shoulder-pushed away from the cinder block wall, each time he touched his eyebrow where it hurt, it was the last time for that too.

He was saying goodbye.

Three and a half cigarettes later, Jory's loop around J deposited him at the front edge of the parking lot, like, if he stood there, insisted, then Mayner would have no choice but to show up, get this over with already.

Instead, it was another jeep, coming in fast, braking hard, sliding to a stop right up against Jory, the driver wowing his eyes across the hood, stepping down to cadge a smoke.

Jory shook one up from his backup pack, passed it over.

"No offense," the driver said, antsy, "but this is all bullshit, right?"

Jory looked to the doorway, where the driver's torch was going to appear.

"The plague?" Jory said back.

"Dead patrol," the driver said, leaning back into the jeep for something. "Preburial. Burning their asses."

Jory looked to the road behind them. When he came back to this driver, the driver had ducked into a nonreg hat. For the sun. Because cancer's such a killer.

Glasses's driver.

Jory dropped his cigarette to the gravel, stepped on it.

"Bullshit?" he asked.

"Collars," the driver said, his cigarette pinched in his fingers to make his point. "Just, each corpse turns up, clip a collar onto it, yeah? Just set it to clamp down on motion, this time. Then let the bonefaces bury them all night and all day. More power to them. Shit. I should write a letter to my congressman."

Jory was studying the doorway again. Studying the doorway and doing the mental Rolodex thing, suddenly sure that nobody who'd gone through torch training with him had been a soldier, just misbehaving civilians. Expendables. Dead weight.

"But there wouldn't be any—there are no accidents like that," Jory said. "With collars."

"What?" the driver said, stepping off, almost insulted. "You mean the brass, they *want* accidents? What are they doing, thinning the herd?"

"No," Jory said, just now seeing it like he should have all along, "not ours," and it was all spread out for him, for a moment—Scanlon wanted the Church gone. And the way to do that was to kill the priests—cut the head off the snake, no matter how many heads it had—and to do that in a way that they'd asked for: Preburial.

Every call, it was *supposed* to go wrong.

It meant one less reject like him, like Glasses, like all of them, sure. But it meant one less priest too, and that was what was important. Scanlon was trading pawns for bishops.

And the board he was trying to control, it was the world. It was the future.

Jory shook his head at the simplicity of it all.

And, because of the document the Church had, and whatever video they probably had of Scanlon playing tic-tac-toe, it had to be like this.

He was calling the Church's bluff. Seeing if they'd keep

feeding their priests to the fire, just to get to bury one or two bodies a month.

So far, nobody'd blinked.

Except all the torches. Right before they died.

How many times had J Barracks been filled and emptied already? Were the handlers ever even *supposed* to function properly?

"Fucking Oppenheimer," Jory said, and before the driver could ask him about that, his torch was in the doorway.

Mark Davies. His cube of armor hooked under the middle finger of his right hand. His boots tied up tight.

"Fresh meat," the driver said under his breath, grinding his cigarette down now. Kind of laughing.

"Like hell," Jory said, pulling deep on his cigarette, watching Mark Davies cross the packed dirt like a fighter pilot. Everybody watching him, nobody saying anything.

Except the driver.

"Care to make it interesting?" he said across to Jory, about Mark Davies. "Even money, he doesn't make it five minutes in the old *casa* of the dead."

Jory blew a tight line of smoke out, and watched it drift.

"What's his name again?" he asked with all innocence, lifting his chin across the yard to Mark Davies, from second period Biology. Mark Davies, who scored twenty-two points that District game, half of them in the fourth.

Jory had listened to it on the radio, on his back porch, and had had to bite his finger with happiness, when that last buzzer went on and on.

"Shit . . ." the driver said, grinning the question away, and then Jory was on him, had him by the shirtfront, was slamming him into the gravel, trying to punch, screaming through his teeth, words he didn't even know the shape of. Just that they were from deeper inside him than he knew he had. Mark Davies just standing there. A couple of the other recruits finally loped over, pulled Jory off, Jory still trying to fight through, back to the driver. He only stopped when different hands hauled him back. Guided him away.

Mayner. His jeep was maybe five steps over. Jory was still trying to pull his shoulders back to himself, his breath coming in deep hitches, his hands already touching his chest, for a cigarette.

In all the versions of this, what Mayner says to Jory here is just a growled *"shut up,"* and then he straps him in, tears away from J Barracks, Jory's hand wrapped around the frame of that fold-down windshield, his knuckles bloody.

Everybody remembers.

Sunset that day, exactly ten years after the plague, it went down chain-link by chain-link for Mayner and Jory.

The jeep was nosed up against the tall fence of one of the restricted zones, Mayner's rigged-together, little CD player spinning out that same teenaged girl's voice for them. It was less about the music, more about that there had once been music.

"We supposed to be there yet?" Jory said.

"They're going to start without us?" Mayner said back, grinding the starter. "You don't have to," he added. "I can, you know. Drop you wherever. People disappear all the time these days. That's one good thing about the postapocalypse."

Jory rocked back and forth slowly.

"It's for the best," he said. "Somebody's got to put a stop to all this."

"I'm not going to code you," Mayner said, backing up all at once, so Jory had to push his hands against the dash.

Jory looked across to Mayner.

"Serious," Mayner added, like it was just a fact, and dropped them into first gear.

Jory studied the city, sliding by.

"You ever hear that Lazarus Complex story?" Jory said.

Mayner caught third, skirted a sinkhole.

"That a Bible thing?" Mayner said.

"You ever wonder how it all started, I mean?" Jory said. "All this?"

Mayner shrugged, concentrating on the road. It was coming up under them so fast.

"You mean was it aliens and all that?" he said.

"All that," Jory said, "yeah."

"It matter?" Mayner asked, hauling the wheel over hard, Jory's hand still clamped to the windshield frame.

"I don't—" Jory started, but then the jeep was sliding. Not out of control, just needing to brake, now.

For the giraffes.

They were crossing the road, the father impossibly tall, looking down at Mayner and Jory, the mother giraffe just moving straight across behind him, a young one crossing last, its legs spindly and knobbed.

The jeep was stalled, so Jory could hear the massive hooves thumping delicately onto the ground. The battery was still pushing that teenaged girl's voice up.

"He was right," Mayner said, about Glasses.

Jory smiled a child's smile, took a mental snapshot—the last giraffes he would ever see, definitely—and in his head, told them to live forever. To never die.

It was his first prayer in years.

CHAPTER THIRTY-FOUR

—1920 New Haven.

This is where it all went down.

Before the plague, it had been a house built for entertaining, a one-story ranch affair, updated through the decades, sitting at kind of a cant from the curb, like the street was accommodating it, not the other way around. The sculpted hedges had gone feral years ago, but the iron-barred windows were all intact. The lightpost at the front edge of the yard looked antique, like it was part of some older place, transported here for sentimental reasons.

The occupants were long gone, of course.

Like some houses you'd find on Disposal, this one had been sealed up since Black Friday, it looked like to Jory. Like the family had left early for a three-day weekend. Or had all been at work, at school.

Inside places like that, the refrigerator wouldn't even smell anymore. There'd be a mummified dog by the couch sometimes, maybe squirrels nesting in the closet, a hole chewed in the ceiling.

And sometimes it would just be quiet. The delicate sound of photographs in kitchen drawers, losing their color. The slick

THE GOSPEL OF Z

paint on the doorframes peeling up, fluttering down in flakes if you pulled your hand across, like you'd stepped into a snow globe.

A good place to die, if you had to.

Jory took it all in, in a glance, Mayner slamming them up onto the lawn, knocking the antique lightpost over about halfway, its smoked-glass cupola drifting up into the air after all this time, shattering across the driveway.

"Was thinking you could, you know, do something dramatic," Jory said, finally letting go of the dash. "Let me know how you feel about all this, maybe."

Mayner craned around to the three missiles mounted on the roll bar. Drawing an obvious dotted line with his eyes from the missiles to the house. That dotted line arced over the house by twenty feet at least, the yard that steep here, where it met the road.

"What?" Jory said, trying to figure out what Mayner was so satisfied about.

"Nothing," Mayner told him, looking around the windshield at this low, wide house from the past. "Just, it's standard procedure to, to 'position the transport such that no inflight correction is required.'"

This was humorous to him. Not quite worthy of a smile.

"You mean they'll miss?" Jory said, looking up to the missiles now.

"They don't know *how* to miss," Mayner said. "But, if I were going to code you, then, *bam,* they'd overshoot, have to circle back, loop down."

"So there'd be a delay," Jory said, getting it.

Mayner shrugged. "Hadn't thought of it that way, I don't guess."

Jory shook his head, hauled the shiny new torch up from the back. He stood by the jeep to get the strap adjusted.

"And you know we're not alone, don't you?" Mayner said, just real casual.

Jory scratched his chin on his shoulder, allowing him to recheck the front door—still shut.

"No," Mayner said, wheeling only his eyes to the rest of the houses in the neighborhood, and Jory, adjusting his strap more than it needed, caught on—unsteady red dots in each window.

Scanlon's men. Backup. Insurance.

Mayner pulled up a water bottle.

"Never done it with somebody watching," he said, spiraling the bottle across to Jory.

Jory cracked it open, drank deep.

"Done what?" Jory said, water coating his chin, the front of his shirt.

"Disobeyed direct orders."

Jory capped the bottle, wiped his mouth. He set the helmet down on his head, rotating it to get it right.

"Think I'll get to talk to him first?" he said, nodding inside.

"Dead guy?"

"Tall guy."

"Your friend in white," Mayner translated, dialing something on the dash. "Far as I'm concerned, the two of you can throw a revival in there. What did they used to call it? Filibuster? Yeah. Filibuster your asses off. I'll stand guard."

Jory looked across the jeep to Mayner.

"I've coded out seventeen of you," Mayner explained, flashing his eyes to a not-empty window across the street, then back to Jory. "Today's not going to be eighteen, I promise you that." Then he turned, holding his arms out, speaking to the red dots. "You hear that? *I'm not doing it!* You're going to have to shoot me too, okay?"

No response.

Yet.

"'Too'?" Jory said, finally.

"I told you," Mayner said back. "No Viking funeral today."

"You know they're going to air-strike this after tonight," Jory said, "right? Claim an old point of infection, that pure strain, fence it off. Hide all the evidence for ten, twenty years."

"Hell's own half acre," Mayner added, not disagreeing.

"Right there in their handbook," Jory said. "Just saying."

"Say it all you want," Mayner cut back. "You're *not* number eighteen. Not today."

Jory watched Mayner fumble with the equipment for some twenty seconds, Mayner's fingers trying to move too fast, doing a lot of nothing. Jory pulled the headset close to his mouth, said, "Got me?"

Mayner opened the channel on the dash, just a hiss coming through at first, then Jory again, standing right there. "Your wife spare one more?"

Mayner reached behind his seat, emptied the cigarette bag onto the seat.

Jory picked the already open pack, pulled one out. He was measuring his life in cigarettes now. And friends.

One of each, he guessed.

"Well," he said, holding the menthol up in farewell, and Mayner held one up himself, put it in his mouth. The wrong end.

Jory left him spitting, walked up the sidewalk like sidewalks still mattered, the ground already shaking with the handler's rust-colored behemoth of a transport grinding up New Haven Street, its headlights on to cut through the dusk.

On the porch, aware of how many crosshairs he was probably standing in, Jory got his torch to spit its flame out, then pulled it back as far on its strap as he could and lit the menthol, his face right in the way if his finger slipped.

Downtown, the fires were still burning. There were probably novitiates up on the ramparts, even, holding buckets of water. Waiting their turn at the pole. One of them with pupils that, because their puddles of iris soaked up different amounts of light, dilated at slightly different rates.

Jory nodded across town to her and stepped inside, careful his torch didn't catch anything dry enough to go up.

Like that wasn't the plan though.

Inside, the air was stale.

Jory clicked his headlight on—same slider button as it had been on Glasses's torch—and the yellow beam swam with dust motes, all of them already adjusting themselves to the door Jory hadn't shut behind him.

Hillford was really going to show up here, after dark like this? On Z Day?

Jory swept the light over the room, keeping the beam at stomach level, his teeth already set for the body he knew was going to be standing there, waiting for him. Hungry, ragged, already launching, leading with its teeth.

Wrong.

This was a grave-robber call after all. Staged, maybe, but still. The corpse had fallen across an oversized white chair, using it like a couch—head on one arm, left leg draped across the other. Chest black with blood, just like the peach smuggler, and—

And tucked in beside the corpse—male, now, and that kind of tall that was really just skinny—was a simple prosthetic leg, from the knee down. But it wasn't simple at all.

Jory let out a sound that had to be a bleat, that told him in a flash what the goats were all saying—*no* and *please.* Both at once.

It was Timothy.

Jory started to step closer, pulled back like this was a trap, shining his light all around, and then did it, cocked his torch back and knelt, one hand to Timothy's leather goggles, his other hand coming up red from Timothy's chest. It was hardly tacky at all. Still slick.

"What the hell?" Jory said, and fell sideways before his body told him why—a ghost was coming up the hall. White, floating.

Jory's finger convulsed on the trigger, the torch sighing its flame out, leaving the carpet at a smolder.

Hillford.

"You," Jory said, pushing away some more, not completely on purpose.

Hillford lowered his head in acknowledgment—*yes, me*—ducked under the arched doorway and into the living room, and Jory's face went cold—the only reason you duck under like that, it's if you know. If you've had to do it before. If you came in the *front* door, not the back.

The same way you step around a weak spot in a tile floor—if you've stepped there before.

And Timothy's wound, it was the peach smuggler's wound all over again. Clean and fast, no joy in it. Just what had to be done.

Dominoes were tipping into each other in Jory's head. Racing to the inevitable conclusion. Falling down into a big picture. After he thought he already *knew* the big picture.

"You, you," Jory said, and stood, the smoldering carpet lighting each of them from below. Like standing on lava crust, a new planet forming under their feet. "Let me see your knives," Jory said.

Hillford cocked his head over, not following.

"I said let me see your damn knives!" Jory said again, angling the torch up now.

Hillford considered, considered, then slid his hands up his sleeves, came up with the black blade, the white blade.

"One of the originals," Hillford said, about the white one.

"Put them here," Jory said, pointing with the torch to the arm of Timothy's chair.

"Would this be a request from the military establishment," Hillford said, "or a personal favor?"

"*Do it!*" Jory screamed, stepping closer, almost nudging Hillford with the flame, a dime-sized circle of the fabric of his white robe glossing up, about to do whatever magic thing it's supposed to in an explosion.

Moving slowly, the blades just between his thumb and palm, Hillford held them both down to the rough white cloth, then, instead of laying them down, flipped them expertly over, pushed them into the fabric, using the arm of the chair like a pincushion.

The white one went in clean, fast. The black one too. But around the black one now, like the chair had been a living thing, was a ring of blood. Pushed up from the blade.

Timothy's blood.

"How'd you get him to meet you here?" Jory said.

Hillford stepped back to get enough distance to see Jory. "He somehow became enamored with the idea you might be here, Jory Gray," Hillford said. "And, as it turns out, he wasn't wrong."

Jory closed his eyes. "But Scanlon, he said, he said that you—"

"The military's fiefdom is not nearly so expansive as it would like to think," Hillford said, his voice so level, so controlled.

"*Why him?*" Jory asked, not controlled at all, and getting worse. "Because he *knew* me? Because of"—turning Timothy over, stripping the shirt from his back, showing his tic-tac-toe tat—"because *you* wanted to be the only one to blackmail the army?"

"Certain rumors were circulating," Hillford said, "that your friend here had been an actual runner, not just one who chose to remember them in ink. It was a mantle he seemed comfortable under, you might say. There being no known runners yet alive."

"You were jealous. He was getting attention."

"A dangerous game to try to play."

"He was *my* age, he *couldn't* have been a runner. And they all died anyway."

"Better that they did, yes."

"For them or for you?"

No answer from Hillford.

"You killed the peach smuggler too, didn't you?" Jory said. "Was he a runner too, or supposed to be? It wasn't enough that Scanlon killed them, was it? Now you have to kill them again?"

"Peaches?" Hillford said, leaning down as if to see Timothy better.

Jory stepped back, aimed at the couch on the other side of the room, and blasted it for a fed-up two count.

The furniture was their candle now. Their campfire to tell scary stories over. Mayner was a steady hum in Jory's ear, reading the thermals on his dash—seeing the light through the window, this call going straight to hell, and fast.

Jory peeled the helmet off, let it drop.

"He said you were doing this, bringing the dead back," Jory said, the torch back on Hillford.

"He's infected?" Hillford said, about Timothy.

"He just, he can't figure out how," Jory said. "But he knows you don't want it to be over. That you like all this."

"'He'?"

"Scanlon."

Hillford nodded, as if this explained everything.

"Fitting," he said. "Fitting that he of all people would deign to judge me, is it not, Jory Gray?"

Jory looked over to Timothy, still dead, then came back to Hillford. "I know you know about the Lazarus Complex," he said. "The gospel."

"The Church is denied very little when it comes to the sordid truths of man, yes."

"But it denies everybody else, right? Dalton never had a chance."

"We all make choices, Jory Gray."

Hillford found reason to look around the room. Jory followed. There was nothing, just flickering light, dancing shadows.

Outside, the handler's heavy door slammed shut, cutting the night in two.

"Heroic General Scanlon," Hillford finally said, like it was already leaving a bad taste behind his mask. "He should know better than to think he can kill me, here. You can't kill an idea. It only gets bigger. But, we should all be thankful to him, should we not? Without him . . . none of this. Without his trials, his double-blind research, the world would still be—well. Your daughter, Jory Gray. Your daughter would still be with you, would she not?"

And now Hillford's right hand was coming up with something. Not a third blade, but . . . the ID card? *Her* ID card?

Hillford flipped it across to Jory, but, being a card, it nose-dived, hit the carpet.

Jory grubbed down into the heat for it, came up with it, the plastic melting into his hand, his fingernails steaming.

Linse's face. The ID he'd lost on that first call.

"Can it be any coincidence, Jory Gray," Hillford led off, "can it be any accident that the arbitrary birth date you listed for her, that it matched so perfectly with your own *daughter's*?"

Jory closed his eyes.

Hillford went on. "Was this one's name even Linsey, or is that just what you chose to call her?"

Jory couldn't look away from the ID.

"Your daughter's birthday was a matter of public record, of course," Hillford said. "And the Church's data banks are, well, extensive."

Drone, drone, like Hillford was far away.

Mayner too, his voice small at Jory's feet.

"But it must have felt like providence, yes?" Hillford ramped up, sidling closer, onto the lava carpet. Onto the bed of coals their floor was now. "It must have, reaching down into the rubble for another victim, another survivor, and, and seeing those *eyes*? The chances of an individual encountering hetero-chromia twice, even in a span of eight years, and in our reduced circumstances, it's, it's—but add to that the natural *associations* you must have made, Jory Gray. The miracles you, who claim to be faithless, believed in, instinctually. Those kinds of, of leaps, Jory Gray, they're reserved for the true prophets, for the . . ."

Jory looked over to Hillford now.

"You were *saving* her," Hillford was saying now, sympathizing, pinching the forgotten menthol from Jory's mouth, flicking it towards the door expertly, better than a priest should know to. "You were saving your little girl. Every father's deepest, most primal fantasy, is it not?"

Jory pressed the heel of his left hand between his eyes. His chin was trembling, his breathing too deep, packing too much oxygen into his blood, so that his head was swimming.

"She could have, she could have just stayed," he said, his voice cracking.

"I know, I know," Hillford said, his hand to Jory's torch shoulder now, "but she's in a better place now, you have to understand. Both of them are, Jory Gray. The way of the chosen is seldom peaceful. No, the elect, such as you, you must endure tragedy after tragedy, as if the world has gambled it can break you, as if—"

Jory lowered his hand. Back to the torch.

"*Both* of them?" he said. "You mean she's—?"

"*Different* better places, Jory Gray," Hillford said, amused by Jory's interpretation.

Jory wasn't amused.

"I'm not your damn angel," he said, the flame bubbling out against the front of Hillford's robe now.

"Not yet, no," Hillford said, stepping slightly to the side, his robe unscorched, just shinier there. Hardened.

"I wasn't hurting her at all," Jory said.

"Yes, I know. You were saving her. Of course."

"*Shut up!*" Jory yelled, pushing a gout of flame past Hillford, down the long hall. Family portraits showed all along one wall, then sucked back into blackness. "If you've really never been coded," Jory said, trying to reel his voice in, "then this should be fun, think? A new experience. What's meant to be always happens, right?"

"Whether we intend it or not," Hillford added, his head repositioning to see behind Jory. To study that darkness, it seemed.

Jory didn't take that bait though. He kept the torch on Hillford. "I didn't know if I was going to do this, at first," he said.

"It may not be as simple as you were led to believe," Hillford said, nodding behind Jory now. "It would appear we have company."

This time Jory did turn around, his hand coming up on reflex for the menthol, so the smoke wouldn't hide whatever was or wasn't there, but then he backtracked to Hillford, pinching it away. Flicking it at the door, the cigarette tumbling so slow through the air.

Those sparks scattering on the stoop.

It was the sign.

Jory pawed down for the helmet—hot—brought the mic up to his mouth. "Not yet! Abort, abort—"

It was too late.

The handler stopped in the doorway, the zombie by its leather-clad tree trunk of a leg, pulling, its head cased in leather—mouth grate, side blinders, strap to its chin, keeping its head tethered.

"Hmm," the handler said, announcing itself maybe, or passing judgment on this dead room, and took another step in, to duck through the doorway, and all its conditioning, its grafts and juice and tech, its fire-retardant armor, none of it mattered at all when what was underfoot was a small entryway rug, dead center in a patch of slick tile, waiting ten years for this very day.

When the zombie caught Jory's scent, started its lunge, the handler set its boots but its boots didn't set.

"Oh," Hillford said, his right arm rising as if to stop this from happening.

In slow motion, almost, the handler fell on its ass, hard enough to shake the whole house, the whole neighborhood, its thick arms flailing back in a most human way, the zombie getting enough slack to gather its legs under it, really pull, the handler spinning sideways from that tight chain.

Jory fell back, dropping the helmet, trying to get the torch between himself and this zombie—blind, just following its nose—and almost had it, his finger digging for the trigger when the handler slapped an ogre hand back, clamped it on to the doorframe, the wood and paneling there splintering, but the stud buried in there was enough. It held.

The zombie came up short, snapping at the air, Jory kicking away from that air. Hillford helped him stand and Jory pushed away from him as well, almost stumbled into the burning couch from the effort.

"Jory fucking Gray!"

It was Mayner.

Jory looked down to the helmet, where his name wasn't coming from, and then to the stoop, where it *was* coming from.

Against every regulation, Mayner was standing in the doorway. When the scene should have been coded minutes ago.

"Everything cool in here?" Mayner asked, the zombie catching his scent now too, trying to turn, come up its own chain. The handler slammed it to the ground, put a boot to its neck, the zombie squealing, clawing at the handler's leg, the handler hardly even noticing.

"No, it pretty much sucks in here," Jory said, just as a bullet splashed through Mayner's shoulder at some three thousand feet per second, spinning him half around, pinning him to the wall for a moment.

"No!" Jory screamed, stepping forward, Hillford taking him by the shoulders now, keeping him from the zombie's reach.

"Mayner!" Jory called across the room, fighting his way to the side, trying to edge around the handler, around the zombie's teeth. Because Hillford wouldn't let go, Jory was dragging him step by step, the zombie cringing away from Hillford enough that the handler staggered forward, letting itself be dragged onto the carpet proper, its small eyes fixed on something Jory couldn't worry about right now.

Scanlon's men, they were shooting Mayner.

"You sons of bitches!" Jory screamed through the doorway, and started to step through, the torch already low and deadly against his leg, only to have the wood beside his face explode, slamming splinters into his face.

"Go, go," Mayner said from the ground, waving Jory back in. A long smear of his blood down the wall behind him. "I got it, man. It's cool, it's cool."

Jory set his feet, opened his torch out into the night, the flame reaching all the way across the lawn, and kept pulling the trigger, even after the flame sucked back, the autocool kicking in, saving the barrel.

And then, with that flame off, it was darker than before. But Mayner was still there, pushed up against the wall now. Trying to shake a cigarette up to his mouth, the cigarette falling again and again, but finally sticking to his lips, to the blood on his lips.

"What do you think?" Mayner said then, to Jory, holding his face up for a light, from the torch, face-on, and Jory shook his head *no,* that he wasn't going to kill him, wasn't going to put him out of this misery, but he clicked the flame back on anyway, just for a light.

The flame didn't come.

"Perfect," Jory said, looking down to the torch, still humming with coolant, "trust the military to—" and another bullet slapped into Mayner, through the same exact hole in his shoulder, it looked like. Then, deeper inside the house, scattering pans in some cabinet.

Mayner kept the cigarette up somehow, pointed it down to the toe of his boot, hot enough from Jory's last burn to, when he held the cigarette there, trail smoke up.

He brought the cigarette up, breathed it red. He coughed it back out like a pro, waving Jory back into the house, away from the porch.

"You know why I'm here?" Jory said then, back to Hillford, Hillford's dead hand still on Jory's shoulder, keeping him alive.

"Of course," Hillford said, distracted again. "Your general, he thinks that if he can wipe away the last of the original three, then that will unmoor the Church's hold on the people he considers his."

"The three from the Dead Sea," Jory mumbled.

"Nothing so grand," Hillford said, "but yes, I believe that's what it's called in the secular tongue. But your general has a poor understanding, a weak grasp, at best, if he thinks this Church of man needs him meddling in our destiny. In the destiny of humankind, what's left of it."

"You sound like him," Jory said, another bullet drilling into the doorframe, just a friendly reminder.

Hillford reached around, swung the door closed without looking. His real attention was behind them, again.

"He can't code us now," Jory said, looking at the dead torch in his hands. But then Hillford was pawing back, his hand stiffening on Jory's shoulder.

"*Jory Gray,*" he said.

It was the first time Jory had heard anything but smugness in Hillford's voice.

He looked up, understood—the handler, that great oversized child. It was hovering its massive hand over the two blades sheathed into the arm of the white chair. The zombie was tearing meat from Timothy's thigh, holding its head back to get its throat straight enough to swallow.

"So—so I guess he's not infected then," Jory said, his voice detached from his thoughts.

Hillford just stepped forward, as if the world were suddenly made of the most delicate glass.

The handler looked up, its eyes the eyes of a dog, considering the lasagna that had just dripped from the table. A dog, thinking it can still slurp most of it up, if it tries. If it's fast enough.

"No!" Hillford said across to the handler, his voice booming with authority, the rest of him stepping closer, his long white hand reaching closer than that, and the handler understood, got the tone anyway, like a dog will, but then, for an instant, it regained that most essential part of its humanity—it disobeyed. It reached down and plucked the white blade up, studying its length, its curve, touching the tip with its other hand, the sharpness piercing the thick leather of the glove, sliding into flesh.

Hillford stopped his approach. Drew his hand up to cover where his mouth would have been. Where it was, behind the mask.

The handler held its cut finger up, so the metal-flaked blood could drop down onto the blade. So it could watch the pretty colors.

"Henh," it said, its zombie still tearing into Timothy's thigh. The zombie's grate was kicked back somehow, its blinders flapping.

This is exactly what was supposed to happen, Jory knew. How Scanlon was going to decommission this purposely defective handler. Along with all the other problems in the room. It was efficient. Very military. One stone, all the birds.

"So . . . so I guess I should burn him now," Jory said, pointing with his torch to Timothy.

"Do you know why *I'm* here, Jory Gray?" Hillford said over his shoulder, palming his boneface mask away, shrugging out of his robe, letting it pool at his feet. His body was just as rotten as his face. No skin left at all, just pain, the kind you have to clean with maggots, if you clean it at all. Like one of the Pharaoh vultures, stripped of its oily black feathers.

Except the fingers, and the lower legs.

They were prosthetics. Like the one Timothy had found. Like the one Timothy had desecrated.

"You were never burned," Jory said, that last domino falling. "Jakarta. Leprosy. Armor—armadillos."

"I'm here for this," Hillford said, not looking away from the handler for an instant, his strangely jointed plastic fingers working the leather straps cutting into his leg stumps, then the rest of him stepping down off the ritual mannequin legs, so that he barely came up to Jory's chest now.

He bit his plastic fingers off, one by one, spit them out.

"This is the hand of man," he said then, flexing his finger stumps, "not the hand of God. If this, as you call it, your virus, if it goes radioborne, as it will in this unnatural host, because it always finds a way, then, then these monstrosities, they and their kin, they *will* devour the world, Jory Gray. Keep the next one from happening at all."

"*Radio?*" Jory said. "But, it's not infected, it can't get—"

"Tell your general about this," Hillford said, standing on his leg stumps now, "tell him how one of us saved his precious world," and then, more agile than made any sense, he was across the room, within reach of the handler, ducking under its great arms for the black blade and rolling through, the stuffing from the arm of the chair hanging in the air behind him.

The handler, still fascinated by its own finger blood, tracked all this a moment too late. Only looked to this disturbance when Hillford was already monkeying up its back, pulling that crusted black blade across its throat, deep enough to draw sparks.

A black line of blood smiled across the room at Jory, the zombie twitching up to this new smell, and then the handler fell, first to one knee, then just forward, the zombie scuttling out of the way at the last instant. Enough slack now to sink its teeth into Timothy's midsection, tear into the guts proper, its chin strap keeping it from taking too much intestine at once. But enough.

Jory, like he was drunk, found Hillford again. The piece of blackened jerky that had *been* Hillford, anyway.

He was behind the fallen handler, his finger stumps to the handler's lower back, as if listening. Communing.

"What do you mean 'radio,'" Jory said. "The virus can't, it couldn't—handlers can't catch it anyway."

"Your torch," Hillford said, cutting Jory off. "How long does your torch's reignition sequence take?"

"My torch?" Jory said, looking down at it like he'd just found it.

Hillford thinned what he had for lips, said, "One blade for life, Jory Gray. And one for death."

Jory tracked down to the white blade on the carpet.

It was curved like a baculum, like a saber tooth, like a toilet bowl.

"No," he said out loud, looking from the white blade to Hillford's white mask, on the floor beside it, "like a rib."

Because bone, it can carry the virus for ten years.

"Scanlon was right," he said to Hillford, in awe. "You have been raising them. With—with an infected . . . you kill them with the, with the black one, then, then you nick their heart with the white one. Not to let the scent circulate, but because the virus won't circulate in a dead, in a dead . . ."

"Your instrument, Jory Gray."

Jory looked down to the torch again. "It's just, you push a button," he said, his index finger suddenly numb, feeling on the stock, just forward of the trigger guard. Turning the headlight off instead, so that Hillford was only lit by the burning couch now. A demon, scuttling around a fallen giant.

"The *flame*, Jory Gray!" Hillford said then, a new urgency to his voice.

Jory felt forward, finally turned the torch over, held it between his legs, couldn't see anything.

"*Now!*" Hillford said, harsh enough that Jory just pushed all the buttons he could find, until the flame burbled on, sent a fountain of incendiary heat into the ceiling, *through* the ceiling, up into the night.

When he lowered it, he understood the urgency in Hillford's voice.

The handler was writhing, its head creaking over. A groan building in its throat. And then the sensors lining its arteries detected the virus, sent out the lockdown alert.

Like it was supposed to, like Jory'd seen in the faith sessions, the handler went into forced rigor.

It was ugly, and looked painful. If they could feel. If it wasn't already dead.

After about ten seconds, though, the handler's massive arm creaked up, fought through the rigor.

The next fail-safe was the one Jory'd done himself, once upon a time—the incendiary device in the handler's skull.

It went with that same muted *pop*.

Black blood seeped from the handler's eyes, then its ears, and it collapsed.

"Gotta love the tech," Jory said to himself.

But the virus was better. The virus didn't give up.

Not this strain anyway. It was straight from the rib of Typhoid Z. From Kitten Man's lost brother.

The handler got its arms under itself, started to rise. It was impossible, but so was the handler.

"What's meant to be, always happens," Hillford said, resorting to scripture for strength, and looked importantly across to Jory, then stepped aside, giving the torch room. But his legs were short now, his steps not as wide.

The handler's hand slashed back, not slow anymore at all.

It crunched around Hillford's stump, pulled him to itself. Then it stood holding Hillford like that, Hillford coming up with the blade, planting it in the handler's left eye socket, the handler stumbling back, falling to one knee, but then plucking the blade out. Crushing it, the massive veins in its forearm standing out like cables. Veins Jory had sculpted, in a former life.

"I will," Jory said to Hillford, "I'll tell Scanlon," and then he raised the torch. The handler stepped forward, onto Hillford's wrist, and pulled straight up on the leg he was clamped on to.

Hillford ripped in half, had been made of old black taffy, his blood sludge, his heart surely massive to have even pumped it once.

And then the handler fell again, was pulled sideways, the zombie screeching away from the scent of the ceremonial leprosy Hillford had been cultivating inside himself. That all the armadillos up the Hill probably carried as well, Jory heard part of himself registering. Little guards, their scent the best wall.

The handler looked along the chain to the zombie, and pulled it into the wall hard enough that the wall didn't stop it. The zombie crashed through, disappeared. But it was still leashed. It anchored the handler there for the moment.

Jory stepped forward, shaking his head *no*, his teeth set, his feet trying to get that way.

"Hey, you," he said, and the handler actually turned its block of a head around.

Jory pulled the trigger, the flame punching hard, driving the handler down, cooking it, the rest of the room baking, melting, drooping into its next shape.

And then it was over.

The autocool kicked on again. Jory let the trigger go, stumbled sideways, half into Timothy, came up with his goggles. He held them to his mouth, just as Timothy's arm jerked back, the bicep contracting.

Jory stood, shaking his head *no*, and directed the torch down, right into Timothy's opened stomach, pulled the trigger.

Nothing. Autocool.

"No, no," Jory said, more of Timothy creaking now. Waking.

Jory looked around the room for something, anything, and there was only fire, enough that he finally had to pull Timothy's stupid goggles on to keep the smoke out.

"Well then," Jory said, and dragged what was left of Timothy into what was left of the couch, left him crackling there, the flames finding him almost immediately, making him the new bright spot in the room.

Jory stood, nowhere to sit. Nowhere to be.

"I'll tell him," he said again to Hillford, his upper half discarded beside the chair. Hillford blinked once.

Jory stepped over him, dug around for the mask, set it back on Hillford's face, then, the torch still humming by his thigh, he collected the prosthetic leg Timothy had found.

It was heavy, solid. Would stop maybe one of the hundred bullets spiraling in for him the instant he stepped out onto the porch.

Unless he stayed here forever.

He laughed once, picturing it—him, moving through the kitchen, studying the pantry; him, ducking under all the laser sights coming through the windows, trying to balance a can of peas across to his new favorite chair—and then he heard it through the hiss of the flames, through Timothy's bones popping, spitting marrow up, and he lost his smile.

He cocked the goggles up onto his forehead, squinted through the heat.

The handler was moving. But—but not on its own.

The zombie on the other side of the wall was pulling on its chain, the welded-shut shackle digging into the handler's fried wrist. Finally pulling *through* that wrist, the thick bones there cracking with a *thud,* the leather and flesh stringing away, the zombie falling back, finally free.

Jory fell back too. The other way.

From the zombie's side of the house now was the sound of breakage, of panic. The zombie was running that domestic labyrinth and doubling back over and over, no system at all.

Jory raised the torch, directed it down the hall, but the auto-cool was still humming, the torch too hot to use.

Jory shook it, slammed the butt on the ground, insisting.

Nothing.

Glass was breaking, back in some bedroom, but there were bars on the windows, on all the windows.

Jory had seconds, less.

He fell forward a bit, weak, and caught himself on the torch, his other hand groping down into Hillford's midsection by accident.

Jory brought that hand up, studied it. Looked down the hall again.

"Henh," he said, the handler's term.

Breathing in once and promising to hold that breath forever, he pulled the goggles back down and applied Hillford's gore to his face, to his chest, and dipped down for more, and more, covering himself in the only religion left to man.

An instant later, the zombie was tearing down the hall on all fours.

Jory waited, calm, defeated, ready if it had to be like this, and the zombie, graceful as any cat ever was, vaulted through the doorway, caught the scent midair and contorted itself around the source of that scent, sliding close enough by Jory that one of its zipper handles *plinked* against Jory's goggles. And then it tumbled into the kitchen.

Jory tracked it, brought the torch's headlight up. Found the zombie on all fours in the narrow passage between the granite countertop and the pantry door.

Its chain was hooked on some wreckage back in the darkness, but it was pulling through, dragging whatever it was into the light.

Until Jory was standing there.

The zombie recoiled from the smell, hissed, lowered its chest to the tile, its legs cocked under it.

"There, girl," Jory said—it was female, had been—"this'll only," and he settled the torch onto the zombie's face. Its leather headgear was all burned off, its shaved scalp crawling with heat, with fireworms.

Before, in another world, Jory had told his daughter that when you stared at the sun, the fireworms would crawl in your eyelids, and you had to look away, rub them out, or they'd stay forever.

But—this was no place to think of her.

Except it was.

Heterochromia. One blue eye from her mom, one brown from Jory, each pupil contracting from the torch's headlight.

This was Scanlon's insurance, to make sure the call fell apart. To make sure Jory did, that he had nothing left to live for.

But Hillford would have to have killed her first. Pushed her through, given her over. Sent her into the tunnel after Jory, to close the circle.

"Linse," Jory said, his hand reaching across for her, the hand he'd painted himself with. "Linsey."

Linse snarled, cowered down farther.

"Baby doll," Jory said, and dropped down to his knees before her. Closed his eyes.

She cringed back, the chain getting enough slack to *tink* onto the tile floor. Whatever it was hooked on was about to let go.

"I'm sorry, girl," Jory said, his headlight tracking up the length of the chain, to the chrome bar stool, tangled in with an unlikely pile of chrome bar stools. The whole pile giving.

And he pulled the trigger.

Still nothing.

Jory shook his head *no*, but reached behind him anyway, for whatever there was—the prosthetic leg. Holding it by the cupped upper calf, his hands looped in the straps, he brought the heel down on the back of his daughter's head, on the back of Linse's head, on the back of *Linsey's* head, into the zipper pull burned into her scalp like a chrome barrette. Again and again and again, until she stopped trying to rise, until the lenses of his goggles were splattered. The chrome stools in the darkness avalanched down at last, the chain letting them go.

Jory reeled the chain in, stood with Linse in his arms.

He made his way to Hillford's robe and used it like a sheet, wound her in it, covering her face last. Kissing her cloth forehead.

It was over.

"Linse," he said again, and heard his own name back.

Mayner.

In the helmet.

"Hey," Jory said, raising the goggles again, to scan the wreckage for the helmet. "You're, you're at the jeep?"

"Old drivers never die," Mayner said, then couldn't find the other end of it. Lost it in some bloody coughing, it sounded like. And laughter.

Jory smiled, smoothed Linse's sheet over her face. Pressed his forehead to hers—this is what he should have done ten years ago—and only looked up when the light in the room changed. The flames crackling in a different way, like somebody else was here.

"No," Jory said, looking up. "No no no . . ."

Rising from the other side of the room, against all logic, against all biology, was the handler. It's skin caking away, ash. Metal underneath. Miles of cable, years of technology, months of effort. An undead juggernaut, finding its feet again.

Jory shook his head *no*, pulled Linse closer, and then lunged forward for the torch, the commotion bringing the handler's head around.

No eyes. Hillford had gored one out. Jory had burned the other. Black tears spilled down into the handler's mouth, the handler tasting them, angling its head up to catch them, try to bite into them. Getting its own lip instead, and tearing it away. Swallowing, the unholy jolt of its own flesh throwing it back for a moment. Expanding its chest. Lighting fire to its hunger. The kind that can burn the world down.

Jory climbed his hand down the torch, clicked the ignite button—nothing.

Again, again. Just the sound, pulling the handler's massive head around.

Jory lowered the torch slowly, Linse still hugged to his chest, and sat there, the handler moving on all fours now, like a gorilla, feeling through the rubble, trying to locate them.

"Shh, shh," Jory said to Linse, to Linsey, rocking her, and the handler ambled over, was right to them now, trying to smell but its nose was burned shut.

Then another shot outside, and another, whipping into metal. The jeep.

Its windshield went next, a very distinct sound, the shattered glass taking forever to settle on the hood.

And now Mayner's voice was coming through the helmet. He was breathing hard, laughing into the mic. Dying, and loving it.

Jory narrowed his eyes, couldn't say anything back.

The handler pawed away a smoldering cushion, uncovered the helmet, that sound. It lowered its face to it but then took a couple of fast, grunting steps to the doorway, more shots out there, drawing it to where it could never go. To where it would never stop. If viruses can have hope, Jory said in his head, to a class that wasn't there, if they can dream, then this is the host it's been waiting all these years for. The perfect killing machine. The one that can never be put down. That doesn't know how to die.

Jory jabbed his hand out, whispered the helmet to him, cupped the headset in his hand.

"Hey, driver," he said.

"Check," Mayner croaked.

"I ever, I ever tell you I'm, that I'm really a Viking?" Jory said.

"Thought you, thought you were Indian or something," Mayner coughed back. From a firing-line cigarette probably. And being shot twice. Maybe three or four times by now.

"No, Viking, definitely. All the way through. Until the end, I mean. The *very* end."

The handler craned its head back to Jory's whisper.

Mayner grunted something that meant he understood. And, *"I said I'm not doing that."*

"You have to, man," Jory said, rolling over to lie alongside the torch, spin the canister off, into his hand. The jelly sloshing in there, cold, pressurized to the moon. "Just count to ten, man, count to ten, and then punch it, I'll be gone before the code ever gets here. There's the delay."

"I told you."

"You have to."

Beat, beat, the world hanging in the balance here.

"You'll be gone?" Mayner said finally.

"Already am. Promise."

"Can I count to seventeen instead?" Mayner croaked out.

Jory settled the canister into the helmet, patted it twice. "Just keep talking," he said, "keep this channel—" but then the handler was there, walking on his knuckles, on his wrist stump, blotting out the hole burned in the roof. Lowering its face to Jory, finding Linse instead. Flinching back from her scent, Jory closing his eyes. And not going anywhere, like he'd promised.

Mayner out there in the floorboard of the jeep, counting into the mic for everybody to hear, "Sixteen, fifteen." Shots drilling through his seats, splintering his dash.

"Fourteen," he said, reaching a bloody arm up to the keypad, a red dot centering on it, blasting that keypad away.

"Fuckers," Mayner said, "*ten*," then, digging the wiring harness out from under the steering column, touching this one to that one, no hesitation at all, he finally answered Jory, what he'd been, before—"Electrician."

Ten counts later, Jory saw it, we *all* could have seen it, if we'd known to watch—three tiny missiles, whistling up into the sky over New Haven Street, twisting through each other's white exhaust, then reaching an apex, hanging there a moment, before slamming back down like judgment, the handler's wide back directly below, its face held down to the small voice in the helmet, to Mayner saying "*run*" over and over. "*Now now now. You promised. Where are you, you goddamn, red ass—*"

Jory heard, but just held Linse closer, snuggled the aviator goggles down into place one last time, and twisted an eyebolt deeper into the four-by-four of his backyard fence, deep enough to hold him this time, he thought. Him and her both.

AFTER

The movies got one thing right, though, the pirate DJ says, his chin still stubbly against that metal screen.

The part about nothing ever being the same again.

The part about how people, we always find a way to live.

None of them ever mentioned the sky though.

That, with the dead crawling over the face of the earth, the skies would be empty again. Just a quiet place to look, always there if you needed to lose yourself for a moment. For a day.

It matters.

And below that sky, all of us.

A hulking young man, say. He's not so complicated. His hair hasn't been shaved down to whitewalls yet. He's standing over his mother's bed, the one she's had since she was a girl herself, *Juliet* woodburned in flourishes into the headboard. Her wrists and ankles tied with shoestrings and thick rope, and they need to be tied. The knots are knotted over and over. An axe is in that young man's hand, and his eyes are red, and the door's closing behind him, because he needs his privacy for this.

Another guy, short and wiry, ragged from days of fighting to live, he's bursting into a church, a zombie priest looking up from its bloody meal, that wiry dude not even hesitating, just tearing a giant cross from the wall, running at the priest with it, the priest's mouth and chin and chest bloody, strings of meat matted in, the wiry dude yelling so that that's all there is to hear anymore.

And more.

A congregation of dusty, headless parishioners, waiting for mass.

A young guy with angry pink hair, shooting flames up a hill, a young girl up there on the wall, touching her own scalp, in memory.

A wife sitting in her living room, the house's windows boarded up, the news on like always, but she can see her husband's reflection in it too. Can see him approaching from the kitchen, soup in one hand, a pistol unsure in the other, but he loves her, she knows he loves her, so she doesn't turn around, doesn't want this to be hard for him.

And there's a hammer, rusting in the tall yellow grass at the foot of a tall silver water tower, the seedheads swaying above it, rustling.

A glass coffin in a dark bar, a drink set on top of it, a slow, desiccated hand reaching up as if to hold that glass, keep it from falling through.

Three tall white priests at night, walking through the tall door of a reinforced fence, a writhing sea of bodies waiting for them on the other side.

There's a mom rushing through school, finding her daughter—it's a Friday, so she's in uniform—a terror rolling up the hall behind them, the mom at the last instant opening a locker, standing her daughter up inside. Kissing that locker after it's closed and then looking up into a sea of death, already splashing at her ankles.

She could have been any of us. She's all of us.

And, and. A tall man in a deep cell, hugging a grimy arm cast to his face, never letting it go, and—and on the *seventh* day, in the upper world, after lights out, a new recruit is rolling through the AM band, the veteran calling down from the top bunk to give it up, that there's nothing tolerable on anymore, this new recruit looking back to the dial anyway, sure he heard something the other night, something good.

It was about before. The past.

And then he pulls it down from the atmosphere, the veteran swinging his legs off the top bunk, his hands clamped to the side of that thin mattress, his shirt tied around his head like a turban.

"No, no, there," the veteran says, and the new recruit turns it up, looks out the open door of their bunkhouse for anybody who might be walking by, a habit that used to get him in trouble at school, and then the pirate DJ who doesn't know the mic that well, he's on again.

The story tonight's a continuation of last time.

A faceless father from the past, impossibly tall, and thin, frail almost, answering the door.

It's two military police, and, between them, a military man, a certain faceless hero of a general, and his neck, it's been torn open in the most crude way, like with a shiv made from a plastic spoon or something, so this general's had to pack it with gauze, then tape that gauze down. But still it's bleeding through.

"He's got long arms, right?" this father says to the general, about his wound. "Can reach farther than you'd think?"

The general's too exhausted for this.

The father leans sideways, eyeing all the olive drab machinery at his curb.

"You brought the army," he says.

"I *am* the army," the general says back, his face grim in the sunlight, the plastic skin around his eyes drawn tight.

The father nods, kind of knew this.

"I don't know where he is," he says, his voice so fake.

"We know he had a, a girlfriend," the general says.

"Heard he might have a special someone," this father says, like offering condolences, then shrugs one thin shoulder. "Beijing?" he asks. "London, Cameroon, St. Petersburg? Edmonton? New York?"

"Son," the general says.

"Sir," this father says back, and, after a standoff that's never going to go anywhere, the general turns, walks back to his convoy, the father's son stepping into the doorway now, to stand in front of the dad, the cast on his arm still new, except one signature—B R I A N.

"Is he there yet, Dad?" the son asks, and the father looks at his watch, out to the east, and says, "Right about now," and goddamn if he isn't right. Halfway around the world, a ridiculously tall, white door is opening for a man just as tall, a dark woman running through, into his arms, one of that place's priests stepping out to chaperone this reunion, his skin mummied in gauze so that there's only his black-rimmed eyes, looking up into the sky. Into the future.

And then the rest.

The planes falling into buildings, the cities burning, a child running into the night for his mother, his back flayed open to the night.

It's the story we all know, except this time, this time it ends with a crater up in Residential, a crater that used to be a wide, low house, the soldiers walking away from it, their red dots scratching the surface of the ground all around them.

This is where the world almost ended again.

And where it begins.

There's a huge white egg buried in those warm ashes, see, its shell shiny, once fabric, a miracle of technology.

A damaged man, a father himself, tears his way up from that shell, stands into the night and peels his antique goggles off, looks around at a world made new, then walks off into it, to spread the gospel, to whisper it into the airwaves, infect mankind with something new—the truth. *That's* what's going radioborne tonight, this DJ says.

"Shit," the new recruit says, looking up to the veteran, this reprobate, who's smiling now, biting his lower lip.

He shakes his head *no* to this baby torch, says, "He wouldn't— he wouldn't want you to talk like that, man."

"What are you saying?" the new recruit says, looking to the door again. Out into the world. "You mean, is he—is that—?"

The veteran laughs, folding his shoulders around it, and slides down from his bunk, stands at the door, his bare back scarred deep and regular, a game he was never supposed to have lived through, a game that makes the young recruit lick his lips, look away.

"Give em hell, Teach," this veteran says out into the night. "Give em hell, man."

THANKS THANKS THANKS

To Bobby Knight in Lubbock, Texas. You were a model. To Brenda Mills, for telling me this was too broken. You were right. To my agent Kate Garrick, for targeting the one broken place that could fix the rest. To Pablo D'Stair and Sarah D'Stair, for navigating some David Bowie/legal stuff. To Robert Gatewood, for working with me on draft after draft of this. To Jesse Lawrence and Christopher O'Riley, for early reads. To Max Brooks and Robert Kirkman and George Romero, for making the world a better place to not be dead in. To Karl Fischer, for relaying something he learned in Paul Youngquist's class, that made me finally understand this story I was trying to tell here. To Paul Tremblay. To Adam Cesare. To Cain Marko, for being Cain Marko. To my colleague Charles Evered, for episode 5.10 of *Monk*. That could be where this whole thing started. But it could have been Bowie, or it could have been Metallica. To Joe Lansdale, for showing me how to be a writer. To Jerry Reed, for getting me through the hard parts of this, and to the Drive-By Truckers, for "Sinkhole," and to Benjamin Whitmer, for introducing me to it. But Bob Seger's "Beautiful Loser" helped as well, as it does with everything. And, without Don D'Auria talking to me in a lobby in New York once, saying I should send him something, then this wouldn't exist, like this. And to Jory, for letting me write about him. I hope I got Linsey right, man. She can live forever now. And thanks to my kids, Rane and Kinsey, for tolerating me talking about zombies over dinner every night, and to my wife, Nancy, for getting up at so many three in the mornings, to walk them back to their beds, because they'd somehow got scared.

Me too, guys. Always and forever.

stephengrahamjones
boulder, co 2008–2013

ABOUT THE AUTHOR

Stephen Graham Jones is the *New York Times*–bestselling author of more than forty novels, collections, novellas, and comic books, including *The Only Good Indians* and the Indian Lake Trilogy. Jones received a National Endowment for the Arts fellowship and has won honors ranging from the Mark Twain American Voice in Literature Award to the Bram Stoker Award. Jones lives and teaches in Boulder, Colorado. Visit his website at stephengrahamjones.com.

STEPHEN GRAHAM JONES

FROM OPEN ROAD MEDIA

OPEN ROAD

INTEGRATED MEDIA

OPEN ROAD

INTEGRATED MEDIA

Find a full list of our authors and
titles at www.openroadmedia.com

FOLLOW US
@OpenRoadMedia